Detour to Agape

A Novel

R. F. Whong

ISBN: 979-8-88904-002-6

Published by Vidasym Publishing
A Division of Vidasym, Inc.
5013 S. Louis Ave., #532
Sioux Falls, SD 57108

Table of Contents

Dedication

I dedicate this book, first and foremost, to my Savior, the Lord Jesus Christ, and furthermore, to my brothers and sisters in Christ who have supported us in our ministry over the years.

Although this is a stand-alone fiction, it is linked to *Blazing China* and *Love at the Garden Tomb.* In that regard, I wish to honor the numerous Christians in China who remain steadfast under tremendous pressure and suffering even today.

Last but not least, many thanks to Hetay Jargalsaikhan of Among Foundation (www.amongfoundation.org), who shared with me his anti-human trafficking activities in Asia. With this, I also hope to bring focus to the many Christian men and women who work alongside different organizations to fight the evil of human trafficking.

Why I Wrote This Book

What do you look for in a fiction book? Besides an interesting plot, I like to be inspired and educated. Also, beauty, imagery, mood, and emotions are important to me. If the book can edify me with a serious theme, it's a bonus.

A few years ago, we spent three months traveling around Egypt, Israel, and Turkey. The idea of this book took shape back then.

I can never write for the sake of writing and entertaining. So, I wrote this with a grievous topic in mind: the evil of human trafficking.

Note: Although this book is a sequel to *Blazing China* and a prequel to *Love at the Garden Tomb*, each of my books stands alone as a distinct and unique story.

To connect with me, please go to www.ruthforchrist.com.

Discussion questions for book clubs

1. "Everyone has a different agenda": Which character's agenda shifts the most over the trip, and what moments drive those changes?

2. Reconciliation or convenience: Does Yao and Ann-Ann's rekindled relationship feel earned? How do class, reputation, scandal, and their shared faith community shape the power dynamics of their reunion?

3. Faith as catalyst: From Josh and Nana Lee's prayers to Shawn's conversion, how is faith portrayed—as comfort, conviction, social pressure, or moral transformation? Which moments make that portrayal feel authentic or problematic?

4. Justice, risk, and complicity: The group's involvement in a trafficking case raises ethical questions—ransom, deception, vigilantism, and sacrifice (e.g., the diamond pendant, Yao's swap). Where should the line be between helping and endangering others?

Chapter One

Hong Kong Kai-Tak Airport
Summer 1981

Why did he agree to come?

Yao Chen fumbled with his limited-edition Patek Philippe watch and waited for the boarding announcement. One of his travel companions, Ann-Ann Lee, stood nearby with her arms crossed as if displaying a stop gesture.

He glanced at her expressionless oval face and dull almond-shaped eyes,

Stop. Stop. Stop what?

What did he expect?

Leaving his conglomerate to his general manager, Susie Han, for an entire month? Crazy. Interacting with Ann-Ann day in and day out? Completely insane.

Nana Lee, Ann-Ann's grandmother, strolled toward him. She placed a palm over her chest, and her still-black eyebrows, a dramatic contrast to her white hair, formed a crease on her wrinkled face. "Are Shawn Han and his girlfriend coming?"

Why did he let Shawn join their private tour group? Yao's eyes tightened at the corners as if he could shut out the jarring mental image of the rowdy hulk standing next to the genteel Nana Lee.

At his silence, the older lady flashed a tentative smile. "Sorry. I shouldn't get annoyed. You probably don't know, either." She guided him to a nearby seat. "Yao, thank you again for coming with us and also for inviting Shawn and his girlfriend."

Josh Ying, Ann-Ann's nine-year-old nephew, scrambled over. "Great-Nana, how about me? You haven't thanked me."

"I've thanked your daddy. He agreed to let you come." Nana Lee chuckled, her gentle voice still laced with a slight Beijing accent. "Otherwise, you'd be at home now." She drew her brows together once more. "If not because of the no-refund policy, we should have canceled the trip."

Ann-Ann Lee took a seat next to Nana Lee. "We've been planning this trip for over six months to celebrate your eightieth birthday last week. Mama and Uncle Duan insisted we should go no matter what."

"Right." Josh retrieved a notebook from the pocket of his khaki shorts. "Uncle Yao, I would like to interview you for my summer project. Is it okay?"

"Sure." Yao twisted his watch into view again. Was the flight delayed? Maybe a good thing since the other two hadn't shown up.

Josh tapped his notebook with a pencil, assuming a pose far too similar to the Hong Kong tabloid reporters who often interviewed Yao. "What made you join this tour at the last minute?"

"Well, um, I've never been to Egypt, the Holy Land, or Turkey." He hadn't pushed out the truth, had he?

The original tour participants included Ann-Ann's mother, stepfather, and maternal grandparents, but her grandmother had a minor stroke a week ago. Although the doctor was optimistic she'd recover fully, her grandpa, mother, and stepfather chose to stay in Hong Kong to take care of her.

But why did he agree to take one of the empty slots when Nana Lee asked him? Could he have said no?

Nana Lee grasped his hand. "Tell me more about Shawn and his girlfriend. What is her name again?"

"Margie Fung." He withdrew his hand, a tingling starting at the back of his neck. "You know Susie Han at our church, right? Shawn is her brother."

"It's kind of them to agree to come with so little warning." Nana Lee checked her watch again. "I do hope they'll show up soon."

2

He hadn't told Nana Lee everything about Shawn and Margie. How could he? The truth wouldn't do the older lady any good.

Three days before their trip, Susie came to see him in tears. Her words echoed even now. "We received a notice from the Istanbul officials. Nathan and his sister, Nancy, went missing. My brother and I grew up with them. A bunch of us in the neighborhood used to eat dinner together every day when our parents were out working late. They're like family."

The PA system announced their flight number. Two people raced toward them. The blond, wearing a pair of ultrahigh golden heels and a tight red dress, trailed her companion.

Nana Lee stood and smoothed her rumpled silver-gray traditional Chinese *qipao* dress. "Ah, must be Shawn and Margie. He looks just like Susie. Let's get in line."

Yao made the introduction, and the group rushed to queue up.

Forty minutes later, he settled into his window seat, Number 46A, in economy class, and gazed at the tarmac as the plane taxied along. Yet, last week's events kept nagging at him.

Susie Han pleaded with him to let her brother and his girlfriend take the two remaining vacated slots. She'd reasoned that, since her brother had contact with the triad, a transnational organized crime syndicate, he might find useful information about their old friends.

Yao sank back against the stiff seat. He should have let Susie take his place. But she was in the middle of completing a huge merger deal for Chang-Ji, his company.

At a loud thump from under the plane, he faced the window. The silver bird took off, and the islands below appeared like black dots on a blue canvas.

He shifted, needing more room to stretch his legs. How long hadn't he flown in economy class? What did he hope to achieve other than touring the religious sites? Well, he needed to leave Hong Kong for a while. So many things to think through.

"Uncle Yao." His seatmate waved a piece of paper.

Yao perked up. "Yes, Josh?"

"Did my mom tell you about my summer project?" He unfolded the paper to reveal an elderly, lanky man dressed in distinctive traditional Chinese attire. "Our teacher told us to have pictures taken with this fellow during our vacations."

Ah, Old Master Q, the lead character in a popular Chinese comic.

Yao squeezed Josh's arm. "What a clever idea. You must have an outstanding teacher."

Josh thrust out his chest. "My teacher is super nice. I like her a lot." He folded up his paper and returned it to his backpack. "Can you take a picture of me with Old Master Q in front of the pyramid? I'm sure all my classmates will envy me."

Yao crinkled up his lips. "Of course. In addition..."

A colossal figure loomed over them. Shawn Han stood on the narrow walkway. "Fine crocodile shirt. Did you buy it from the Wing-On store?"

What was Shawn up to? "Your polo shirt looks even better."

Shawn glanced down at his shirt, then spoke in Cantonese. "You and Daisy Dong are engaged, right? It's nice to marry *into* the Dong family."

Yao chuffed out a breath and suppressed the urge to roll his eyes. "Don't believe the tabloids."

"He-he-he, whatever." Shawn leaned against Josh's seat and lowered his voice. "That beautiful young lady traveling with us, Ann-Ann Lee. Do you know her well? Does she have a boyfriend?"

What? He must be joking. Yao peered toward the seats a few rows ahead.

"Don't worry about Margie." Shawn's low chuckle rumbled deep in his broad chest. "We're in sync about an open relationship from day one."

"But—" Yao scratched his cheek, his mind clouding. Was it jealousy or confusion? "You and Ann-Ann Lee are so different."

"Hey, opposites attract." Shawn brought his voice even lower into a whisper. "I'm big everywhere, including *there*. For sure, she'll like it very much."

Josh's mouth formed a perfect *O*, and Shawn winked.

Must Shawn always speak vulgar nonsense? Was it his compulsive habit? Yao pinched his brows tight, then kneaded the groove with one hand. "You shouldn't talk like that in front of a child."

"It's never too early to start sex education, right?" Shawn jabbed Josh's shoulder. "Now, be serious. Does Ann-Ann Lee have a boyfriend?"

Yao drew his brows even tighter. "I have no clue. Why don't you ask her yourself?"

"Shawn, what are you doing over there?" Margie called from her seat. People nearby turned their heads.

Shawn waved in reply. "I'd better go. Talk to you later."

After he strode away, Yao closed his eyes, imagining his time with Daisy, his girlfriend for the past eleven months. A lovely girl with all the right connections. Did she love him for who he was? Did he love her for who she was?

No. He ground his teeth. Stripped of her family name, she wouldn't have attracted his interest.

But a marriage liaison with the powerful Dong family would raise his company's status to the next level. Was success more important than love?

"Uncle Yao." Josh tugged at Yao's sleeve. "What did Uncle Shawn mean by 'I'm big everywhere, including there?' Why will Auntie Ann-Ann like it?"

"Shush. Keep your voice down." Yao tapped the boy's lips with a finger. "Ignore him. He was yakking nonsense."

Josh spoke again in a hushed tone. "What is sex education?"

A mistake, a huge mistake, to have Shawn traveling with them. The heat turned into a flame, and Yao remained silent.

"Uncle Yao, are you blushing?"

"I'm not—"

Margie, clad in a tank top and shorts, walked by, offering a perfect reprieve. Her high heels caused her buttocks to sway with each movement.

When did she change out of her red dress? So tall and muscular. Did she lift weights every day like Shawn?

A few pairs of eyes, including Josh's, followed her.

"Uncle Yao, isn't Auntie Margie Chinese? Why does she have golden hair?" Josh whispered. "And why does she wear a top like that?"

Margie must have heard him because she turned back to stand by him. "See how all those men look at me?" She lifted her chest high. "That's why."

At the sight of another perfect *O* on Josh's mouth, Yao slid his lashes down to feign sleep. Yet his shoulders remained tense.

A group of them, including Susie, her neighbors, and Yao, used to operate vending carts in Hong Kong's busy streets, selling anything and everything from food like fish balls on a skewer to clothes. Shawn, one of the triad forces in Mongkok, the Kowloon side's major shopping area for locals, took them under his wing, although they all had to pay him monthly protection fees.

Later, they dispersed. Shawn moved to Macau to operate a casino there. Susie came to work for Yao after his business took off. Her neighbors went to Turkey to work.

Yao's chest ached at the potential danger to his old friends' lives. The disappearance of expats from Hong Kong, many of them on work visas in Europe, had been recurring news lately. Interpol had launched investigations, to no avail. What made Nathan and Nancy, the apples of their parents' eyes, leave home and go to Turkey?

He twisted his body and massaged his cramped legs. Boy, he'd forgotten how unbearable the economy class could be. Maybe he shouldn't have agreed to put himself in this uncomfortable situation.

"Ha, Uncle Yao, you're still awake." Josh touched his arm. "I forgot to tell you. I also need to keep a journal every day and write all the unusual things I hear or see."

Yao slit his eyelids open and peeked at Josh.

The boy still held that notebook. "Want to hear what I've written?"

"Maybe another time." He shut his eyes again. "I'm tired. Let me take a nap."

With Josh, May-May's second son, sitting next to him, Yao couldn't block the memories of his past and the Beijing courtyard house where he and May-May grew up together. Such a long time ago. Still, thoughts of it created sorrow mingled with gentleness. Let bygones be bygones, they said, but those precious memories refused to depart.

May-May and he spent most of their after-school time together, swimming in the nearby river, playing games, growing vegetables, and raising chickens in the yard. He'd heard her mother and sister lived in Hong Kong, and he'd even seen their pictures. The girl, May-May's identical twin, looked just like her.

Josh tugged at his sleeve. Wouldn't the kid leave him alone?

"Uncle Yao, my great-nana wants to talk to you."

"Yao." Nana Lee handed him a card when he opened his eyes. "Sorry, I forgot to give this to you. It's from May-May."

He tore it open and stared at the familiar neat handwriting. She thanked him for allowing Josh to share a room with him and asked him to keep a close watch on the boy. So thoughtful, like always.

As Nana Lee strolled away, Josh peered at the card. "What did my mom say?"

"She said you're unruly and asked me not to let you out of my sight." Yao pressed his lips together, hiding the urge to laugh. The unruly one wasn't Josh, but Shawn Han.

Josh pursed his lips as if to match Yao's, dipped his chin, and returned to his writing.

Good. The boy might leave him alone for a bit.

Yao shut his eyes. *May-May*. All along, he'd intended to marry her. After he escaped to Hong Kong amid the height of the Cultural Revolution, China shut her door to outsiders, and he and May-May lost all contact for years. Still, his goal to get her out of China drove him to start his textile factory, real estate business, and finally, his conglomerate. He realized his get-rich dream, but May-May married someone else and bore three children before she turned thirty.

When he lost her, all he'd left was his business empire. Yeah, he still strived to turn his business into something that would be the envy of everyone in his circle. Yet, if he died today, who would enjoy what he'd amassed over the last decade?

Was everyone an accidental existence in an accidental world?

Lord, please help me find my path during this trip.

He drifted to sleep.

Chapter Two

Ann-Ann Lee gazed past her nana at the cloud outside the porthole. Nana would be devastated if they'd canceled the trip.

Lord, thank You for things coming together.

Nana meant so much to her.

After Mama and Uncle Duan's wedding ceremony, she felt so alone and afraid. The entire world, including Mama, had abandoned her. Then Nana walked into the room where she was hiding and helped her establish a genuine relationship with God.

Her wild days ended.

How strange all those years now seemed. Before Nana and May-May immigrated to Hong Kong eight years ago, for a long while she'd harbored a dislike or even hatred of them.

A sigh whooshed over her ear.

"Are you all right?" She patted Nana's hand.

Nana smoothed her dress as if trying to dust off invisible troubles. "I'm worried about May-May's family."

"You mean Charlie?" Ann-Ann tilted toward Nana. Both her nephews had inherited her brother-in-law's mixed-race good looks with fine bone structure and a straight nose, but Josh's health far surpassed his brother's. The day before their departure, Charlie suffered another asthma attack, and May-May had to take him to the emergency room again.

Nana rubbed at her temple. "We must pray for Nian-Rong. Instead of overcoming his asthma, he gets worse and worse."

Tenderness softened Ann-Ann's posture over the boys whom Nana habitually referred to by their baby names. Only one year apart, the boys always played together and often fought over trivial matters. Two years after May-May's daughter was born, Charlie started having asthma attacks. Josh soon outgrew his older brother, and the two didn't fight anymore.

"I've been praying for him. Everybody in the family is praying for him." Over her seat belt, she cuddled Nana into a half-hug, pressing her cheek to Nana's wispy white hair. "By the way, Josh doesn't like people calling him Si-Rong."

"True." Nana dipped her head and whispered like in a prayer. Holding back her shoulders, she perked up again. "Praise the Lord, we could fill the slots in time to take this trip. It seems half my life, ever since becoming a Christian, I've been wanting to visit the Holy Land. I can't wait to trek the roads our Lord once walked on and see the places He used to visit."

Ann-Ann nodded along but wasn't so sure she shared Nana's excitement.

Oh, Lord, why did our carefully planned family tour turn into a makeshift ensemble?

Would her active nephew run into trouble? How about that unmarried couple sharing one room? Her spiritual and uptight nana hadn't raised an issue about their living arrangement. Did Nana truly follow Paul's statement in 1 Corinthians chapter five, "What business is it of mine to judge those outside the church?"

Ann-Ann tipped her face up at the ceiling and resisted the urge to roll her neck back and forth to release the tension claiming her body. "Nana, why did Yao decide to come with us?" She let out the troublesome question. "Didn't recent tabloids mention he's dating a socialite, the Dongs' youngest daughter? The news even hinted they would become engaged soon."

Back then, Yao and she had been dating. In her last one-on-one encounter with him, he'd taken her to his Palo Alto ranch house in California, and they debated what a Christian was. Since she was a child, she attended church with Mama and considered herself a Christian. Yet, Yao commented she wasn't one because a Christian wouldn't do what she did. She'd scoffed and told him to get lost.

"Ann-Ann," Nana chided, "don't believe the tabloids. I worry about him. Sometimes, ambition blurs our vision. To a determined young man like him, the shortest route to break into Hong Kong's top-tier social circle is through marriage."

Ann-Ann kept quiet, a jittery heat surging through her. Since that irksome night, she'd avoided him. Still, after she moved back to Hong Kong, they attended the same church, and he joined her family for lunch every Sunday.

How was she going to face him, day in and day out, for an entire month?

Nana's cold touch prodded her arm. "Yao told me you two dated when you were in California. Your mama and I always treat him as one of us. It would be great if you could be together. Why did you break up?"

"I–I—" Ann-Ann forced a smile. "He isn't my type."

Nana crossed one arm over her chest and cocked her head. Wisps of white hair fell onto her left brow. "And Stanley? Also not your type?"

How irritating that Nana knew everything about her! The smile slid from Ann-Ann's face.

After she returned to Hong Kong about two years ago, she met Stanley at a Christian conference, and they courted over the next year. They didn't do much other than hold hands with occasional timid kisses. That was how Christians dated—no sex until the wedding night.

Stanley proposed last Christmas Eve, and she said yes. One week later, she mustered up her courage to tell him she could never conceive. The next morning, he broke off with her. She understood. No decent Christian man who wanted children would marry her.

"Right." She sucked in a deep breath and rubbed at the tightness gripping the back of her neck.

Nana's shoulders slumped, and she raised her chin. "When do you plan to settle down? Your mama and I are concerned about you."

Without thinking, Ann-Ann waved. "I'm doing well being single. I have you, Mama, Uncle Duan, May-May, and all the surrounding others."

Nana's lips wobbled. "We can't be with you forever. Eventually, we'll leave you one by one. When you grow old, who will take care of you?"

She resisted the childish urge to roll her eyes and, instead, patted Nana's arm. "How do you know someone would take care of me? Maybe I'd be the one taking care of him."

"How about your job? What happened to your company?" Nana touched her fingertips together.

"They filed bankruptcy." She puffed out a breath, attempting to brush aside the unpleasant topic.

"You've been out of a job for over six months."

"If I still had my job, I wouldn't have had time to come with you. Right?" She examined her manicure. "Don't worry. As soon as we get back to Hong Kong, I'll find another job."

"Your argument always wins."

The seatbelt signs went off, and Ann-Ann stood up. "Time to go pee. Let's talk later."

She sat on the toilet and blinked back a rush of heat from her eyes. Did Nana know about her past with JT, her true love at one point?

They spent so many wonderful nights in the apartment he bought for her. She'd revealed some of her innermost thoughts, even how her family struggled. Her mother never bought her anything because they had to scrimp to send food to her nana and twin sister in China.

JT's words echoed even now. "You didn't know your nana and twin. They're strangers to you. Even though you can't see them, they're always present, like some phantoms who keep stealing from you. You have no way to fight back."

She fell in love right there. But that liaison didn't last. JT belonged to someone else.

An announcement broke into the small space. "We invite all our passengers to check our in-flight duty-free goods...."

After returning to her seat, to avoid talking about marriage, she put on her headphones and watched the movie throughout the meal service.

The seatbelt signs lit up again, and her head jerked up. What was going on?

The PA system sounded above her head. "We're experiencing turbulence. Please return to your seats and fasten your seat belts."

Oh no, she got motion-sick easily. *Lord, please don't let the turbulence trigger it.* She bit her lower lip, her nails digging into the armrest.

From her aisle seat, she glanced outside at a blanket of fluffy white clouds outside the window. So peaceful. It gave no hints as to why the plane rocked and bounced. Next to her, Nana's snores rumbled like an eighteen-wheeler truck. How could she fall asleep so quickly?

Another jolt lifted Ann-Ann off the seat. Then the captain's voice rose. "We're entering a turbulence zone for an unknown amount of time. Cabin crews, please stop all services and return to your seats."

Ann-Ann's stomach churned. She rubbed her temples to suppress her queasiness.

Uh-oh. She'd better rush to the lavatory.

As she stood up, a harsh announcement attacked her ears. "You must take your seat and fasten your seat belt."

Before she sat back down, she coughed, and vomit gushed onto the back of the man sitting in front of her. "Mr. Han, I'm—"

Another bout of regurgitation cut off her subdued apology. This time, the contents of her stomach sprayed all over Shawn's polo shirt.

She must have spewed up her entire insides. It smelled like fermented stinky tofu sold on Hong Kong street corners.

Odd. After she sat, her nausea disappeared.

The plane no longer jolted and swayed. Then the seatbelt signs went off.

Shawn stood up and surveyed her body up and down. "How did you avoid splattering your beautiful teal shirt and matching pants while not missing an inch of mine?"

"I–I..." She straightened her shoulders. "I'm so sorry. Tell me how much your shirt costs. I'll reimburse you. Or should I buy you a new one?"

He lifted one eyebrow. "You think money will make up for this?"

"What else can I do to compensate you?" She fidgeted, another type of churning in her stomach. What did this gorilla want?

"Let me go clean up first." He pulled a fresh shirt from his bag. "We'll talk again."

He strolled away, and she sank into her seat.

Margie stood by her aisle. "Shawn is interested in you."

"What do you mean?" As the churning intensified, Ann-Ann swallowed hard. "I thought he was your boyfriend."

"We're in an open relationship." Margie raised her index finger. "He's quite a man, lots of fun to be with. Don't miss your opportunity."

With a wink and a smile, she trod away in Yao's direction.

What was an open relationship? Quite a man? Lots of fun to be with?

Ann-Ann slouched against her nana's shoulder. Was it time to date a non-Christian?

But it was so risky in the secular world. Unscrupulous men had injured her heart and soul. She shuddered, letting her eyes slide closed.

Oh, that beach house on Lantau Island, the largest island in Hong Kong. In that handsome bungalow surrounded by white fences flush with climbing purple flowers, she lost her virginity to a playboy. Vincent opened Pandora's box for her. Her church always taught her sex was a dirty subject. Yet, she'd never experienced so much pleasure and went with him to the beach house every day during her summer vacation. Two months later, she found herself pregnant, and he disappeared into Europe. An abortion in her neighborhood's cheap clinic landed her in a hospital. She could never conceive.

Lord, I know You have forgiven me. Please help me walk on the right path.

Another PA announcement disrupted her contemplation. She sat up straighter and grabbed the water bottle from her seat pocket. As her fingers unscrewed the cap, a shadow loomed over her.

"Okay, I know how you can compensate me." Shawn gripped her seatback, then leaned into her space. His lips quirked to one side, and his eyes twinkled. "Treat me to an outstanding steak dinner in one of Cairo's nightclubs. How does that sound?"

So simple? She huffed a breath. "Have you been there before? Do you know which club to go to?"

"I haven't." With him so close, his warm breath fogged over her. "My connections are vast, and my resourcefulness is never-ending. I guarantee it'll be one of your most memorable experiences."

She tilted her head to study him. Like his sister, he owned a pair of large, luminous eyes with a deep dimple on each cheek. But the same features on him didn't look feminine.

"Why are you staring at me like that?"

She stood up, heat rising to her throat. Was the air dry in the cabin? "Excuse me. I need to go freshen up."

He turned sideways to let her pass.

Yet, she walked a few steps and paused. Her memory wouldn't relinquish its hold.

After the abortion, she vowed to allow no man to take advantage of her and trampled the heart of any guy who dared to get close. Having casual sex, drinking, shopping excessively... She'd indulged in all activities to numb her heart and soul so she could smash the intruding profile of a baby, her baby that she'd murdered.

Then, once Nana helped her establish a relationship with God, she'd understood what Yao told her on the night they broke up: "I can't tell you what a Christian is. I can tell you what a Christian isn't. A Christian isn't someone who receives baptism, attends church regularly, or even serves as a pastor in the church. A Christian isn't someone who reads the Bible often or even memorizes the entire Bible. If it's that simple, all the Pharisees at Jesus' time would be Christians."

Was it too late? Could she start all over again? Her wild days were like the indistinct fine lines around her eyes. When either was examined closely, decent Christian men pulled away. Meanwhile, weren't the marks on her face like signs of a trail map, waiting for another lost soul to follow them and hike into her heart?

She shook her head hard, a feeble attempt to brush aside her memories of Yao and the other men in her life.

"Auntie."

She turned to the soft call. "Yes, Josh?"

He pointed beside him. "Shh! Uncle Yao is asleep, but I can't sleep. I don't know why." He stood and grasped her hand. "Why are you standing here? Are you going to the toilet? I'll go with you."

As they approached, individuals queuing in the area shifted to let them pass.

Josh pulled her to the back of the line. "Auntie Ann-Ann, did my mom tell you about my summer vacation assignment? I need to record all the unusual things I hear or see every day."

He retrieved a notebook from his pocket and flipped to a page. "Listen to what I wrote so far. 'Auntie Margie is the most unusual person I see today. She's Chinese but has golden-colored hair. Also, she has big melons on her chest.'"

The young mom standing next to them started giggling. Her daughter, a tad younger than Josh, frowned. "Mommy, why don't you have melons like her? You have pears."

The woman's cheeks turned crimson. She pulled her girl with her and hurried away to another line.

Did they understand Cantonese? They must.

Unconcerned, Josh resumed his reading aloud. "'Uncle Shawn said something I didn't understand. He told Uncle Yao he was big everywhere'—"

"Shush." Heat crawled up to Ann-Ann's face. She scanned around and hitched out a breath, her shoulders loosening. Good. Nobody heard Josh. Or if they did, they kept it to themselves. "I don't think your teacher will appreciate what you've jotted down. You should replace it with something else."

Josh raised his head. "Why?"

"Er..." She rubbed her temples. "Why don't you write about our food on the airplane?"

"But there's nothing special about what we ate."

The lavatory door opened.

"Josh, can I go in first?" Without waiting for a response, she rushed in and shut the door.

How could Shawn Han speak like that in front of a nine-year-old? What would he say to her during their steak dinner in Cairo?

Chapter Three

Ann-Ann checked her watch as her steps scuffled along the smooth linoleum. Six a.m. In less than an hour, they'd passed through customs. Not bad at all.

Her stomach rumbled like an alarm with its own will. After her motion sickness, the light meal before landing didn't help much. She'd never been so hungry, not even when Mama pawned her jewelry to buy food in their first few years in Hong Kong.

As they strolled into the crowded waiting area, a dark-skinned man came forward. "How do you do?" He spoke in Mandarin, then switched to English. "Sorry, my Chinese is rather limited. Are you the Lees from Hong Kong?"

Nana halted. "I'm Su-Ann Lee. Are you Mr. Ahmed?"

Wow. In college, Nana majored in English. At age eighty, she hadn't lost her ability to speak perfect English. Also, her back remained erect, and she maintained a slim figure. The edges of Ann-Ann's mouth turned upward. Good thing she and her twin took after Nana with that tall, slender build.

"Please call me Darius." Mr. Ahmed made a slight bow and took the large suitcase. "Are you guys ready for breakfast? Do you want to try our local food?"

"Yeah." Setting her suitcase down, Ann-Ann tucked bouncy curls back from her face. "I'm famished."

Shawn Han gave out an enormous yawn. "What kind of breakfast are we talking about?"

Ann-Ann scrunched her nose and waved away flies swarming her. Did she smell so bad the flies admired her? Yuck, traces of vomit smeared her sneakers. Maybe she did emit a scent to attract those pests.

"Ful medames," Darius responded, "is our most common traditional breakfast. We simmer fava beans with oil and salt for hours and serve it with a boiled egg."

Yawning was contagious. Nana covered her mouth while the rest risked having insects fly in.

"I need some vegetables," Margie grumbled.

Yao nodded. "Me too."

"Me three." Josh raised an arm.

Ann-Ann resisted the temptation to speak and swallowed her unspoken, "Me four."

"No worries." Darius's white teeth flashed with his grin. "Let's go to one of our best local breakfast joints. They serve cucumbers and tomatoes with ful."

They walked into the early morning sunshine, and a gray minivan with another dark-skinned man in the driver's seat awaited.

Darius jumped into the van, and the gang followed. "My colleague, Mostafa, will be your driver in the next few days."

The van pulled onto the main highway but stopped for people to cross.

Odd. Pedestrians roamed the busy road as if it was a sidewalk.

Beyond the tinted window, patches of dirt and sharp-edged rocks broke up the land. A harsh, unfriendly region. Wasn't the Nile River nearby?

Twenty-five minutes later, Mostafa stopped before a stand-alone hut in an empty field. Ann-Ann trailed Nana inside the restaurant, then halted in the doorway.

Argh. People and flies everywhere. Two insects and a few men's greedy gazes fell on Margie's body.

Josh flapped both arms like in a butterfly stroke swimming competition. "Auntie Ann-Ann, didn't the plague of flies in Moses's time end three thousand years ago? You taught us in Sunday school recently, right?"

He spoke in Cantonese. The others in her group cracked up, but the Egyptians gaped in silence.

The hostess, a young woman with a narrow forehead and a pair of painted eyes, greeted Darius as if he was her long-lost brother and guided them past the back door into an empty yard full of climbing vegetables. Plump green cucumbers and overly ripe red tomatoes basked in the sun, and Ann-Ann's stomach growled again. Boy, she was hungry.

They settled into a round metal table, but as soon as their orders arrived, six flies touched down. Unconcerned, Darius and Mostafa dipped their forks into ful.

Poor guys. They must've gotten up super early to go to the airport and were hungry like her. The men in her group also dug in, while she, Nana, and Margie leaned back.

"It's better than I thought." A mouthful of food muffled Shawn's voice.

"Auntie Margie, didn't you say you need vegetables?" Josh attacked the dish of sliced tomatoes and cucumbers. "Very delicious."

Margie rolled her eyes but didn't move a finger.

Nana bent over and whispered into Ann-Ann's ear. "Josh may get sick. We need to pray for him."

As a finance major and a chief financial officer for her now-defunct company, Ann-Ann had gotten used to estimating risks and returns.

Should she or should she not? Oh, why not? She'd eat now and worry later. Waving away the flies from her plate, she raised her fork and charged forward.

***

Yao dropped his fork. The typical Egyptian breakfast suited him well. He'd loved fava beans since his childhood. In their Beijing courtyard house, he and May-May had grown them by a fence. "Darius, what's next?"

"It's a private tour. You can tell us where you want to go, and we'll take you there."

Josh picked up the last marinated cucumber from his plate and plopped it into his mouth. "The pyramids. I want a picture taken in front of the Great Pyramid with Old Master Q."

"Josh, don't speak when your mouth is full," Nana Lee chided with a smile. "I would love to see the pyramids as well."

"Me too." Ann-Ann squinted as if to study the remaining pickled peppers.

Shawn exchanged a glance with Margie. "You guys enjoy yourselves. Margie and I need to take care of some errands."

"What's the name of our hotel again?" Margie retrieved a pen and a notebook from her pink purse. "We will go there directly this afternoon."

"Shepheard's Hotel." Darius jotted down the name and address, then scooped up another spoonful of ful.

Shawn leaned toward Ann-Ann and pretended to whisper. "Don't forget the steak dinner you owe me. Will six p.m. work for you? See you in the lobby."

But since he spoke in such a loud voice, everybody must have heard him.

After Shawn and Margie sauntered away, Nana Lee patted Ann-Ann's hand. "Why do you owe Shawn a steak dinner?"

Yao cocked his head at the older woman's softly spoken Mandarin. Indeed, how did Shawn secure a date with the proud Ann-Ann Lee in mere hours?

Before Ann-Ann responded, Darius urged them to stand up. "Let's go to the pyramids. Soon the sun will get boiling."

They returned to the highway. Even from afar, the top of the Great Pyramid peaked over the landscape.

Wow, the world's Great Wonder was situated so close to the town center.

As they approached the ancient burial sites, three monumental structures emerged. After the van stopped, Josh got out and ran forward. "Uncle Yao, take a picture of me with Old Master Q."

Yao ambled over to Josh, who stood in front of an enormous granite boulder, much taller than the boy was.

Ann-Ann spoke behind him. "Look over there. Some smaller pyramids too."

"Truly a sight to behold." Nana Lee raised her camera. "I'm so glad we came."

They heeded Darius's suggestion and climbed down a steep ladder to the bottom of the Great Pyramid.

The guide's voice echoed around them. "We acknowledge this chamber as the spot where Khufu, the most powerful ruler of our Old Kingdom, was laid to rest."

Not much to see other than an empty vault lined with stone after stone... Yao rubbed sudden shivers from his arms. In 1968, he'd visited the graveyard where Confucius and his descendants were buried. Was that trip just over a decade ago?

The greatest pharaoh, like China's most-admired teacher, Confucius, didn't even have a trace remaining at his burial site, attesting to Solomon's statement in Ecclesiastes: "Utterly meaningless! Everything is meaningless."

A dismal feeling hollowed out Yao's chest until he felt as empty as the chamber.

1968.

How could he erase that year from his memory? The year amid the height of the Cultural Revolution. The year Red Guards murdered his father during a denunciation meeting. The year he escaped to Hong Kong as a freedom swimmer.

What was life for?

He'd asked that question on the Pearl River bank in Macau. Had he found his answer?

Since he returned to church six years ago, he no longer frequented nightclubs and cut his liaison with one of his business partners. Although the darkness entwined in his heart drifted away, he still struggled as God's child walking in the light.

Young beautiful women flocked to him as soon as they found out who he was. None of them would take a second look at him if he wasn't the CEO of Chang-Ji, his holding company that oversaw the operations of all its subsidiaries covering Japan, Hong Kong, the US, and even Europe.

Where would he find a girl who loved *him*, not his money?

If only May-May were still single. He'd marry her in a heartbeat. But she viewed him more like a brother than a lover and wouldn't have agreed to be his wife. At least the love of his life was happily settled with a wonderful husband and three well-behaved children.

The guide's voice sounded, breaking into his meditations. "Legend has it that the remains of the pharaoh's sarcophagus are still there." Darius pointed at a fractured mass of red stone. "It'll ring like a bell when struck."

Josh raised a hand. "May I try?"

"It's merely a legend."

Yao's belly rumbled like an airplane about to take off. A faint yet distinct sound escaped from his lower extremity, and a foul smell filled the vault.

Josh sniffed, then scrunched his nose. "Who farted? Was it you, Uncle Yao?"

With his neck heating, Yao stepped toward the ladder.

"Josh, it's not polite to speak like that." Nana Lee ruffled the boy's silky hair.

"I'm sorry." Josh scooted over and followed Yao up the ladder.

Yao stood under the bright morning sunshine and massaged his stomach. Good. The churning subsided. Must've been the suffocating air down there.

The rest of the group soon emerged from the abyss.

"One more thing to do." Darius scanned around them. "You must ride the camel around the pyramids. At a certain angle, you can take a picture that will appear like your palm is touching the tip of the Great Pyramid."

Nana Lee patted her dress. "I think I'm too old for that."

Josh eyed the camels nearby, then Old Master Q in his grip. "Old Master Q is older than Great-Nana. I'll stay here with him."

Ann-Ann glanced at Yao as if checking his intention. Right, she still tried to avoid him.

What made him date her all those years ago? Was it because she was May-May's identical twin? Was it her confident demeanor, so unlike May-May's? Or was it how she wore makeup on her eyes and lips with such a flair, while May-May never bothered?

They'd spent many wonderful dates together until that troublesome evening. Afterward, he'd tried to reach out to her, but she rejected him as if he'd betrayed her.

Now, was she beckoning him to ride the camels together?

Yeah, why not? He'd never come to this part of the world again. "Okay, let's do it."

Darius waved at a teenage boy standing to their left. The young fellow nodded and pulled two of the camels forward. Their guide helped Ann-Ann get on the first one. "The camel will sway. Don't sit up straight. Try to relax and move with the animal. The less tension you hold in your body, the more comfortable your ride will be."

Sounded easy enough. Yao threw his leg over the middle of the humps and mounted the second one. After the camel stood up, his shoulders stiffened. The beast was much taller than he'd expected.

The teen guided them away from the crowd toward behind the pyramids. As the animal rocked from side to side, Yao's stomach churned, then boiled. He needed to poop really bad. The kind of bad where he'd drop everything to find the nearest bathroom.

To their right stood the Great Pyramid. To their left? Not much to see other than a landscape of sand and harsh sunlight. Sure. The Sahara.

"Hey, you!" he yelled, sweat beads forming on his forehead.

The teen looked up but kept walking alongside his two camels.

Great. He didn't understand English.

Ann-Ann, riding along his right-hand side, turned. "Are you talking to me?"

He tried to steer the camel to the open field. The beast refused and continued to follow its young master.

His mind raced. What to do? He groaned. *Forget good manners*. "Ann-Ann, my stomach hurts. I must take a poop. Right now."

She went silent. Next came an ear-piercing scream. The lanky boy halted his two pets. She flailed her arms in a frenzy like a mad woman, sending her curly hair bouncing. Somehow, the teen understood and uttered a command.

Both camels kneeled.

Getting off was much easier than getting on. Yao swung one leg over the hump and jumped off.

Before he bolted toward the nearest dune, Ann-Ann yanked a pack of tissue paper from her bag. "You may need this."

Minutes later, the killing sensation in his belly vanished.

In his whole life, he'd never felt so relieved as he covered his watery poop with sand.

Yeah, for thousands of years, people in the Sahara must have carried out the same routine every day. Or maybe not quite the same unless they had diarrhea.

Fava beans, cucumbers, pickled peppers? No. The culprit must have been the flies. But why didn't other people get sick?

He trod back to the four, now all sitting or kneeling.

Ann-Ann raised an eyebrow. "Are you all right?"

"Much better." He gave out a sheepish grin. "I owe you a favor."

Boy, he'd love to offer to take her for a steak dinner. Whoa. Where'd *that* thought come from?

Rumbling roars escaped one camel as if to cheer his reply. He cupped a palm to his mouth, grateful his travel companion was smarter than he was. The twins would achieve identical IQ scores from an intelligence test. During his old days with May-May in Beijing, no matter what Nana Lee taught them, May-May always memorized it faster than he did.

"Our time with the camels is up." Ann-Ann stood. "Let's go."

Too bad he'd spoiled their chance to have pictures taken that would appear like their palms were touching the tip of the Great Pyramid.

Chapter Four

Yao slouched on the opulent sofa. Should he change into his pajamas and go to bed? With his earlier stomach problem, skipping dinner might not be a bad idea.

But after a light lunch and a two-hour nap, maybe he should wait for his regular bedtime to improve his jet lag.

He twisted his watch into view. Still early, not even seven. With the six-hour difference between Cairo and Hong Kong, Daisy would be sound asleep or enjoying herself at a party. He'd promised to call her as soon as he arrived, despite the excessive cost of an international call from the hotel. Well, money shouldn't be a concern, right? He dialed her number. The phone rang for like an eternity. When no one picked up, he replaced the receiver, and an eerie hush stretched across the room. He stifled a groan. *Okay, remember to call her tomorrow morning.*

Josh emerged from the bathroom, clad in an adult-sized robe. He shuffled sideways and then forward like a hermit crab in an outsized shell. "Uncle Yao, take a picture of me with Old Master Q."

Yao crinkled up his lips. "Sure." He surveyed the room with its blue-and-white checkerboard carpet and floor-to-ceiling purple draperies over the enormous window. "Where do you want it done?"

Josh wobbled toward the sunny yellow wall and a magnificent painting of the old Shepheard's Hotel in its glory days. He lifted Old

Master Q and turned the old man's gigantic head to face the camera. "How about here?"

Yao pressed the shutter a few times to ensure at least one negative would turn into a fabulous picture.

"Are you ready to listen to my diary for today?" Josh stripped off the robe and hopped onto the bed.

Someone tapped on the door.

"Who is that?" The boy shoved the notebook back into his pants pocket and leaped from the bed.

The knock persisted, followed by Margie's voice. "Me."

Josh ran to let her in.

A tight red qipao dress highlighted her every curve, a string of round white pearls hung around her neck, and a ruby ring glared from her right middle finger.

She sat on the corner of Josh's bed. "The night is still young. Let's go out for dinner."

Josh's hair slipped forward as he shook his head. "I can't. Great-Nana wants me to have dinner with her downstairs." He glanced at the radio clock on the nightstand. "Six forty already? I'd better leave now."

Once Josh jogged out, Margie cocked her head, her eyes bright as a bird about to pounce on a worm. "Well?"

So, this must be how the worm felt wriggling and trying to hide from the eager bird. "Well, what?"

"Don't tell me you came all the way from Hong Kong to sleep in a hotel room." She hopped away from the bed to grab his arm. "Let's go to a dinner show."

Hmm. Let the worm become a snare to the hungry bird. "Under one condition."

Her eyebrows spiked up, then landed back down. "Yeah?"

"Answer a few of my questions." He returned to his previous position on the sofa.

"Deal." She squeezed in and snuggled close to his side. "But no more than three yes-or-no questions and no guarantee my responses will satisfy you."

Such a shrew. And she dared to challenge him. Didn't she know he'd handled many tough issues in his business?

He straightened his spine and tapped his fingers in his contemplative pose. "First, are you a triad member like Shawn

Han?"

Her body went still. "What if I tell you I'm not? Will you believe me?"

"Okay." His first defeat slumped him against the sofa's plush back. He clucked his tongue to release the steam building up inside of him. "You and Shawn Han left us to run errands. Were those related to our missing friends?"

"Yes... and no." Mimicking him, she let her naughty tongue peek between her lips.

She was more interesting than he originally thought. And quite charming. Undeterred, his gaze flitted about her body. "Are you in a sexual relationship with Shawn Han?"

Her cheeks flared crimson, and she shifted her body away. "Maybe."

Maybe? What happened to her yes-and-no answers? Hadn't they set clear guidelines?

She pulled herself up. "Well, I've answered your three questions. Let's go."

"A promise is a promise." He lifted his dog-tired body out of the cushy zone. "Do you know where to go?"

"Trust me." She sauntered toward the door, swaying her hips.

Who taught her to walk like that? She portrayed herself as a seductive goddess. But why did she blush when he asked about her relationship with Shawn Han?

Without finding an answer, Yao tipped his head to one side and followed her out.

A taxi and twenty minutes later, he trailed her through a dark alley into a cabaret. A half-naked pharaonic mural hung behind the stage. Pictures of belly dancers and Arab princes on horses adorned the walls, while disco lights swirled around the vast dance floor.

In the far-left corner and under the colorful dancing beam, Ann-Ann's smooth shoulders appeared like carved white jade.

Years ago, they'd shared dinner in a French restaurant. He'd changed his return ticket to Hong Kong to spend more time with her in San Francisco. That night, she also wore a black, off-the-shoulder dress. With her hair down and a red lip, she became a version of beauty on his mind. He hadn't expected a bitter fight after their romantic dinner.

"Yao." Margie tapped his arm, breaking into his contemplation.

"Let's take a table and eat. I'm famished."

A band with a drum, a clarinet-like instrument, a lap harp, and mandolins whirled an Arabic tune.

The PA system announced, "Next is our gorgeous Adara from Damascus."

In a bead bra top and a chiffon skirt, a young dancer, shaking her breasts and buttocks, glided up to the wooden stage. She lifted her skirt, pushed out one leg, and gyrated her rear end.

Margie dropped the menu before him, diverting his attention from the near-naked flesh. "Shish tawook, chicken kebabs marinated in yogurt and the special tomaya sauce, is popular here. Oh, kofta is outstanding too."

"What's kofta?" He glanced at the menu.

"A skewer with minced lamb, sumac, and red onion in a tahini sauce."

"Okay. I'll have that." His gaze returned to the performance. The dancer had left the stage.

What? Each performance lasted less than a blink of an eye?

When the food arrived, Margie carved her chicken into squares and speared one with her fork. "Most folks in Hong Kong eventually adopt English names to make themselves more memorable to the surrounding British. Why do you keep your Chinese name?"

Yao shrugged. No way would he share private information with an almost stranger. "How about you?"

"Margie is my given name since birth." She pushed her shoulders back. "According to the tabloids, you're thirty-two, right? Is there any merit to the story that you walk with a slight limp because you got shot by a gangster in one of your fortune-hunting adventures?"

Kofta tasted better than he thought. "What if it's true?" He chuckled at his typical response.

Margie examined her broccoli. "Tell me."

"You guessed it right. The tabloids lie. I got shot, more a life-and-death situation rather than a fortune-hunting expedition." He described his escape from China to Hong Kong as a freedom swimmer but didn't bother to say the tabloids were off by a year on his age.

The PA system crackled again. "Please welcome our goddess Penelope from Seville."

A new dancer floated in. With willowy arms framing her face, she turned her head sideways and went down on her back while pulsing her belly as if it had a life of its own. Thunderous applause broke out as she rose to her bare feet and sprinted from the stage. In a few graceful steps, she shifted to their table side, bumped her hip against Yao, and gestured for him to stand.

He flitted his gaze to Margie. Her mouth widened in a bewitching smile, and she rose, pulling him up.

With her five-inch stiletto heels, Margie, a tad taller than he, towered over the petite, barefoot beauty. They moved together with the rhythm of the Arabic night. The performing artist drew their hands on her belly and rippled her hips. Then she pushed them back into their seats and vibrated her breasts in their eyes. She pulled her top down slightly, displaying the word *auxilio* below the top rim of her bra.

What did the red tattoo mean?

Margie retrieved a hundred-dollar bill from her purse and slipped it into the dancer's bra, covering up her tattoo.

*****

Ann-Ann eyed the man sitting across from her. Quite an attractive physique. The shirt's thin navy fabric highlighted his broad shoulders and bulging six-pack. Shawn probably worked out with weight lifting every day.

The problem? From her experience in the dating world, the personalities of such men didn't often measure up. Plus, he wasn't a Christian.

She'd trampled men's hearts, and hers had been crushed. How many times did she have to try before she found a suitable man to spend her life with?

"Tell me where you've been hiding. Why didn't I meet you before?" Shawn leaned over the table, his elbows mussing up the white lace cloth, and extended a hand to her.

She swallowed her last bite of the chicken kebabs, savoring the killer yogurt marinade. Ignoring his arm, she raised her water glass as a barrier. "Tell me why you came on this tour. You and Margie don't seem interested in tourism."

He drew back, a smirk curving his lips. "Come on. Your eyes have been all over me."

Water sloshed the tablecloth as she replaced the cup and resisted the urge to roll her eyes. "Don't flatter yourself."

"Okay, okay. I'll be serious." He snapped his fingers. "My sister told me about Yao and May-May Lee. She neglected to tell me May-May Lee has an identical twin sister. Did you also grow up in Beijing?"

"I grew up in Hong Kong. My mother and I left Beijing when I was two." Mama seldom talked about her past. Yet, a tidbit of gossip at church mentioned her mother left Beijing because a local scoundrel harassed her.

Heat seared Ann-Ann's eyelids. Her beautiful mother, an intellectual educated in the US, a young widow with two daughters, became the target of sexual harassment by a laborer. Under communism in China, with the working class rising to power, she had no place to seek help. But why didn't Mama flee with both her girls?

"Must be quite a wild tale." He gave her a teasing wink. "Care to tell me more?"

The PA system announced a new dancer—Penelope from Seville.

Ann-Ann shifted her legs in her chair. Brushing aside her tangled emotions, she refocused.

The performer left the stage and moved to dance with their friends across the ballroom. Shawn stretched his neck like a giraffe, eyebrows jogging up his forehead. "Are Yao and Margie training for the next Olympics or what? When did they add belly dancing to the competition?"

She narrowed her eyes. "Are you jealous? Aren't you and she in an open relationship?"

"We are." He scratched his forehead. "Still, since we travel together, I'm responsible for her conduct."

She dipped her chin to hide a smile. "Why did you and Margie join our tour, anyway? You two didn't even go to the pyramids with us this morning. How could you miss the world's greatest wonder?"

Penelope flounced away.

"I–I—"

The next performer, Lydia from Corinth, drifted from the stage toward them. She danced a few faltering steps as if ready to drop on the floor. Then she swept the hair away from her face and yanked both Shawn and Ann-Ann upright.

Were they supposed to place their hands on her belly like Yao and Margie did with the last dancer?

Lydia advanced toward Shawn and gestured for him to gyrate his hips. He raised both arms to mimic her. With one unexpected swift turn of her body, the dancer grabbed Shawn's right hand and deposited it on Ann-Ann's chest.

What in the world? Ann-Ann jerked one hasty stride back.

"I'm sorry." Shawn carried himself to the side.

The dancer's lips crinkled up. She winked and glided away.

Whew. Ann-Ann had never been so happy to see someone leave.

As she took her seat, a man wobbled over, holding a clay jar. He hiccupped and plonked the container in front of Shawn. "Here it is."

Shawn waved. "Thank you, but I don't need it."

The drunkard turned around, and his eyes opened wide, his vaporous breath hitting Ann-Ann's nostrils hard. "Ah, with a companion like this, no wonder you declined."

He advanced and puckered his lips toward her mouth.

Without thinking, she turned away her head and rubbed at her chest to ward off the rush of disgust. The next instant, the man dropped his entire length flat on the charcoal carpet, his legs twitching.

She gawked. "Did you do something to him?"

"You probably know acupuncture points can do magic to our body. I helped this poor guy relax. He'll recover soon and feel refreshed." Shawn bent to lift the fellow off the floor, then carried him back to his table.

Wow!

Ann-Ann remained in her seat, her arms hanging loosely at her sides. She'd heard and read about the effectiveness of Chinese martial arts but always considered them legends.

They weren't legends.

When Shawn returned, he didn't sit. "Enough adventure for the night? Ready to call it quits?"

"What martial arts do you practice?" She grabbed her purse.

He winked. "Shaolin."

She stood and smoothed her long silk aquamarine gown. "And what is the jar for?"

"Curiosity will kill a cat." Gripping her elbow, he led the way toward the other side of the ballroom. "Let's go fetch Yao and

Margie."

The four squeezed into a taxi with Shawn in the front seat. She and Margie flanked Yao in the back.

"What a night." Yao chuckled. "I wonder why that dancer had a tattoo on such a weird place. And what does *A, Y, U, D, A* mean?"

Ann-Ann couldn't help asking, "What tattoo?"

"Curiosity will kill a cat." Shawn glanced back at her.

"It wasn't a tattoo. That girl wrote the word there using her red lipstick pen. She's in serious trouble." Margie raked a hand through her dyed hair. "Auxilio means help in Spanish."

"What? Do you speak Spanish?" Ann-Ann scooted to the edge of her seat and craned around Yao to see Margie better. "How do you know she's in trouble?"

"Margie speaks four languages," Shawn chimed in. "Spanish is one of them."

Ann-Ann's mouth slid open. No one would guess that from Margie's appearance.

"Why do I know she's in trouble?" Margie waved. "By logic, reasoning, and indirect evidence. Who would take the trouble to *draw* the word *auxilio* on her chest below the bra rim?"

"You asked me the purpose of that clay pot." Shawn reached over his seat. "Do you still want to know?"

Must've been something embarrassing. Ann-Ann sat still and kept quiet.

"All those dancers are for sale." His bass tone sounded lower than usual, so convincing that Ann-Ann hung on every word. "Men put their bid and the name of their target girl into the jar. The highest bidder gets to spend the night with her."

Head tipped to one side, Ann-Ann covered her mouth with a palm.

"Is she the only one in trouble?" Yao asked. "How about the others?"

"She must have done something that displeased the person above her." Margie fixed a stern look. "As long as the others obey and don't cause trouble, they should be okay for now."

Ann-Ann overcame her shock and moved her hand enough to speak around it. "Is there anything we can do for her?"

Both Shawn and Margie shook their heads.

Yao scratched his chin. "Can we notify the police here?"

"Useless." Margie pressed her palms together. "Aren't you two Christians? You can pray for her."

Ann-Ann flipped her lashes down and folded her hands in her lap, weighed down by the heaviness of her heart. Why did those girls end up where they were now? What desperation drove them from their family and friends? Didn't anyone love them and try to look for them? *Oh, Lord, have mercy on those poor women.*

After they exited the taxi, Shawn tapped Yao's back. "Tell Darius we won't join you tomorrow morning. Margie and I have more errands to run."

Chapter Five

Ann-Ann took her time to apply a smoky shadow, making her eyes appear even larger and brighter, then scowled at her reflection. Why did she bother? Whom did she try to impress?

"Ann-Ann, you don't need makeup." Nana braced her elbows on the table, her eyes gleaming.

Nana's admiring gaze warmed her heart, but mischief edged it out. She scrunched her nose. "What do you mean? Am I so old that cosmetics can't cover my blemishes anymore? Maybe I need plastic surgery."

Nana burst into laughter. "You're thirty. Youth is your best makeup."

"I'm no longer young." Ann-Ann tilted her face up and squinted. "Look here. Crow's-feet." A weight pressed down on her levity. Men still showed interest in her. How long would that last? Besides, guys who focused on the outside seldom cared to delve into her inner world. Where would she find *the one* to share her innermost thoughts?

An incessant knock on the door rattled her.

"Who is that?" She twisted her Cartier watch face into view. Not even eight. At the sight of the old scar on her wrist, the constant reminder of her suicide attempt, a pang of sorrow rippled through her.

"Me." Her nephew's high-pitched voice sounded.

When Nana opened the door, Josh dashed in. "Guess what? Uncle Yao just taught me how to make babies."

Ann-Ann stopped applying lipstick with a brush, and Nana arched a brow. They asked in unison, Mandarin and Cantonese blending. "What did Yao teach you?"

"He said to change *Y* to *I*, then add *E* and *S*. Now I know how to turn baby into babies."

Nana exhaled a deep breath. "That's great." She shared a smile with Ann-Ann over the boy's head. "We'd better go down. Darius said we have a full itinerary today."

In the lobby, new arrivals, current patrons, and their guides sent an almost electrical current of anticipation through the air. Darius, standing in a corner with Yao, waved them over, and she followed Nana through a group all clad in matching yellow T-shirts. The red words *You can't buy happiness, but you can buy plane tickets to Cairo* arched over the pyramids stamped on their chests.

Darius took out a sheet of paper. "Today, we'll take you to the bazaar, the synagogue, and the Hanging Church. Since time is limited, tell me where you want to spend most of your day."

"The Hanging Church? Is it also called Saint Virgin Mary's Coptic Orthodox Church?" Nana placed a palm on her chest, and her eyes sparkled. "That's one of the oldest churches in Egypt, dating to the third century. Ann-Ann and Yao, what do you think? Should we spend more time there?"

Ann-Ann cupped an elbow with one hand while tapping her lips with the other. "The name sounds interesting. How did they hang the church in the air?"

Darius chuckled. "We named it the Hanging Church because it's hung on two towers of Babylon fortress."

Heat rushed to her cheeks. She glanced at Yao. Good. He wasn't laughing.

"I want to go to the bazaar." Josh moaned, his shoulders sagging.

"We'll have time to shop." Yao patted the boy's head. "Tell you what—rumor is that the church has something special. When you look at the icon of St. Mary there, her eyes follow you from any angle."

"Really?" Josh slackened his jaw. "Let's go."

Nana smoothed back her already smooth white hair. "Where are

Shawn and Margie?"

"They need to run errands again." Ann-Ann led them toward the door. "They're not interested in today's itinerary."

Even at this hour of the morning, as she stepped outside, heat rose in waves from the street, and dust drifted around. They followed Darius to their first stop, the bazaar. The air on those narrowed streets became stiller, filled with the mystery of ancient history, antiquities, and sweet spices.

Josh halted in front of a stall displaying lanterns. "Great-Nana, see that golden one? It looks just like Aladdin's lamp. Can I buy it?"

Ann-Ann trailed behind them and giggled. Yeah, Nana would give in.

Yao bent to her ear, crowding into her space. "What do you think about last night?"

She shuffled back a step, conscious of his intent gaze. Her smile faded. He still wore the same cologne—woody and spicy. With a deep breath, she drowned in his scent, returning to that night years ago until the bazaar's clamor intruded.

She folded her arms across her chest, debating whether to stay or leave.

As if reading her mind, he stretched out a palm. "Don't go. I owe you a big favor. If not for your quick wits while we were riding the camels, I don't know what would have happened."

She squinted. Why did he bring *that* up? What did he want? She stood her ground—waiting.

The edges of his mouth turned upward. His gaze locked with hers. "Honestly, what do you think about Margie's comments? Is that dancer in danger?"

Her hair slipped forward, curls tickling her cheeks as she shook her head. "I don't know. Do you believe her? Why did Shawn and Margie join our group? They don't seem interested in sightseeing."

"That I know. I should've told you earlier." He slid his hands into the pockets of his khaki shorts. "They are here on a special mission."

When he related his friends' disappearance, she huffed and swept the hair away from her face. "Are they going back to that club? Do they think it has anything to do with your missing friends?"

"I have no clue." With hands still in his pockets, he rocked back on his heels. "The triad retains many secrets and mysteries. No outsiders can ever figure it out."

As a triad member, Shawn must have mastered Chinese martial arts. "Is Margie also a triad member?"

"I asked, but she didn't give me a straight answer." He ducked his chin and nudged one of his sandals along the street, sending a pebble rolling. "After last night, I think she is not."

"So, she *isn't* Shawn's girlfriend at all."

He cocked his head, his thick eyebrows drawn together. "The question remains—who is she?"

"Maybe a private investigator?" She wiped at her mouth, turning a laugh into a snort.

"Quite possible. Shawn stunned me when he said she speaks four different languages."

"Uncle Yao." Josh skipped over, his enormous smile displaying a missing upper canine tooth. "They had some weird toys. The whole bazaar *is* bizarre."

Darius approached and clapped. "Are you all done shopping? Let's go to the synagogue and the Hanging Church."

***

Yao trekked out with the group from Ben Ezra Synagogue into the winding alleys.

Ann-Ann huffed an audible sigh. "I don't know whether the synagogue truly marked the spot where the basket of Baby Moses was found. Seeing such a unique place turned into a tourist attraction saddens me."

Yao remained quiet as she spoke. He couldn't deny he still found her attractive. Yet, no doubt, some tension existed between them. At least, today she hadn't shunned him like before.

His mind shifted toward another thought. When he called earlier today, Daisy inquired whether his Palo Alto house was available for visitors because her brother planned to visit the Bay Area. He'd given her his property manager's phone number. Were their conversations always so superficial? Had they ever talked about something deep, something with essence? Could he have told her about his past?

Darius halted and clutched a piece of paper against his chest. "My friends, before we enter the Hanging Church, I have to say something."

They formed a small circle around him. He coughed and laced

his hands together, holding the paper. "You must've seen last week's news about how firefights broke out between Copts and Muslims in the El Zawya el Hamra neighborhood of Cairo?"

Yao nodded. "This morning, the news showed further clips of the incident."

"I've been a guide for over ten years. Tourists don't like to get caught in unpleasant situations." A flush mottled Darius's cheeks. "The designated guide at the Hanging Church may try to engage you in political discussions. Please let him know if you aren't interested."

What a warning. How serious could it be?

Nana Lee exchanged a glance with Ann-Ann. "Darius, thank you for letting us know in advance. Before this trip, I read a book about the Coptic community in Egypt and learned the Coptic Church was established by Mark, the author of one of the four Gospels. Aren't they the largest population of Christians in the Middle East?"

"Yes, we are." Darius touched his forehead.

"So, you're a Coptic Christian?" Nana Lee moved one step closer to him. "Tell us what's on your mind. Even though we met you only two days ago, you've taken good care of us. I consider you a friend."

"We've been suffering violence and discrimination since President Sadat embraced Islam. He rebuilt the Nasserist police state to promote Islam. Our police, instead of protecting us, prey on us." Darius narrowed his eyes to slits. "We're barred from positions of leadership and jobs deemed sensitive to national security."

Nana Lee touched his arm. "Even facing suffering and persecution, you don't waver from your faith?"

"People in our country consider changing one's religion a shame." His voice wobbled. "Plus, we're proud of our heritage. Our ancestors made significant contributions to Christianity. Without us, there would be no Nicene Creed. Emperor Constantine called the Ecumenical Council of Nicaea after our patriarch, Pope Alexander I, requested a meeting to respond to heresies."

Persecution... Goosebumps puckered Yao's skin. He rubbed his arms, forcing them to subside. Nana Lee's image during her denunciation meeting, amid the height of the Cultural Revolution, flashed across his mind. In the middle of a circle, Nana Lee kneeled. The Red Guards swarmed up to spit on her and pummeled her with fists and feet.

Now, her gentle voice rose. "Darius, we're also Christians. Yao"—she hooked her arm with his—"and I went through similar hardships in China. When the government's policy confronts our Christian beliefs, to follow Christ means to put our life at risk. Before the Cultural Revolution, I never fully understood what Jesus said in the Sermon on the Mount, 'Blessed are those who are persecuted because of righteousness, for theirs is the kingdom of heaven.'"

Heat swelled Yao's throat, and he swallowed hard. "I'm not worthy of Mrs. Lee's praise. Under tremendous pressure, while she remained steadfast in her faith, I questioned God's care and love for His children."

Moisture gathered behind his eyelids. He turned his head away, holding back his tears and painful emotions. "My ma died when I was four. After the government eliminated private property ownership, my pa and I moved into a magnificent estate that once belonged to Mrs. Lee. She led Pa to Christ, and we went to church with her until the government shut down our church building. Then the Red Guards murdered Pa because of his Christian faith."

Yao shut his eyes and rubbed the taut point between them. He wasn't present when Pa died. When he'd learned of Pa's death, he'd raised his fist toward the sky and shouted, "Are You there? If You're powerful, wise, and loving as they say, why can't You let Pa live?"

Those questions and the feelings stimulating them burned inside of him for years.

"Oh, Yao." Nana Lee hugged him. "You'd endured much more than I did."

"Thank you." He dipped his chin, not fully trusting himself. He seldom cried and for sure wouldn't do it now. The last time he lost control was when Nana Lee showed him his pa's letter.

Josh wrapped his arms around his waist. "Uncle Yao, I love you."

Ann-Ann made a silly face with crossed eyes. "Josh, do you understand what we're talking about?"

"Must be something serious." The boy tilted back his head. "It made Great-Nana and Uncle Yao sad."

Nana Lee ruffled the boy's short hair. "You're such a sweet child."

"I'm sorry to have caused the distress." Darius clasped his hands. Then his countenance brightened. "It's amazing how we Christians

38

connect right away, even though we're from different parts of the world. The apostle Paul was right in his letter to the Galatians. 'There is neither Jew nor Greek, slave nor free, male nor female, for you are all one in Christ Jesus.'"

Under her breath, Ann-Ann muttered, "'Whoever finds his life will lose it, and whoever loses his life for My sake will find it.'"

As Yao's gaze met hers, he crinkled up his lips.

Why did he have such a wild mood swing today? One moment, sorrow engulfed him. The next moment, he felt like laughing. Yet, how could he not grin when reminded of his conversation with Ann-Ann about memorizing Bible verses?

He'd told Ann-Ann that, after the government put their pastor in prison, their pastor's wife assigned different books of the Bible for each of them to memorize in case the government confiscated their Bible. He and many others eventually memorized most books in the New Testament. Ann-Ann had widened her eyes and claimed she could recite quite a few Bible verses too.

Josh loosened his hold on Yao. "Let's go to the church. I can't wait to check out how Saint Mary's eyes look at me from any angle."

Chapter Six

The elevator dropped to the ground floor. Yao's toes tingled inside his sneakers, the heaviness in his chest refusing to lift. Last night, sleep eluded him. Scene after scene from long ago flew across his mind like a movie on fast-forward.

Josh tugged at his sleeve. "Uncle Yao, I heard some people call this an elevator. Isn't it a lift?" His eyes sparkled, lashes flicking up. "Come to think about it. Both names are wrong. This thing goes up and down, right?"

Yao's shoulders loosened up somehow at his companion's cheerful voice.

The door opened, and the boy dashed into the lobby. "Come, Uncle Yao. Uncle Shawn and Auntie Margie are already waiting."

Margie left the plush sofa and handed over a copy of the *Egyptian Gazette*, the oldest English-language newspaper in the Middle East.

Okay, what game was she playing now?

Shawn gestured with his chin, compelling Yao to turn the pages. "Flip to the local news section."

Buried in a corner was a paragraph about the death of a belly dancer named Penelope from Seville, Spain.

Yao rubbed his brows, at a loss for words. How much did Margie know about those poor women?

Josh grasped his hand. "Uncle Yao, are you all right?"

He nodded, but his heart hollowed out.

Would their friends suffer the same fate?

"Are you guys going to Alexandria today?" Margie reclaimed the newspaper. "Shawn and I still have errands to run. Come to our room tonight. We can talk more."

As they walked away, Yao's mood plunged further, and his old friends' images lingered in his mind. Once, years ago, the police came by, the street hawkers scrambled to hide, and Nathan hurt his left hand. A deep cut slashed across his index finger. Afterward, he carried a visible scar.

Were Nathan and his sister okay?

Their guide, Ann-Ann, and Nana Lee strolled in. Darius waved a fresh paper. "We'll drive to Alexandria today." He grinned at Nana Lee. "You haven't grown tired of Coptic churches. No worries. We'll visit the St. Bishop Coptic monastery first, then tour the Citadel of Qaitbay, the Montaza Palace with its extensive gardens, and the famous library."

"Ah, the Great Library of Alexandria, one of the largest and most significant libraries of the ancient world." Nana Lee smiled back. Then, craning her neck, she raised the same question as yesterday. "Where are Shawn and Margie?"

Unable to meet her gaze, Yao picked at the cuticles on his thumb. "They have businesses to take care of."

Nana Lee mumbled under her breath. "I wonder why they come with us. They've been keeping to themselves."

After entering the van. Nana Lee sat with Josh in the last row and, perhaps purposefully, let him sit with Ann-Ann.

Years before, when Nana Lee led him back to God's family, Yao had confessed all his affairs, including his liaison with Ann-Ann. Did Nana Lee think he and Ann-Ann could get back together?

Now, Ann-Ann's jasmine perfume and her shapely legs, inches away, brought a tingling sensation to his body.

Had he become supersensitive because of his edginess? Should he tell her about the belly dancer's fate? No, not with others around.

"Great-Nana,"—Josh called out in his soprano-like voice—"in the lift, somebody mentioned TGIF. What does it mean?"

"It means 'Thank Goodness It's Friday.'"

"Oh." Josh went quiet—but only briefly. "How about SHIT? Does it say something about Thursday?"

While Nana Lee remained silent, Darius burst into laughter. "Yeah, it means 'Shout Hooray It's Thursday.'"

Yao couldn't hold back his smile. How nice to be with his family of friends.

***

Ann-Ann gripped the van's door handle, then lowered her arm. Her fingertips prickled as Darius's joke rang in her ears. She tried to smile, but a tight knot remained lodged in her stomach.

Why did Nana want her to sit with Yao? She stole another glance at him. The TGIF conversation softened his I'm-despondent-and-not-in-a-mood-to-chat expression. Did he feel uneasy sitting by her? The feelings must be mutual.

"Here we go." Darius pointed at the bridge. "We passed the Nile again."

Outside the window, green fields stretched into the horizon.

She muttered under her breath, "When there's water, there's life."

Yao shifted his body her way. "Did you say something?"

"Oh, nothing." Mimicking him, she turned her shoulder to face him, the seat belt cutting into her lap. "I was thinking about the information Nana told me concerning the Saint Bishop Monastery."

"Nana Lee did her homework well. She read so much about all the different sites in Egypt."

Ann-Ann loosened the seat belt across her cerulean pantsuit and smoothed her fingers over the rumpled slacks. "She said St. Bishoy founded the monastery in the fourth century. His relics remain there. Supposedly, his whole body is preserved via incorruptibility."

"Sorry, what is incorruptibility?" He crossed his long legs, and his shoe bumped hers.

She tucked her feet beneath her seat. Still, at the contact, a quiver in her stomach squiggled up to her throat, and she swallowed. "Incorruptibility is an Eastern Orthodox belief. Divine intervention allows some human bodies to avoid the normal process of decomposition after death as a sign of their holiness."

"Indeed?" He cocked his head, edging further into her space. "Do you believe such a thing?"

"I—" Why did the van suddenly feel so small and his scent so strong? She tucked her hair behind her ears and sucked in a deep breath. "I think miracles do exist. At the same time, it's difficult to know whether St. Bishoy's body remains intact since nobody is allowed to open his coffin. Do you believe in miracles?"

"I do." After an awkward pause, he smiled, crinkling up his smooth face. "Once, someone told me that a miracle is an extraordinary happening attributable to God's presence and action. In that sense, *our* returns to God's family should be considered miracles. Don't you agree?"

What did he mean by "*our* returns to God's family"?

The van hit a pothole, bouncing them in their seats, and he gripped her headrest to brace himself, moving closer. "I overheard your prayer with Nana Lee on the day your mother and Uncle Duan got married. Since you moved back from California, I noticed you've changed a lot."

Had he been watching her from the sidelines? Was he still interested in her?

Don't be ridiculous. He'd been busy dating Daisy Dong and wouldn't care about her. Even if he did, she should run as far away from him as possible. She'd vowed to never again get involved with a man who belonged to someone else.

"I've changed a lot too. If it's not because of God's presence and action, then what is it?" His finger tangled in her hair, and a shiver coursed up her spine.

She pulled her hair free.

"Nana Lee told me you've been learning piano. How is your progress? I picked up playing the violin a few years ago and have enjoyed it very much."

Did he also feel uneasy enough to cover up his embarrassment with small talk?

"Neither the family nor the tabloids ever mentioned you playing the violin." What else had he been doing? She repositioned herself in her seat, making sure she was far enough away he couldn't snag her hair again. "Josh is gifted in piano. When May-May is busy, she asks me to take him to his lessons. I decided to take lessons from the same teacher."

He smiled. "I'm also learning Chinese painting and tai chi."

The self-made business executive was branching into nonmaterialistic realms. "Isn't tai chi a form of qigong? I've heard they're influenced by Buddhism and Taoism and sometimes are

43

linked to the evil spirit. Aren't you concerned?"

"You do have to be careful when practicing tai chi or qigong. I try to avoid their chants." He pushed himself away from her seat and waved. "By the way, Margie wants to talk to us tonight."

Good. He'd moved his hand away.

Wait. What had he said? Ann-Ann jerked up her head. "Margie? What's it about?"

He glanced back at the last row. "It's something about that belly dancer. Let's not go into details now. Margie said she'll order us room service. After we get back, please go to their room at six p.m."

***

Yao left Josh at the restaurant downstairs with Nana Lee, then strolled to Shawn's and Margie's room. Inside, food spread across the coffee table, together with two bottles of wine.

Ann-Ann, planted on the sofa, a glass of red wine in hand, twisted the glass with a frown as he approached. "Margie just told me about the dancer's death."

Margie gripped her wineglass stem, her red nails garish against her honey-toned chardonnay. "We went to the police station to find out more about the incident but without avail."

He cocked an eyebrow.

"Red or white?" Shawn gestured for him to sit on the plush sofa.

Yao glanced at Ann-Ann. "Red." During their last date, did they drink red wine or martinis?

Shawn leaned forward to pour the drink. "The government here is as corrupt as anywhere else. No bribe, no information."

Smooth and full-flavored, the wine relaxed Yao. He took another sip but kept his expression somber.

Ann-Ann set her glass on the table and picked up a crispy deep-fried ball, likely falafel, an Egyptian version of taamiya. "Shawn and Margie need our help."

Yao eyed the pita bread stuffed with minced meat, his stomach rumbling. Though excellent, the fish he'd been served at lunch in Alexandria came in a skimpy portion. "How can we help?"

Shawn pointed at Yao's limited-edition Patek Philippe watch. "This will do."

"What?" He retracted his hand. "I went through a tedious application process to buy this watch. I can never get a second one."

"Is the watch more important than our friends?" Shawn frowned.

Yao hid his watch hand behind his back. "You haven't convinced me what you're doing has any use in uncovering their whereabouts."

While Shawn lapsed into silence, Margie passed a piece of paper to Ann-Ann. "Please read this aloud."

After a frown at their companion, Ann-Ann recited it in a monotone. "'The famous French writer Gustace Flaubert wrote in 1850 about his encounter with dancing girls in Esna, Egypt. He described them as learned women, which meant prostitutes. He detailed how he had sex with a tall, splendid creature from Damascus...'"

Bile rose to Yao's chest, and he clenched his teeth against the urge to vomit. Yet images of his past encounters with numerous "learned women" flooded him, sneering at him, accusing him. Wasn't he like that French man a hundred years ago?

Lord, I claim Your forgiveness once more. Satan, get away from me with your deceptive allegation.

Margie tapped his shoulder. "Yao, are you all right?"

"I'm okay." He sipped his wine and calmed. "I'm sorry, but the watch is out of the question." He put down the glass, rummaged through his pocket, and retrieved a black case with the word *Hermès* on it. "I can give you this business card case. Maybe it's sufficient?"

Shawn drew his brows tighter. "I don't think so."

"Where did you get this article? It disgusted me." Ann-Ann handed the paper back to Margie. "What information are you looking for? Are you sure you can get it with a proper bribe?"

"We copied it from the local library, a historic account about belly dancers involved in the sex trade even back then." Margie brushed her bangs aside. "I want to know the condition of the dancer's body. And I'm sure we can get that information with a decent bribe."

Yao tucked the case into his breast pocket. "Why are you interested in knowing the corpse's condition?"

"Well, in all the cases involving the death of an expat, either the body was badly decomposed or the upper part went missing." Margie pressed her sensual lips into a thin line. "If, as I suspect, this dancer's death is related to the other cases, the information will help me evaluate my hypothesis."

"Such a poor, unfortunate girl. So young and so beautiful, but so cruelly murdered." Ann-Ann reached into her blouse to pull out an object—a pendant with a sparkling, transparent stone. "This is a two-carat natural diamond. D color and flawless."

Margie received the pendant, her eyes glistening. "It's more than enough. Thank you very much."

Shawn stared at Ann-Ann. "I know Yao is rich. I didn't know you were also loaded."

Yao winced, and he swallowed hard to keep down the bile. Why did he still value materials more than people? And Ann-Ann... She used to be selfish and materialistic, even more than he was. Did her return to God's family bring about a total change in her heart and attitude?

Shawn speared a piece of chicken with his fork. "Let's eat."

Forty minutes passed while they consumed the food with occasional chitchat.

Ann-Ann dropped her fork. "I'd better get back to our room lest Nana worry." She stood up. "We'll be leaving for the Faiyum Oasis tomorrow morning. I suppose you two plan to stay in Cairo to continue your investigation?"

Both Shawn and Margie nodded.

"I'll tell Darius." Yao also stood. "My friends, please be careful. I sense this country seems dangerous."

Shawn wagged a finger at him. "Not any more problematic than Hong Kong or other parts of the world."

Yao followed Ann-Ann into the hallway and released a weighty breath, but couldn't ease the heaviness in his chest. He stilled her by stepping in front of her. "You're so kind and generous. You don't even know Nathan and Nancy."

"Don't blame yourself." A slow smile uncoiled her lips and loosened the tightness in his chest. "I know how difficult it is to get a limited-edition Patek Philippe watch."

A tenderness spread through him as they resumed walking. "As soon as we get back to Hong Kong, I'll buy you a diamond pendant to replace the one you gave Margie."

They halted in front of her room. She took out her key. "Once I find a job, I can buy one for myself if I want to."

She unlocked the door, stepped inside, and closed it behind her, leaving him staring at the mahogany wood. He swallowed hard at a similar image, except it concerned May-May, Ann-Ann's twin.

After he'd escaped to Hong Kong, he lost contact with everyone in Beijing because China shut its door during the Cultural Revolution. Then Nixon visited China, the country opened up, and Ann-Ann's mother, Leesan, received a letter from May-May.

He'd rushed to Auntie Leesan's apartment, excitement pulsing through his veins faster than he could move through the city. On the coffee table lay a picture of three adults and two boys—Nana Lee, May-May, her *husband*, and their two children. The bottom fell out of his world. With a hasty excuse, he took leave. But once the lock clicked behind him, he slumped against the wall next to the elevator and stared at the mahogany wood.

The door opened, and Yao jerked back a step into the hotel hallway.

"Ha, you're still here. Auntie Ann-Ann said you're back in our room." Josh rushed out and grasped Yao's hand. "Do you want to hear what I've written in my diary today?"

"Sure." He forced a smile as Josh swung their arms with more energy than Yao ever remembered possessing. If he'd married May-May, Josh would be his son. But it wasn't meant to be. "Let's go."

Chapter Seven

Ann-Ann surveyed the van, then the barren landscape outside the window. With her mood as dismal as the scenery, a lump lodged in her heart as the baby's fuzzy profile in her dream from last night lingered in her mind.

She always assumed the baby was a *she*, a cute little thing like May-May's youngest, Audrey. In her dream, the baby never showed herself clearly, but Ann-Ann could sense she was smiling, enticing her mother to embrace her, hug her, and love her.

"Darius"—Nana's gentle voice reached her ears—"please tell us more about this oasis we're going to."

"Ah, Faiyum Oasis." In the front passenger seat, Darius turned his head back as far as he could. "Unlike typical oases, the fertile land in the Faiyum doesn't depend on water from springs, but on canals branching off from the Nile. The drainage water flows into Lake Qarun."

Nana's soft nod ruffled her white hair. "The book I read claimed the region has the earliest evidence for farming in Egypt."

Ann-Ann sank back into her dream. Why did the baby come to her again? Why did Satan keep accusing her?

Maybe the diamond triggered it? Yao had praised her kindness and generosity. Had she changed after establishing a relationship with God? She must have. Before that, she wouldn't have cared.

Nowadays, she tried to seek God's guidance in everything she did. And yesterday, when Margie mentioned their need, Ann-Ann received a command from the Holy Spirit to give up her pendant.

A Bible verse flashed across her head. "If we confess our sins, He is faithful and just and will forgive us our sins and purify us from all unrighteousness."

Lord, I claim Your promise of forgiveness once more. No matter how many sins I've committed, You've forgiven me.

Seated to her left again, but this time in the van's far rear seats, Yao straightened his broad shoulders, then crossed and recrossed his long legs. "Besides the lake, what is there for us to see?"

Was the space too tight for him?

Darius smiled. "I'll take you to see the waterwheels first. Next, we'll go to Lake Qarun, then visit Tunis Village."

She tucked loose curls behind her ear, trying to calm herself. "What's so special about Tunis Village?"

"Good question." The guide waved his paper in the air. "In 1962, the famous poet Sayed Hegab with his Swiss wife, Evelynne, came to the village and built a house and a pottery workshop. The locals have been refining the art ever since. Now its pottery products are famous in Egypt."

"Are we going to the pottery workshop?" She kept the conversation going. At least, it distracted her from another grievous soul-searching.

"Of course." Their guide beamed. "You can watch the young artists work and buy their wares."

When nobody raised any more questions, Darius winked at Josh over his shoulder. "Josh, didn't you buy a lamp from the bazaar the other day? Have you found out whether a genie lives inside?"

"Mr. Darius, you must be joking." Josh crossed his arms, snorted, and lightly kicked Darius's seat in front of him. "I'm nine years old. Aladdin and his genie don't exist."

"I'm so sorry. I forgot you're not a little boy." Chuckling, Darius pointed at the parched land. "Look at that. Do you want to hear a joke about the genie and the desert?"

"Sure," Yao chimed in. "Keep us entertained."

"Here it goes." Darius wiggled his brows. "Once upon a time, a businessman from Hong Kong, a lawyer from Japan, and a homeless man from San Francisco got lost in the Sahara Desert. They traveled together and found a lamp."

Josh leaned forward. "Yeah? What happened?"

Darius made a rubbing gesture. "The businessman rubbed it, and a genie popped out. 'What's your wish?' he asked."

Josh tapped the back of Darius's seat. "What did he say?"

Ann-Ann's mouth curled up. The guide and her nephew were a perfect pair for comedy.

Darius pressed his lips together, his expression serious. "The businessman replied, 'I miss the bustling streets in Hong Kong. Please send me home.' Poof! He was back home. The genie turned toward the lawyer. 'What do you want me to do for you?' The lawyer said, 'I miss the cherry blossoms in Tokyo. Please send me home.' The genie waved a hand and whooshed him back home. Then the genie approached the homeless man. 'As you may have guessed, your wish will come true.'"

Darius's voice dropped so low Ann-Ann couldn't hear him.

Josh kicked the front seat again. "Could you please speak louder?"

The guide raised his voice. "The homeless man gestured to the vast and empty desert. 'I have no home, and I'm a bit lonely. I wish you bring my friends back here with me.'"

"Bravo." Yao laughed aloud and clapped. "Truly, bravo. Darius, you'd make an outstanding comedian."

Ann-Ann cracked up. "Such a silly joke." Yet, it lightened her mood. *Lord, thank You for friends and family. Through them, You confirm Your love toward me.*

"Thanks." Darius clenched his fists together into an appreciation pose. "Tomorrow, we will fly to Luxor. Shawn and Margie must come with us unless they want to pay for their hotel room in Cairo." He smirked. "Are they on their honeymoon or what? I once guided a tour with a newlywed couple. After checking into their room, they never stepped out until the day they were ready to fly out."

***

Yao pretended to adjust his seat belt and used the excuse to study the woman on his right. Today, Nana Lee asked him and Ann-Ann to sit together in the last row.

She glanced at him from time to time. Before this trip, she'd avoided him. During the past few days, she no longer turned away when he initiated a conversation. Was she softening toward him?

The scenery outside changed. Instead of dry, parched land, peaceful green fields now lent their soothing palette to the view. Then the van passed through a gate.

"Here we are." Darius grabbed his piece of paper once their driver parked. "Let's go see the waterwheels."

They strolled along a canal to a four-meter-wide black wheel.

Darius pointed at the ancient structure, easily marked as something from antiquity. "For years, this was what we used to carry the water up from the Nile. They disappeared in all of Egypt long ago except here. Faiyum still owns over two hundred of them."

Nana Lee let go of Josh's hand. "Do they still function? How do they operate?"

"Yes, they still work." Darius halted. "Moving water drives the wheel. It lifts water and drops it onto land. Believe it or not, the invention of waterwheels can be traced back to the Ptolemaic times."

Ann-Ann gathered her curly hair as it blew in the breeze. Still, dark wisps teased her cheeks and caught on her full lips. "What kind of material is the wheel made of?"

"Wood coated with a protective black tar."

Nana Lee bopped her head. "Ah, that explains their black appearance."

Yao thought of a movie from years ago. Was it an adventure story? He couldn't remember the details. Yet, a scene etched in his mind. Somewhere in Egypt existed a region full of crocodiles. "Darius, are there crocodiles here?"

Darius widened his eyes. "How do you know? Our ancient literature, *The Book of the Faiyum*, celebrates the crocodile god Sobek and his special relationship with this region."

"Look. Is that a fish?" Josh leaned toward the canal.

Yao shifted one step forward, and his throat seized up as he yelled. "Watch out!"

Too late. The ground slid out from under the boy, and he tumbled into the rapid current.

"Josh!" Both Nana Lee and Ann-Ann screamed, their eyes bulging from their pale faces, but they remained rooted as if stuck in cement.

The boy disappeared. Then his head resurfaced.

Yao dashed forward. His foot pushed off the bank, and he leaped into the canal. For a second, he felt like back in the Pearl River, struggling for survival. The water was warmer. But the current swirled around him, and the weight of his clothes, the high-end sneakers, the custom-made leather belt, and even his precious Patek Philippe watch, all seemed to pull him under.

Stay calm.

Darius's shout reached his ears. "In front of you."

Yao kicked his legs hard to propel himself toward the silhouette of a body. As his hand almost touched his target, the boy flipped.

"Oh no!" the women screeched in unison.

Darius's voice rose again. "To your right."

Heart thudding, Yao scanned around. How did it happen? The kid was now behind him to his right.

He turned and swam against the current, battling the water as it rushed forward.

At last, he seized Josh's shoulders before the boy sank again.

"Hooray!" the three on the shore cheered. "Praise the Lord."

He threw an arm across Josh's chest and let the boy's weight hang upon him as he swam. Then he hefted the boy back onto the bank, scraping his own knees as he scrambled up the muddy slope behind him. Was Josh breathing? Why was he so still? Surely—*surely*—he'd gotten to him in time?

"Jesus, please..." Nana Lee whispered.

Yao dropped beside Josh, placed the child on his back, tilted his head, and lifted the chin. He pinched Josh's nostrils shut and covered his mouth with his to give two rescue breaths.

Ann-Ann's sobbing voice cried out. "Josh's chest moved!"

Good. No need to do chest compressions.

The boy opened his eyes.

Nana Lee bent down to touch Yao's shoulder. "Josh is all right. Praise the Lord."

Whew! Yao released his hold on the boy and exhaled a deep breath. *Thank You, Lord.*

Josh sat up, wiped his wet face, and whimpered. "Great-Nana, I'm sorry. I didn't do it on purpose."

Nana Lee pulled him into her arms, moisture glistening in her eyes. "Of course, you didn't do it on purpose. My baby, it's okay now. Don't cry."

"Well, happy ending. If Mr. Chen didn't jump in, I would." Darius looked Yao up and down. "Believe it or not. This happens all the time, especially with children. That's why I have spare clothes in my van. Maybe they'll fit you."

Ann-Ann scraped a hand through her hair. "How about Josh?"

"Will an adult T-shirt do? At least for now." Darius led them toward the van. "His clothes should dry out before we get to Tunis Village."

As previously planned, they went to Lake Qarun, then visited the pottery workshop in Tunis Village. Despite the exquisite products, nobody was in the mood to buy anything.

Yao stood in the quiet green garden outside the demo room. For years, he hadn't thought of his escape from a thicket near Pearl River in Guangdong to Macau. Yet, this experience triggered a full-blown memory of the night he fled from China.

How many hours did he float with a log in the Pearl River? Such a long time ago. The details faded somewhat. But the sensation of eerie darkness closing over and embracing him remained vivid. He shivered as if hearing anew that the Red Guards had seized his father and five others from a Christian gathering, then beat his pa with a hammer in a denunciation meeting. Pa died on the spot from a strike to his neck. Afterward, the Red Guards searched everywhere for Yao.

He'd had no choice but to become a freedom swimmer and leave China.

"Thank you for rescuing Josh." Ann-Ann's clear, modulated voice roused him from his dismal reverie. "The tabloids said you swim in your Olympic-size swimming pool every day. Now I believe them."

"Don't believe what you read in the tabloids." He scratched his forehead, a feeble attempt to brush away those unpleasant images from his past.

"Darius's T-shirt fits you well." A tiny grin tugged at her mouth. "The pants are a tad short."

Yao looked down at his feet with a heightened awareness of being scrutinized. The tabloids would go crazy if they caught him now. The always-impeccably-dressed Mr. Chen Yao wearing high-water pants.

"Should I take your picture?" She reached into her purse.

"Absolutely not." Odd. His gloomy mood diffused. He smiled back. Oh, for sure, they were identical twins. For a breath, he was back in the Beijing courtyard house, and May-May was standing in front of him.

"Is your Patek Philippe okay?" Ann-Ann ran a hand through her curly mane.

Yao raised his wrist and twisted the watch into view. "Should be fine. It's waterproof."

After peeking toward Nana Lee and Josh, Ann-Ann reached as though to touch him before drawing her hand back. "Do you think Shawn and Margie will find more information today?"

Caught by surprise, he let his arm drop to his side. "Sorry. What did you say?"

"Oh, nothing important." She fussed with her hair again. "Nana asked once more why Shawn and Margie didn't come with us. I didn't know what to say."

He chuckled, the heaviness in his heart evaporating. "Maybe Darius's joke about the honeymooners would have answered your nana's question. Anyhow, tomorrow, they'll go with us to Luxor."

She took one step forward. "I've been wondering about Margie's hypothesis on those expats' terrible fates."

A pleasant jasmine scent drifted into his nostrils. Boy, she smelled so good. Unlike May-May, Ann-Ann always wore makeup. Today, she'd carefully lined her eyes and applied a smoky shadow. Blusher highlighted her cheeks, and the bright-red gloss on her lips would entice any man to get closer and...

Heat rushed into his loins. Huh, Darius's pants were tight, not comfortable at all, especially now. Since returning to God, he'd abstained from sex in all his relationships. Even his current girlfriend had commented that she admired his discipline.

Yet, when he was awake at night, Ann-Ann's gorgeous body and their previous tryst taunted him. They'd sat together on his plush white leather sofa and proceeded from kissing to heavy petting. After she loosened her dress straps, he froze, got up from her, and told her he had herpes. Did he regret not making love to her on that night? If he didn't move away from her, would they be married by now? No. Unlikely. Both of them had too many issues in their lives back then.

"Tomorrow." He swallowed and feigned calmness. "Let's talk to them again tomorrow."

Chapter Eight

The nonstop flight from Cairo to Luxor took less than two hours. While Ann-Ann stood by her nana and waited for their luggage, Josh came over, his eyebrows squished together. She patted his shoulder. "What's the matter?"

He tilted his head to one side and pursed his lips. "Uncle Shawn said God doesn't exist and there's no heaven. Is he right?"

She exchanged a glance with Nana, then stooped to Josh's level. "Tell me what happened."

"Uncle Yao told him I almost drowned yesterday. After Uncle Yao left, Uncle Shawn asked whether I was afraid. I said I wasn't because I'd go to heaven if I died. He laughed and asked me where heaven was. When I answered heaven is where God is, he laughed again and asked me how I know God exists." His expression crumpled anew, and he tugged on an ear. "He said he didn't believe in God and heaven."

Ann-Ann's hands fisted, her fingernails biting into her palms as she straightened to her full height. What right did Shawn Han have to speak such rubbish to a nine-year-old?

Nana drew her and Josh to a corner. "Josh, you answered him well. Heaven is where God is. We'll need to pray for him that he can see and know God."

"Nana Lee." Yao pushed a cart piled high with their suitcases toward them. "The other bags are on Darius's cart. Let's go."

Outside the airport, the daybreak sunshine cast a rosy hue across the morning sky. A different gray van and a new driver awaited them. The first rays of sunlight warmed Ann-Ann's face, and anger loosened its clench on her muscles. Still, either she or Nana had to talk to Shawn about his improper behavior.

Darius helped load all the luggage into the trunk. "We still have a few hours before boarding our riverboat. I'll take you to the Karnak Temple Complex and the Luxor Temple. Both are on the UNESCO World Heritage list."

While walking up to the Luxor Temple, Ann-Ann tilted her head back and fixed her gaze on the tall, four-sided, narrow tapering monument with a pyramid-like shape at the top. "Wow. How did ancient people build such an enormous structure?"

"The obelisk is impressive, isn't it? Eighty feet tall, it has cast a shadow over this land for over three thousand years since they moved it here during the reign of Ramesses II." Darius pointed at it. "A pair used to stand here. We gave the western one to France about a hundred years ago."

"Ah, I read about obelisks in my book." Nana took out her camera and snapped pictures. "Pharaohs tried to honor gods with them and took pride in the number of obelisks they erected."

Shawn also grabbed his camera for a few shots. "What kind of stone is this made of?"

"All obelisks were quarried from pink granite in Aswan. I'll take you to a quarry site once our riverboat stops there. You'll see an unfinished, abandoned obelisk left in the parent rock, likely because of a crack. From studying that, our scholars have concluded workers used hammers or dolerite balls to cut the stone by hand." Darius's mouth crinkled up. "Mr. Han, do you want me to take a picture of you and Ms. Fung?"

Margie peeked at Shawn. The crimson on her tan face deepened. "Sure." She tucked a loose strand of hair behind her ear. "Thank you."

"Okay." Darius received the camera from Shawn. "You two stand closer. Mr. Han, wrap your arm around her waist."

Ann-Ann studied the couple. Both were tall, muscular, and beautiful, quite a remarkable sight. But why was Margie blushing? Ann-Ann shook her head and brushed aside her suspicion. "Darius, you haven't answered my question. How did your ancestors erect such an enormous stone?"

Instead of responding, Darius gestured to her. "Ms. Lee, would you care for a picture with Mr. Chen? You two look awesome together."

As Yao flicked his eyes between his camera and her as if checking her intent, she scuffled back a step, heat flaring through her. "Oh no. I'm more interested in knowing how people set up an obelisk without our modern technology."

"We still haven't figured it out." Darius returned Shawn's camera. "Even just moving them was difficult. A record by Queen Hatshepsut narrated she had her two giant obelisks transported by twenty-seven boats. But she didn't say how they erected the monuments."

"Did it take a long time to quarry such a huge stone?" Yao moved forward to study its foundation. "How did they secure the structure?"

Ann-Ann stole a glimpse of Yao. Was he upset because she didn't want a picture with him?

"Ha, our Queen Hatshepsut said her obelisks were completed in just seven months. Inconceivable, right?" Darius waved his paper in the air. "Our ancestors pinned this to the ground with nothing but its weight. It must be put up at just the right angle and position."

"Incredible and mysterious." Yao smiled at Josh. "Where is your Old Master Q? Let me take a picture of you."

Afterward, Darius guided them through both the Luxor and the Karnak Temples.

Ann-Ann surveyed the temples, pylons, and chapels. Quite an unbelievable sight. Karnak must be the largest religious building ever constructed.

***

Yao sat by the floor-to-ceiling window in their riverboat's dining room and chuffed out a breath. The visit to the two temples justified all the trouble they'd gone through, even the brutal four-o'clock flight.

"May I sit here?" A large shadow appeared across the pristine white fabric of his dual-seat table.

"Shawn?" Yao raised an eyebrow. "Are you here by yourself?

Where is Margie?"

Shawn set his plate down. "She's in our room, napping."

"I suppose Nana Lee and Ann-Ann are also too tired to come for lunch." Yao picked up a piece of beef stewed with onion, carrots, green beans, and an unknown spice. Egyptian secret ingredient? Perhaps.

Shawn cut into his fish fillet. "Where's Josh?"

Wow. The juicy meat melted on the tongue. So tender. "He went to Nana Lee's room. They ordered room service."

Shawn nodded, his expression somber. "Before I came here, Nana Lee cornered me and talked to me for almost thirty minutes about God and Jesus."

Yao stopped chewing and stretched his eyes wide.

"Why do you look surprised?" Shawn pushed green beans around his plate. "My sister warned me Nana Lee would try to make me into a Christian. Susie is right."

"And did she succeed?" Yao swallowed his mouthful of food, warmth creeping into his heart.

"Are you joking? Of course not." Shawn forked a chunk of fish into his mouth. "But something she said puzzled me."

Yao held his breath, waiting.

"If God didn't exist, then why would a whole ethnic group of people for generations claim to be God's chosen people? I couldn't answer her question." Shawn waved his empty hand in the air. "The descendants of the Jews who compiled the Old Testament are still with us today. I acknowledge it's a fact."

Was the Holy Spirit working in Shawn? "So, you believe God exists?"

Shawn huffed. "I don't know. Somehow, I've never pondered the God stuff like how she portrayed it. Have you?"

"Yes," Yao replied without hesitation. *Lord, please give me wisdom.*

"Even if God exists, why do I need to believe in Jesus?" Shawn clattered his utensils as he scooped another bite of fish. "In history, quite a few people claimed to be God." He spoke around a mouthful, then swallowed. "We have so many religions. What's so special about Christianity?"

Yao sucked in a breath. "According to studies, over three hundred prophecies from the Old Testament were fulfilled in Jesus

Christ. I don't think anyone else in history could point to ancient books that prophesied his coming. That alone makes Jesus unique."

Shawn squinted. "How do you know those were not inserted into the Old Testament by Jesus' disciples?"

"Good question." Yao dropped his fork and held his hands together. "Soon, we'll visit the Qumran Caves, the place where a group of shepherds found the Dead Sea Scrolls. The Book of Isaiah, with many prophecies about Jesus Christ, is one of the original seven scrolls discovered there, dating from about one hundred and twenty-five years before the birth of Jesus. It's also the largest and best preserved of all the biblical scrolls, the only one that is almost complete. When one compares those manuscripts with the editions we have now, the difference is negligible, less than one percent."

Shawn paled. "I—"

Margie's tall figure strolled toward them. "Ah, you two are hiding here." She cocked her head. "May I join you?"

Of all the moments for her to show up, she had to come now? If he wanted to speak with Shawn more about the Bible, Yao would need to find another time.

"Sure." He moved to grab an upholstered dining chair for her from an empty table nearby. "Go get your food."

He shook his head when she returned, holding a plate piled high with meat and desserts. "No veggies?"

"On vacation." She rolled her eyes and slid into the chair he'd pilfered. "So, what are you two talking about? You looked rather serious."

Shawn rubbed a hand down his pants. "Yao was asking whether Ann-Ann's diamond pendant did its magic and what information we found."

Why did the big fellow feel uneasy? Okay... Since the guy mustn't want Margie to know his interest in Christianity, Yao had to play along. "Tell me again. What have you discovered?"

"Food here is splendid." Margie picked up an enormous piece of rib and bit into it, then wiped her mouth with a napkin. "Wow, nice. So juicy. Our contact person loved the pendant and showed us photos of the corpse. As I suspected, the upper body went missing, and the remaining body parts were gruesome...."

She took another large bite while describing the details. How could she say those things and keep eating as if discussing the weather? A shiver ran up Yao's spine, and a sickening sensation crept up from his stomach to his throat. The delicious beef lost its appeal.

"We confirmed Margie's hypothesis," Shawn chimed in. "This case is linked to all the others."

"So... what? Have you figured out what's going on?" Yao massaged his neck to calm himself. "Do you think Nathan and Nancy may encounter the same fate? I hope it isn't too late to save our friends."

With her teeth, Margie peeled the last strip of meat from the bone. Then she tossed it aside on a napkin. "Have you heard about human trafficking?"

"Human trafficking?" He moved his hand up through his hair, raking the bristly parts at his nape the wrong way. "Are you referring to smuggling people into a foreign country?"

"Not quite." Shawn shook his head. "That's human smuggling. We're talking about the recruitment, transportation, transfer, and receipt of persons by force, fraud, or coercion."

"Sometimes human smuggling may turn into human trafficking." Margie grabbed another rib. "But they're two different things."

Yao pushed his seat away from the table. "What has this to do with the dancer's death?"

"I suspect she was a victim of human trafficking." This time, Margie used her knife to trim the fat away from the rib.

Darius passed by, holding a plate. "How is lunch? Are you guys enjoying it?"

Shawn raised a thumb.

"Ah, I can see Ms. Margie loves the ribs. Yeah, this riverboat is famous for its barbequed meat." Darius pulled a chair over. "Tomorrow, we have to get up early again. We will tour the Valley of the Kings, then spend a night at Esna. In the remaining days, we'll visit the Temple of Edfu."

Esna? The town where that French writer detailed his sexual encounter with a belly dancer about a hundred years ago? Yao's stomach churned. He stood up. "Excuse me. I need some fresh air."

After leaving the dining room, he walked up to the upper deck with a heaviness on his chest. He couldn't help but dread his friends' fate. Was the triad involved? If yes, what were Shawn and Margie's roles if they were triad members?

"Hi, Yao." Ann-Ann, shaded by a huge umbrella, tucked a magazine beside her on the lounge chair as he walked over. She lifted a glass of ice water, and condensation dripped from it onto the blue top she'd tucked into her crisp white shorts.

"You wouldn't believe what I've just heard." He plopped down on the chair next to hers. The sun shone into his eyes, and he squinted against its atypical brightness in this country. "Margie told me she saw the pictures of the dancer's corpse."

Ice tinkled as she replaced the glass on the table between them. Flicking the condensation from her fingertips, she sat up straighter. "Did the news upset you? Why do you look agitated?"

"It's—" He swallowed hard and relayed his conversation with Margie. "It's the way she said it. While tearing meat away from ribs, she talked about it as if engaged in casual chitchat."

"Hmm." Ann-Ann removed her white-framed sunglasses. "Remember our discussion the other day about her relationship with Shawn?"

"I do. Tall, muscular, speaking four different languages." Yao scraped his chin. "You suspect she isn't Shawn's girlfriend."

She tucked her sunglasses in her hair, using them to pull the curls back from her face. "She blushed when Darius wanted to take a picture of her and Shawn in front of the obelisk."

He shifted his weight and leaned forward. For sure, Ann-Ann was smarter than he was. "You're observant. Come to think of it. They don't behave like a couple. Why did Susie tell me Margie is Shawn's girlfriend?"

She wrinkled her nose and rubbed at the indentation the sunglasses left behind. "Maybe Susie didn't know it for sure. Maybe that's what Shawn told her."

All his previous fondness for Ann-Ann rushed back, and a new feeling emerged. What was it? Admiration? Endearment? Affection? "You said she might be a private investigator. Do you still think so?"

"If she's a private investigator, who hired her to come on this trip and why?" Ann-Ann touched her fingertips together. "Maybe she's something else."

"Ha, Uncle Yao, I found you." Josh emerged from behind the umbrella. "I left my key in the room. Could you please open it for me?"

Yao wet his lips, his stomach tightening. Must the kid always pop up when he was enjoying his time with Ann-Ann?

Josh tugged at his sleeve. "Uncle Yao, let's go."

"Okay." Yao pressed his lips into a thin line and followed Josh down the stairs.

Chapter Nine

Ann-Ann hooked her arm with Nana's and walked out of Tel Aviv's customs area. "I enjoyed the Nile River cruise. Those tombs in the Valley of the Kings were impressive. But as the saying goes, it can be too much of a good thing. After the third one, I became desensitized. Can't wait to see the Holy Land. I hope our next guide will be as good as Darius."

"Ah, the Holy Land. We're finally here." Nana glanced at Josh, then frowned. "Are Shawn and Margie going to run errands here as well?"

"No. They'll join us." Ann-Ann stifled a sigh. Shawn was coming. Would he be argumentative like before? Would his taunts and sneers about the Bible rouse doubts in Josh's young mind?

Nana patted Ann-Ann's arm. "Let's continue to pray for his salvation. The work of the Holy Spirit will soften his heart. I'm sure of it."

A middle-aged fellow stood outside holding a sign welcoming the Lees to the Holy Land.

"He must be our guide." Nana withdrew her hand and stepped up. "Are you Mr. Cohen?"

The man smoothed his russet beard. "Please call me Adam." He directed them toward a minivan parked beyond the sliding door.

"Did you all have an enjoyable flight? Ready for your adventure?" He glanced at his notes. "We'll go to Jaffa and stay the night there."

The midmorning sun cast a glare across the white van's tinted windows, a long shadow reaching toward them on the walkway.

They'd be visiting all the amazing areas described in the Bible!

Ann-Ann nearly clapped to release the emotion rushing through her. Here she was, ready to discover where Jesus Christ and His disciples used to live and tread.

Only a few years ago, she wouldn't even read the Bible. What a long way she'd come. So much grief mingled with joy.

"Jaffa?" Nana's eyes sparkled. "Is it the same as Joppa?"

"Yes." Adam's smile spread out on his tousled beard. "It's the biblical town of Joppa. In Hebrew, it's Yafo, and in Arabic Yafa."

Nana touched her cheek, laughing out a delightful sound. "So, we'll be where the prophet Jonah fled after the Lord told him to go to Nineveh and where Peter saw the heavens open and a great sheet being lowered to the earth."

Adam opened the van's door for Nana. "Absolutely. I'll take you to the very house where Peter saw his vision."

Ann-Ann's chest warmed as she settled into her seat. *Lord, thank You for Nana. If not because of her, I might be still wandering in the wilderness.*

Shawn, sitting behind her, tapped her shoulder. "So, whatever the Bible talked about wasn't just a legend? People can still go see the places nowadays?"

"Yes. I can't wait to visit all the sites I've read about in the Bible." Nana glimpsed past her at Shawn. "Are you interested in learning more about Jonah the Prophet and Peter the Apostle?"

In front of them, Josh cried out, "Great-Nana, I want to hear the stories."

A playful mood getting the best of her, Ann-Ann scrunched her nose to tease her nephew. "You should do it. Haven't you heard about them in your Sunday school class many times?"

"Yes, ma'am." Josh raised a hand to his temple and saluted. "I'll talk about Jonah, and you tell the story about Peter."

The boy sucked in a quick breath. "God told Jonah to warn the people in Nineveh to repent, but he didn't want to do it. He got on a ship, trying to hide from God. The ship ran into a storm, and his shipmates threw him into the water." He stretched his arms wide.

"A fish this big swallowed him. After three days, the fish spit him out. So, he went to Nineveh."

Ann-Ann curled up her lips at his childish tone and gesture. Her effort in teaching the Sunday school wasn't in vain.

"Nice job." Yao patted Josh's arm. "Now, give us more details. Why did Jonah refuse to follow God's command?"

"Because... because..." Josh threw her a pleading glance.

She chuckled. "Think about what happened between Jonah's country and Nineveh during that time."

"Ah, yes." He scrunched his forehead. "There was a war going on between them. Jonah didn't want his enemies in Nineveh to repent. Because if they repented, God would forgive them."

Yao applauded. "Excellent."

"It sounds like a legend to me. Margie, don't you agree?" Shawn's bass rose in volume, mockery souring its sound. "How could a person survive for three days inside a large fish? It's not scientific."

While Margie kept quiet, Ann-Ann bit down on the urge to ask why Shawn always behaved like a juvenile.

"Well, don't pass judgment too soon." Nana twisted backward in her seat to him. "Wait until you hear Peter's story. Ann-Ann?"

Ann-Ann cringed her shoulders, getting ready for more taunts. "Well, if you don't like what Josh said about Jonah, you won't appreciate what I'm about to say."

"Humor me." He crossed his beefy arms over his chest.

Tension stiffening her shoulders, she flitted her gaze at the van's ceiling. "Now, I must first introduce some background information. Peter was a Jew and followed strict Jewish traditions. He wouldn't eat unclean food like pork and wouldn't mingle with Gentiles, the non-Jews."

Shawn's mouth dropped open. Not bad. So far, so good. But she'd get a neck ache if she didn't loosen up.

Ann-Ann shifted against the back of her seat to make space for her legs. "One day in Joppa, the city we're heading to now, at noon Peter went up on the roof to pray and became hungry. He saw heaven open and something like a large sheet being lowered down to earth by its four corners. It contained all kinds of unclean food, like four-footed animals, reptiles, and birds."

She paused on purpose.

Shawn's warm palm rested on her shoulder once more. "Ha, besides pork, Jewish people also don't eat frogs, snakes, and pigeons, all the high-end delicacies we pay lots of money to eat in Hong Kong?"

"That's right." She scooted forward in her seat to dislodge Shawn's hand. "Back to Peter. A voice told him to kill and eat them, and he refused, saying that he'd never eaten anything unclean in his whole life. The voice spoke to him a second time and asked him not to call anything impure if God had made it clean."

"Did he eat them?" Shawn hissed out a breath. "What's the moral of the story?"

At least he showed some interest. She bobbed her head. "What happened next was crucial in the Christian church's history. God used that vision about food to prepare Peter for some Gentile visitors, sent by a centurion of the Roman regiment named Cornelius who lived in Caesarea."

"Ah, Cacsarca," their guide chimed in. "We'll go there tomorrow."

Nana smiled. "I can't wait to visit the ancient city built by Herod the Great with its Roman amphitheater. It's also the place where Apostle Paul spent two years in prison."

Ann-Ann tucked tickly strands of hair behind her ear, her shoulders loosening up. "Without that vision, Peter would never agree to go with the visitors to Caesarea. But he went, and Cornelius and many others there accepted Christ as their personal Savior. That event marked the beginning of a new era for Christianity. For the first time, the Holy Spirit descended on Gentiles."

"Bravo." Yao applauded. "You're such a wonderful storyteller. I'm sure your Sunday school students love you."

She hugged her arms, heat rising to her face. Since when was Yao so generous with his praises? So unlike him.

"My classmates all love Auntie Ann-Ann." Josh's high-pitched voice echoed in the van.

Shawn tapped the back of her seat. "A vision? The Holy Spirit? They all sound like fairy tales. If you can convince me those things still happen today, I may consider putting aside my skepticism."

"The Holy Spirit is still working today." Yao touched his fingertips together. "People still see visions. I read an article about many Muslims with no knowledge of Christianity experiencing dreams and visions of Jesus Christ."

"Those may be rumors." Shawn waved the words away. "You mentioned the Holy Spirit. What is it? How does it work? Give me an example."

Yao cleared his throat. "First, the Holy Spirit is not an *it*. He is one of the three persons in the Triune God."

"The three persons? The Triune God?" Shawn snorted. "You confuse me even more."

"Let's not go into the theology side." Nana turned sideways, then dabbed her glistening forehead with a handkerchief. "The most important work of the Holy Spirit is to let us recognize our sins. I, like most people, think I'm a decent person. But when the Holy Spirit enters my heart, I begin to see all the sins within me."

"It must be a form of autosuggestion."

Nana leaned toward Adam. "Can we turn up the air-conditioning, please?" Then she refocused on Shawn. "Unlike autosuggestion— wherein one taps into his own strength to become more confident or to feel better—the Holy Spirit points out our sins. All Christians share the same experience."

Ann-Ann's toes tingled inside her sneakers, her chest feeling lighter. Nana said it so well. That happened to her. Before her conversion, she'd thought her abortion wasn't a sin and being a tycoon's mistress was a smart, profitable decision. Yet, how could she describe her interaction with the Holy Spirit to Shawn? She might as well try to tell him the flavor of a special drink. Since he'd never tasted it, he wouldn't understand.

The van stopped before a stone structure with an ancient-looking door.

Adam raised a hand. "Sorry to interrupt your interesting conversation, but we've arrived where Peter saw his vision."

***

In the historic Tel Aviv neighborhood, Yao strolled up to the Hotel Nordoy's rooftop. Was it like this when Peter climbed up to the rooftop of Simon the Tanner in Joppa about two thousand years ago?

Unlikely. The stone structure he saw earlier wasn't the original house. Back then, a tanner could only afford a scanty earthen hut at best.

Whatever it was, God showed Peter that salvation would be extended to Gentiles, even ones like him, a guy who used to visit call girls. Yao hung his head. He'd changed, and so had Ann-Ann. Did it matter? With their troubled pasts, maybe they weren't meant to be together.

"Hi, Yao." Margie's husky voice called his attention to the corner on his left.

Three of his travel companions sat together, basking in the late afternoon sunshine. Ann-Ann's rosy cheeks glowed, and her smiling mouth drew his gaze.

He rubbed the back of his neck. "Oh, you're also here."

"Yeah." She pushed her sunglasses onto the top of her hair, loose wisps poking out around them. Her eyes seemed brighter than usual. "Believe it or not, this hotel was built in 1925, the oldest continuously operating hotel in the city. Its rooftop is famous."

Shawn pulled a chair over. "For you. Care for some wine?"

Without waiting for a response, he filled a glass with merlot.

Yao took a sip to moisten his dry throat. The three looked serious. Was Ann-Ann trying to tell Shawn more about the Holy Spirit?

"Dinner won't be ready for another twenty-five minutes." Margie put down her glass. "I must say this place is gorgeous."

A soft breeze teased strands of Ann-Ann's curly mane against the sweep of her cheeks. With delicate fingers, she tucked the locks behind her sunglasses. "Margie was telling me she and Shawn can't do their investigations in Israel. So, they'll be with us the whole time."

"Nice to have a break." Shawn gestured to Margie. "Yao and Ann-Ann are here. Perhaps you ought to talk more about the human trafficking issue."

Ann-Ann arched an eyebrow. "Yeah?"

Yao scratched his chin, his chest tight. "You weren't present when we chitchatted in Egypt."

"What had I said?" Margie squinted. "Ah, yes, the difference between human smuggling and human trafficking." She reached into her purse and retrieved a piece of paper. "Some intriguing statistics I gathered from that library in Cairo. Every year, millions are trafficked worldwide, and a majority of them are women."

Maybe also irritated by the warm breeze? Margie swept her yellow-gold hair away from her face. "Dealing drugs is profitable.

But it pales in comparison with trafficking women. With drugs, you have to grow, cultivate, distill, package, and then smuggle them. With women, you can skip all those troubles, and they can be used by the customers again and again."

Like last time, disgust crept up from Yao's stomach.

Ann-Ann's smile disappeared and her face paled. She rubbed her temple. "Why can't the government do something to help those poor women?"

"Corrupt governments and problematic policies contribute to this problem. They're more severe in some countries than in others." Margie's gaze lingered on her notes. "There are also cultural differences. In India, selling girls may be the only way of survival. In some countries, having sex with a prostitute is a legitimate form of entertainment, like going to the opera or museum."

"Ah, I remember visiting the red-light district in Amsterdam." Oh no. An unfortunate slip of the tongue. Yao didn't intend to reveal that part of his past.

"So, you had sex with a pussy blonde in Amsterdam?" Shawn's mouth contorted into a rigid line, and his eyes narrowed into a sarcastic glare. "And you tell me you're a Christian?"

Yao remained quiet, heat rushing up from his neck to his ears. The painful memory of his wild days hollowed out his heart.

"Shawn, I don't appreciate what you've just said. It's offensive." Ann-Ann raised a finger. "At our age, who doesn't have a bit of history? You aren't a saint yourself. The important thing isn't what you used to do before you became a Christian, but whether you stop once the Holy Spirit tells you those are sins."

Yao stole a glimpse of her, appreciation edging into the hollow spaces of his heart. She looked sincere. But why? Was she no longer mad at him? For sure, they'd both changed since their last date.

"Ha, you mentioned the Holy Spirit again." Shawn swung his body to the side with a scornful twist of his mouth. "I'm almost certain it's Christians' pure imagination. If it exists, why doesn't everybody know about it? Don't you agree, Margie?"

Margie didn't respond but picked up her glass for a generous sip of wine.

Ann-Ann gripped her seat's armrest. "Don't be so confident of yourself. Many facts hide in plain sight. You don't know them unless you use your heart and soul to search for them."

Familiar quick footsteps sounded, and Josh emerged from the staircase. "I've been looking everywhere for you, and you're all here. Dinner is ready."

"Thank you, Josh. Let's go." Yao stood, glad for the distraction.

For sure, Shawn was improving. Susie had mentioned that, whenever she tried to tell her brother about God and Jesus, he made an excuse and took leave. He still sounded obstinate, but at least he showed a willingness to listen.

Shawn rubbed his hands together. "Tonight, the four of us are still going to the club for some fun, right?"

Yeah, what else could they do? Yao didn't want to stay in his room to watch television. Neither did his three travel companions.

Chapter Ten

Ann-Ann followed her three companions into Mash Night, Tel Aviv's most popular clubhouse. With shiny streamers, the disco ball flashed. Colorful lights lit up the dance floor, strobing in a fantastic show.

After the serious talk about Christianity and human trafficking, she could use some downtime. As long as Shawn didn't hurl insults at her or Yao tonight again.

The host guided them to a corner table, and Shawn ordered their drinks. She took a sip, a tangy sensation burning her throat down to her chest. "Wow, what is this? So strong."

Shawn uttered a long name. With the surrounding noise, she failed to catch it. The powerful taste brought back a memory from her wild days. Was she seventeen? She'd attended her best friend's birthday party. Originally, she worried nobody would dance with her because she was the only girl in a simple dress with no jewelry. But her friend's older brother rescued her and danced with her all night. Afterward, she went out with him every day. That was... until she told him she was pregnant.

"Let's dance." Margie sprang from her seat and hauled Shawn away.

Music pounded into Ann-Ann's ears, and a thousand beams beat on her body. To blot out the scenes from her past, she tossed down the remainder of the drink. Then she shut her eyes, opened them again, and blinked.

Yao was staring at her, a gentle smile parting his lips. "Are you all right?"

"I'm fine. Thank you." Heat flushed her cheeks, and she traced a finger along the gold-rimmed edge of her glass. Their make-out years ago flashed across her mind. Despite the push and pull in their relationship, on this trip, she was knowing him anew day by day.

When she raised her gaze again, he was still looking at her. Perhaps he, too, was thinking of their previous time together.

The live band played a waltz, "The Blue Danube."

His eyes sparkled. "Care to dance?"

Before she responded, he twirled her onto the floor and pulled her closer. As his large palm molded her back, a pleasant sensation, like a feather, tickled her inside. Odd. Tonight, her emotions fluctuated, spinning out of control. Maybe it'd been too long since she'd visited a club.

His breath was warm on her ear. "Thank you for coming to my rescue when Shawn taunted me."

"Shawn can be brutal." She dipped her chin, her skin tingling as sweat formed on her neck. "Did you visit the red-light district in Amsterdam? What was it like?"

"I'm embarrassed to admit that, although it was a slip of my tongue, I did go there." He swirled them around in a different direction. "On our last date, you accused me of sleeping around. You're right. Before returning to God's family, I thought a man needed to sow his wild oats. I bought into the mainstream culture and considered sex like food that a man couldn't live without. It's nothing more than a deception from Satan."

She wetted her lips, an expansive sensation rising in her chest. He was sharing some of his innermost thoughts. "Didn't you grow up in a Christian family? You told me you've memorized almost the entire New Testament. What caused you to go your own way?"

"I suppose it was a mixture of different factors." His deep voice vibrated. "After Red Guards murdered my father because of his Christian faith, hatred and anger burned in my heart. I asked God why He couldn't prevent it from happening if He was the Almighty."

As they turned again, the light fell on his face, highlighting the shadows in his eyes. But even as a tenderness crept into her bosom, a warning sounded in her head: *Watch out. Don't make the same mistake. He belongs to someone else.* "I probably would have asked the same question. Did you get an answer? How did you overcome the barrier between you and Him?"

"For many years, I focused on making money to numb my soul." He guided her toward the center of the dance floor. "My goal was to become rich so I could get May-May out of China to Hong Kong. Your mother invited me to church almost every week. I always declined. I told myself, once May-May and I got married, we would go together."

Goosebumps spread over her body. She turned her face up at him. "Nana told me you've loved May-May since you were a child. But she didn't wait for you. She married Jie. Do you think she's betrayed you? Are you angry with her?"

He shook his head. "May-May never said she would wait for me. She always treated me more like her brother. Still, I spiraled into depression after I learned of her marriage to another man. I had money, sex, and all the other things my heart desired, but I was miserable. Then your nana moved to Hong Kong with May-May's family. She came to talk to me and showed me my pa's last letter to her. That was the turning point."

She blinked, taking in a deep breath before exhaling. "What did your pa say in that letter?"

"He asked your nana to tell me not to worry about him, no matter what. He'd already received words from the Lord. 'Be faithful, even to the point of death, and I will give you the crown of life.'" His lips curled. "Your nana then mentioned she'd made an astonishing observation. Those who walk closely with the Lord always learn in advance their journey on earth is coming to an end. Nana Lee told me my pa must be a beloved child of God and wanted me to know it."

She swallowed hard, heat swelling her throat. Yao's father, a beloved child of God, would rather die than give up his faith. Through an unfortunate turn of events, he lost his only blood relative in this world.

The waltz ended, and a burst of applause broke out. The band started another tune, this time a quick-paced song.

People around them lifted both arms into the air, tucked their hands into their underarms, and flapped like a bird. Another pair nearby locked arms, facing opposite directions, and spun.

Shawn and Margie emerged. He shouted, "Let's switch partners."

He pushed Margie toward Yao and pulled Ann-Ann toward him. "It's the chicken dance. Let's hold hands, lean back, then rotate."

She still had questions for Yao. But as the rhythm kicked up, she couldn't speak much.

A couple next to her hopped and waggled.

Shawn bellowed, "Come on. Join in."

The dazzling movements were contagious. For the first time in years, she let go and moved her body with the music in whatever way she felt right. Soon, all thoughts left her brain. She hadn't felt so free and alive in a long time. Shutting her eyes, she let the pounding beats guide her.

A warm hand fell on her bum. She opened her eyes and kneaded her brows together. "Shawn, what are you doing?"

"So sorry. You're bumping in my direction." He gave her a sheepish grin.

The magic spell broke. Her body was sweaty, and her throat felt like closing in. The alcohol in that drink caught up with her. "I need to sit down."

***

Back in their hotel room, Yao slouched on the pearl-white sofa, his focus drifting away from *War and Peace*. He loved Tolstoy's fiction book, though this title seemed more like a historical chronicle than a novel. Maybe someone would take the initiative to capture the painful experiences of the Cultural Revolution in a book?

He stared at the phone. Too late to call Daisy. He'd do it first thing in the morning. His stomach twisted into a hard knot. They'd been dating for almost a year. She, a Christian, attended a different church. They prayed together from time to time. Yet, unlike tonight with Ann-Ann, he and Daisy never talked about something so intense, so personal.

He closed his eyes, rubbed his temples, then whispered into the empty room. "Why did I share those secrets and innermost thoughts?"

Someone knocked.

"Who is that?" He sat up straight.

"Uncle Yao, it's me. I forgot my key."

He opened the door. "You're out late. Were you in your great-nana's room?"

"Yeah." Josh laid Old Master Q on his bed with great care. "I'm so happy you took a picture of me and Old Master Q together with the enormous fish in that town we visited earlier. What's the name again?"

"Jaffa."

"Yes, Jaffa." The boy pulled him to sit on the sofa. "Want to hear a joke I've just learned?"

"Sure." Yao chuckled and drummed his feet against the plush carpet. The more he spent time with Josh, the more he loved him. May-May and her husband did an excellent job of raising their children.

Josh put his fingertips together as if trying to concentrate. "A boy argued with his teacher about whether a whale could swallow a person. His teacher said it was impossible because whales had small throats. The little boy said, 'It's possible because Jonah got swallowed by a whale.' The teacher laughed at him. 'That's not even a true story.' The boy retorted, 'How do you know? When I go to heaven, I'll ask Jonah myself.' The teacher replied, 'What if Jonah didn't go to heaven?' The boy answered, 'Then you ask him.'"

Yao laughed aloud and elbowed Josh. "Such a marvelous story. Where did you find it?"

"From the newspaper in the lobby." Josh's lips crinkled up. "Want to hear another joke?"

"Of course."

"This one is a bit sad." Josh coughed, clearing his throat. "John was telling his friend, 'Isn't the story of Jonah and the whale awesome? Imagine being in the whale's belly for three days.' His friend replied, 'So what? My uncle's been in the belly of an alligator.' John was stunned. 'Really? For how long?' His friend answered, 'It has been three years by now.'"

"Well done." Yao applauded, then jostled the boy into a side hug. "Keep up the good work. I'm certain you'll receive the highest grade from your teacher for your summer project."

"You think so?" Josh thrust out his chest, then pricked up his ears. "Wait. Someone knocked on our door."

The boy rushed to open it. "Auntie Ann-Ann!"

"You left this in our room." She handed him a backpack.

"Oh yes." He let her in. "Thank you. No wonder I laid Old Master Q on my bed."

"Well, it's late. I'd better leave." Her teeth flashed white, her cheeks turning rosy.

At her blush, a spiny sensation zipped through every inch of Yao's body. He stood before knowing what he was doing. "I'll walk you back to your room."

She arched an eyebrow but didn't say anything.

"Go, Uncle Yao." Josh returned to the sofa. "I'm fine being alone here."

Yao accompanied her down the hallway, racking his brain for something to talk about. "Do you have a few minutes? Could we go to the rooftop for a chat?"

She gave him a questioning glance.

Okay. At least she didn't say no. He led the way up the staircase.

Moonlight filtered through the tree branches, casting strange shadows on the yard. As another similar scene flashed across his mind, he gripped the back of a chair and gazed into space. Was he eighteen? He and May-May had sat in their favorite corner of the courtyard house in Beijing. He told her he doubted whether God answered his prayers. When their discussion deepened, he drew her into his arms, but she pulled away.

"Do you want to discuss some issues?"

Ann-Ann's confident tone interrupted his contemplation. He slid into his chair. "Oh yes. I'd like to know what you think about our earlier conversation."

Odd. In front of her, he could just be himself. With Daisy Dong, he had to put on the air, acting out his CEO role. Was it because he'd confessed his past to Ann-Ann?

A smile softened her expression, and the moon's reflection glowed in her dark eyes. "About how you returned to God's family?"

He thrust his hands into his pockets to suppress an urge to hug her. "Did my confessions disturb you?"

"Not at all." She sat and leaned against the headrest. "I appreciate your testimony. I was in the wilderness for a while myself. Your sharing has a special meaning for me. We once were lost but now are found. It's by God's mercy and grace."

Tonight, after their dance at the club, her gentleness had been a calming tonic for his spirit. He couldn't deny he still desired her as much as he used to long for May-May. The difference lay in the experience. Back then, he was a teenager with nothing and didn't know much about love. Now, he had quite a history with women and was a successful business executive.

What was the issue at hand? Didn't he want to focus on Daisy and his dream of elevating his company to the next level?

Ann-Ann stood and yawned. "It's getting late. We'll need to get up early tomorrow morning."

As she approached the stairs, she slowed her steps and waved. The moonlight shone on her, casting a long shadow of her slender body on the gray cement floor. Yao couldn't turn away. The entire world seemed frozen in an instant.

Oh, Lord, what's going on with me? Why does she affect me so?

Chapter Eleven

Yao sat with Josh in the hotel lobby the next afternoon and darted his gaze toward the elevator door from time to time. They were supposed to meet Ann-Ann and Nana Lee with their guide at five p.m. to go to the Sea of Galilee.

"Uncle Yao, I need your help." Josh flipped to a blank page of his notebook. "Could you please help me spell out those places we visited earlier today?"

"Sure." Yao drew back his attention and, at the sight of Josh's serious face, gave out a light chuckle. "The first town is spelled *C, A, E, S, A, R, E, A*, where we saw the ancient theater and the sea."

He waited for the boy to finish writing. "Next, we went to the site where Elijah had a confrontation with the prophets of Baal. It's called Mount Carmel, *C, A, R, M, E, L*. Then we visited the town where Jesus grew up. The spelling is *N, A, Z, A, R, E, T, H*."

"Got them." Josh turned over a page. "And the village we're in now?"

"Capernaum, *C, A, P, E, R, N, A, U, M*. We're by the Sea of Galilee. Well, it's actually a lake, Tiberias." Yao bent forward to check the boy's neat, small handwriting. Quite a smart lad. He had gotten all of them down correctly.

Josh drew a bunch of flowers on the page's remaining space, then closed the notebook. "Great-Nana is super happy we've got to visit all the sites described in the Bible."

His simple statement warmed Yao's heart. He grasped Josh's hand. "Your great-nana is always so cheerful, full of thanks and appreciation for everything."

One colossal figure loomed over them. "What's so special about the shoreline we're going to this afternoon?"

"Ah, that I know, Uncle Shawn." Josh perked up, his eyes bright and his shoulders straight. "I've just learned about it before our trip. Jesus and His disciples came here, and many followed. To keep them from crowding Him, He asked his disciples to have a boat ready for him, and he preached from it to thousands of men and women on the shore."

"How could you believe such a ridiculous story?" Shawn's chin jerked up. "Did they have electricity? Did Jesus use a microphone? How could He give a speech to thousands of people from a tiny boat? Absurd. Laughable."

Tears welled up in Josh's eyes, his lips quivering. He gave Yao a pleading glance.

Yao drew in slow breaths to suppress his irritation over Shawn's harshness. Josh was only nine years old. Yet, Yao also had doubts when he came upon that Bible passage in the Gospel of Mark. He cleared his throat to calm the tightness gripping it. "Josh, Uncle Shawn raised an interesting question. Let's wait until we visit the site. We can ask our guide."

Shawn pivoted his heels to face the elevator door. "Here he is."

Adam walked out, followed by the rest of their group. "Great. Everybody is here. Let's go."

A short drive later, the van dropped them off, and they strolled down a gravel pathway. Odd-shaped boulders lined the bank while water lapped the shore. Decaying leaves piled up on the ground, and birds chirped on the branches.

Adam halted before a cove shaped like a natural amphitheater and gave each of them a handout. "This is an article published in 1976 in *Biblical Archaeologist*."

Yao flipped open the booklet. "Ah, an amateur archaeologist and a sound engineer conducted an experiment to test the location's acoustic effects." *Thank You, Lord. This is what we want to know.*

Josh tugged at his sleeve. "Uncle Yao, can you explain it to me?"

Yao pointed toward the steep slope behind them. "Two researchers observed how bursting balloons ascended the slope and took readings at assorted intervals until one hundred yards out." A glance at others told him everyone, including Shawn, became engrossed with the information. "At the end of the study, they concluded that, because of the cove's bowl-like setting, five to seven thousand people could see and hear Jesus in a boat a short distance away with no problem."

"So, the Bible is correct?" Josh's high-pitched voice echoed in the vast space. "Even without a microphone, people could hear Jesus' words clearly."

Nana Lee chuckled. "Josh, I'm afraid people a hundred yards away heard what you just said."

"Awesome." He cupped both hands around his mouth. "Hello, I'm Josh Ying visiting from Hong Kong."

Shawn trod over and slapped a hand on Josh's shoulder. "My smart little buddy, I'm sorry. You and the Bible are right."

"It's okay." Josh flashed a bright smile. "I'll pray for you so you can know Jesus."

A surge of joy mingled with gentleness washed over Yao. He stooped to hug his kindhearted companion. "I'm so proud of you."

He stood up, shifted one step forward, and came face-to-face with Ann-Ann. As their gazes locked, a gentle grin crooked up a corner of her mouth. With her so close, he could see the dark circles surrounding her irises. For a moment, his surroundings faded to gray. His soul connected with hers in a way beyond comprehension. He didn't understand why but sensed his life wouldn't remain the same.

***

Ann-Ann eyed the fried whole fish on her plate. The combined aroma of ginger, garlic, and lemon made her mouth water. "What's it called again?"

Nana, sitting on her right side, cut open the fish. "Adam said it's the St. Peter's fish, the kind that Peter and his fellow fishermen used to catch from the Sea of Galilee."

"It looks just like tilapia in Hong Kong's wet market." Yao, on Nana's other side, leaned over to talk to her.

Heat crept up to Ann-Ann's face. Lately, he seemed to grab every opportunity to interact with her. When they locked eyes an hour ago on the lakeshore, her heart had trilled like a high key on the piano reverberating within her. Her assumptions about Yao seemed wrong. Maybe there was more to him than a self-made man about to become engaged to a wealthy socialite.

"I agree." Nana pulled apart her fish, then tilted her face toward Shawn. "What do you think about the acoustic study in the handout today?"

"The Bible may have its merits." Shawn took a sip of Sauvignon Blanc. "Boy, this wine is excellent for our fish."

Yao glanced at Ann-Ann. "I thought most Jews are against Christianity. I was surprised Adam took us there to show us that the Bible's description was accurate."

He was paying her attention again. Something stirred in her core, brushing against her rib cage. What was it? Unease? Possibly tenderness? Or...? Scared by the unidentifiable emotions, she ducked her head.

Ann-Ann, you're thirty. You haven't many years to waste on a man who belongs to someone else.

Nana scooped a spoonful of rice. "He also told us about the Sea of Galilee's ever-changing condition. Because of its low-lying position and its surrounding hills, the sea is prone to sudden violent storms. The writings in the New Testament about Jesus calming the storm are as accurate as they could be."

"Adam mentioned Jesus' walking on the water." Shawn put down his wineglass. "Do you guys really believe that? How could a man walk on the water?"

"Hmm." Nana stopped her spoon's movement. "You don't believe in miracles at all, right? Before, you thought the stories about Jonah and Peter were legends."

Shawn squinted. "In this modern age, who would believe in supernatural things?"

"A lot of us do." Nana stared into his eyes. "The difference lies in whether you believe in God. If the Almighty God exists, then, of course, He can make miracles happen. We discussed God's existence the other day. I hope you've thought more about my question for you. If God doesn't exist, then why would a whole ethnic group for generations claim to be God's chosen people?"

"But—"

Margie coughed and nudged him. "Your fish is getting cold. Fried food tastes better when it's still hot."

"Ann-Ann, you're quiet tonight." Yao tipped his head at her. "What do you think about Adam? Why did he take us to the shore?"

Heat rushed back to her cheeks. She tucked her hair behind her ears before speaking. "Could he be a Messianic Jew?"

Josh, on her left side, touched her arm, his voice muffled. "What's a Messianic Jew?"

She pointed at her mouth and didn't reply.

Her nephew swallowed. "Oops. Sorry. I forgot. I shouldn't talk with food in my mouth."

She ruffled his short hair, her chest welling. Josh was such a well-behaved child. "A Messianic Jew is a Jewish person who believes in Jesus Christ as the Messiah and his personal Savior."

Nana tilted her head to one side. "It's quite difficult to lead a Jew to Christ. That's why we haven't met too many Messianic Jews."

"Jesus and all his early disciples were Jews." Yao's skin wrinkled around his forehead as he frowned. "My friends often ask me why so few Jews are Christians."

Nana flattened her palm on the silver tablecloth. "In early church history, Christians suffered most from their fellow Jews. When a Jew accepted Jesus as his Savior, the Jewish community and even their families considered him no longer Jewish."

Ann-Ann fumbled with her glass of wine. When Nana spoke, were Yao's eyes on Nana or her? Why did she become sensitive to his attention?

"Most Jewish people are taught that Jesus couldn't be the Messiah because He didn't fulfill the job requirements." Yao waved, late afternoon sunlight glinting on his Patek Philippe watch. "God called Abraham from the beginning with one clear goal. In the future, all nations and people would receive God's blessings through Abraham's one offspring, the Messiah. But because of intense persecution in history, Jews gradually developed different thinking. This Messiah is only for them. He has to lead them out of suffering."

"True." Nana inclined her head. "That was why when Jesus first started his ministry, many jews followed Him. Those same people later demanded Pilate crucify Him when Jesus refused to be their king."

Shawn pushed against the table and stood. "I'm done with dinner and also with all the religious talk. Good night, everyone."

"Wait." Josh swung his arm out. "Before you go, do you want to hear a joke about fishing?"

Shawn's eyebrows flicked up.

"Here it is." Josh sucked in a quick breath. "Dad and Jonny are searching in the yard for worms to use as bait. They find many different insects, but nothing is suitable. Then Jonny holds up a long dangling thing. 'I found some bait.' Dad took a look. 'Sorry, Jonny. We can't use that. It isn't an earthworm.' Little Jonny scratched his head. 'Well, if it's not from Earth, what planet does it come from?'"

Shawn laughed aloud, his forehead smoothing out again. "Kiddo, you're such a funny child. Where did you find all your jokes?"

A smile overtook Yao's face. "Did you find it in the newspaper like your last ones?"

"Yeah." Josh bobbed his head. "Uncle Shawn, I've been praying for you. I hope you can pray to Jesus yourself. He will answer all your questions if you ask Him."

Shawn rolled his eyes but kept quiet.

Ann-Ann laughed, with moisture gathering behind her eyelids. What a blessing to have a child like Josh by her side. A gentle soul, funny, kind, considerate, and forgiving.

Even though she could never bear children, her nephews and niece were so dear and lovable, as if they grew out of her own body. Maybe because she and their mother were identical twins?

Chapter Twelve

Ann-Ann yawned and followed her friends out of the minivan. Today, Adam would take them to climb Mount Arbel, the most iconic viewpoint over the Sea of Galilee.

She strolled along the narrow gravel pathway, suppressed another yawn, then blinked. Last night, she'd tossed and turned after her dream. The baby visited her again. One moment her profile was indistinct. The next instant, she morphed into Audrey, then grew up like Josh.

Josh tugged at her sleeve, blunting her contemplation. "Auntie Ann-Ann," he whispered, "could I ask Adam whether he is a Messianic Jew?"

Before she said anything, Adam halted at the bottom of the hill. "The hike may not suit everyone." He glanced at Nana and Josh. "Some sections are steep and exposed."

Nana ran her fingers over her silk pants. "I shouldn't do it. You young people go ahead."

Josh put down his backpack. "Great-Nana, I'll keep you company. Old Master Q can't climb either."

"Okay, no problem." Adam clapped. "For those of you who want to do it, please follow the markers and climb steadily until reaching a place with a black sign. At the junction, take a quick detour to visit the Arbel fortress built inside the rock. On your way down, make sure to visit the ancient synagogue and hike down the wadi under the cliffs."

"Let's go." Margie waved. Athletic, she moved with ease toward the hill.

Shawn trailed her and bellowed, "We'll see you at the top."

Never one to enjoy athletic activities, Ann-Ann shaded her eyes and surveyed the landscape.

"Are you coming?" Yao took a step toward her.

She lowered her arm and smirked. "I'm trying to decide if *any* view can justify the sweat and exhaustion."

"You and I, we always analyze things as if making a business deal. The path is safe and not difficult." Yao patted his knee. "Even though I walk with a slight limp, I'll give it a try. Come. Let's do it together."

Shocked by how he'd read her mind, she glanced at Nana. Then, at her nana's encouraging nod, Ann-Ann gave Josh her purse. "I'll leave this with you."

"The hike will take you a few hours." Adam handed over two water bottles. "I'll drive Mrs. Lee and Josh to other sites around the lake and come back to pick up you guys."

Ann-Ann followed Yao toward the trail. The road wound uphill and became steep. After twenty minutes, she broke a sweat.

"Need to take a break?" He stopped and hovered over her, his breath hot on her cheek. Sandwiched between him and an enormous boulder, she couldn't move and swallowed hard.

He unscrewed the water bottle and took a sip. "Nice."

She tried to do the same, but her fingers failed her.

"Let me." He opened it with ease.

The summer breeze must have shifted, sweeping a familiar smell into her nostrils. Likely from his aftershave. As he gave the bottle back to her, their gazes met. The lakeshore moment of yesterday rushed back. Unable to look away, she inhaled his woody, spicy scent.

His hand trembled, and the water bottle fell to the ground. "Oh, I'm so sorry." He bent to pick it up, his hair brushing against her bare legs.

Her skin tingled. She shouldn't have worn shorts. But with the weather so hot, all four of them were clad in shorts today.

He surveyed the bottle, then furrowed his thick brows. "Yours is almost empty. Have mine."

The fallout from his look touched a sensitive part in her heart, a feeling she hadn't experienced before. Something warm and sweet and unidentifiable.

"It's okay." She forced calmness into her tone. "I'm not thirsty yet. Maybe at our next stop."

An unnerving silence lurked as they strolled through the flat level, heading to the next climb. When she stepped on a sharp stone, her feet slid out from under her. Yao's large hand caught her forearm, and they toppled together against a vertical mass of rock, her body leaning into his.

Their gazes tangled again. His so dark and unreadable...

She tried to wiggle her body away, but he didn't let go.

"Ann-Ann." His whisper echoed in the space, tenderness softening his expression.

No. He belonged to someone else. She was no longer twenty-one and couldn't afford to make the same mistake.

She broke their eye contact and freed herself, shattering the magical moment. "We'd better hurry. Shawn and Margie are waiting for us at the top."

Yeah, it was better this way, keeping a safe distance from him.

They trudged to a clearing. The sun was high in the sky, nowhere near its base of disappearance.

From the top of the cliff, a joint view of both the sky and the Sea of Galilee spread before her. The ever-changing glitters of water reflected the gigantic rocks. "It's gorgeous. Are we at the top yet? No, I don't think so."

"Did you hear the birds chirping in the nearby bushes?" Yao took out his camera to snap a few shots. "Do you want a picture?"

The wind grew stronger than down below, whipping her curls across her face. She brushed the hair away and shook her head. "Let's go to the top."

As she ascended, Shawn's and Margie's tall profiles came into view. Her chest swelled. "Hurray, we've reached the top."

"Ha. What took you two so long?" Shawn waved. "Nice view here. Let's take a picture together."

Ann-Ann hesitated, but Margie had already set up her tripod.

Oh, what was the harm? A group picture didn't mean anything.

"Let the ladies stand in the middle." Shawn directed Yao to Ann-Ann's right side while he wrapped his arm around Margie's waist.

As the shuttle clicked and the sunshine beamed into her eyes, the moment etched into Ann-Ann's mind. Yes, she would treasure this hike in her heart.

"On our way up, Margie was still talking about that belly dancer in Cairo." Shawn helped Margie put the tripod away. "We're thinking maybe we can do something in Jerusalem."

Yao gave him a questioning glance. "What do you mean?"

"There's a business side to human trafficking." Margie shoved the folded-up camera stand into her backpack. "Although Israel's government exerts tight control over many crimes, we wonder whether their banking system has leaks and loopholes."

Exhausted, Ann-Ann plopped onto a smooth rock and buried her fingers in her hair. "What kinds of leaks and loopholes?"

Margie sat by her side. "Certain hallmarks exist in accounts used by human trafficking groups. For example, multiple accounts are established for different businesses or persons with the same signatory powers on each account. In some cases, the accounts show frequent outbound wire transfers to countries active in human trafficking, inconsistent with the business's nature."

"How are you going to find out?" Yao sat on Ann-Ann's other side, sandwiching her in between. "Can you walk into a bank and request to review their clients' accounts?"

Shawn squatted before them. "Well, it's worth a try. We don't have much to do in Jerusalem."

Yao's eyes opened wide. "Not much to do in Jerusalem? Are you kidding me? There is so much to do and see there."

"Whatever." Shawn stood and shrugged. "Enough rest? Let's go down. Adam said we'll go take a boat ride on the Sea of Galilee, then drive to the Jordan River at Yardenit, right?"

Ann-Ann yawned again. An afternoon nap on the minivan to the Jordan River baptism site would do her a lot of good.

***

Back at the hotel room, Yao shaved, then smoothed back his hair. Still pondering whether to go down to the bar in the lobby for a drink, he dropped onto the sofa next to Josh.

Josh finished his writing. "I asked Adam whether he's a Messianic Jew, and he said yes." He drew a bunch of lilies across the bottom of his page. "Uncle Yao, with so many sites we've visited today, which one do you like most?"

"The hike up to the top of Mount Arbel." Oops. Maybe he shouldn't have said that since Josh didn't get to go.

"Yeah?" The boy closed his small notebook and tucked it into his pocket. "What's so special about your hike?"

"We—" Yao shook his head. He couldn't tell a nine-year-old his special moment with Ann-Ann. His lips tilted up at the thought of her jasmine-scented body pressing against his when they fell together. But then she'd broken the moment and hurried away. Why? "Well, the scenery was gorgeous. How about you? Where is your favorite site?"

"The Jordan River." Josh bent to retrieve Old Master Q from his backpack for a close survey. "Awesome. I had nice pictures taken with him there." He returned the paper man to his storage. "But I don't understand what Uncle Adam said about the dispute between Jordan and Israel. Could you explain it?"

"Oh, that." Yao shifted, leaning further into the sofa. "Did your auntie Ann-Ann teach you about Jesus' baptism?"

"Yes." Josh stood and sat back down, sitting on his left foot to face Yao. "The baptism took place in Bethany, right?"

"For centuries, Bethany, located north of the Dead Sea and east of Jericho, was important for pilgrims. People set up monasteries and other religious structures there." Yao squeezed his hands together. "Do you know the Six-Day War?"

"I'm thirsty." Josh shifted to the coffee table. "What about the war?"

Yao's throat itched, and he followed Josh to pour a cup of water. "Israel fought with a coalition of Arab states, mainly Egypt, Syria, and Jordan. Israel won the war and occupied the west margin of the Jordan River, including the area opposite Bethany in Jordan. Then the Israeli government established Yardenit this year as another baptism site."

"Wow. That sounded complicated." Josh pushed his cup away. "I'm going to see my great-nana. She promised to tell me a story. Do you want to come with me?"

Maybe he could ask Ann-Ann to join him for a drink? Yao's legs seemed to have their own will to propel him out of the door with Josh and into the other room down the hallway.

"You're here." Nana Lee came forward to hug Josh.

Ann-Ann hid in the sofa's corner and flashed a smile.

Yao took a step forward. "Are you taking a nap? Am I interrupting?"

She shook her head, her lips still curling up.

Nana Lee gestured for him to sit by the coffee table. "Ann-Ann and I were talking about how much this trip has helped us better understand the biblical settings."

"Yes?" He couldn't take his gaze away from Ann-Ann. "What did you tell your nana?"

"Oh, chapter eight in Luke mentions that quite a few women who were with Jesus and His disciples helped to support them out of their own means." Ann-Ann straightened up. "Before, I always wondered how those women traveled with the Lord and where they stayed at night."

"And?" He went to sit by her, giving in to the magnetic pull.

She lowered her lashes and remained quiet.

Nana Lee chuckled. "Now that we've seen how small this region by the Sea of Galilee is, it becomes evident that they probably all went home at the end of the day. It would take them less than thirty minutes to walk home from where Jesus was."

"Ah, it makes sense." He tapped his fingers against his knee, and a warmth tingled in his chest as Ann-Ann peeked at him from time to time. "May I call it a form of physical theology? Knowing the geography of the Holy Land for sure helps me better appreciate the Bible."

Josh pulled Nana Lee to sit down together. "Great-Nana, are you ready to tell me your story now?"

"Hmm." She shifted her gaze to Ann-Ann. "Why don't you two go for a walk while Josh and I enjoy our daily story time?"

Nana Lee probably sensed something. Maybe she thought he and Ann-Ann could get back together. Yao stood and stretched a palm toward Ann-Ann. "Will you come?"

She didn't take his hand but pushed herself out of the plush sofa.

He stifled a huff and guided them into the lobby. "Want to go to the bar?"

"Not tonight." She pointed at the leather armchairs near a small library, complete with writing tables and antique lamps. "How about there?"

He could take a drink or two, but having the chance to sit together with her in a cozy nook tickled his heart.

They took their seats in silence.

She raised a finger, breaking the tranquility. "I want to ask you something."

He leaned forward, searching her face in the ambient lighting for a clue to her true intention. "Yes?"

The light caught the loops of her curls as she tilted her head. "What do you think about our earlier conversation with Margie and Shawn?"

"Their plan to crack the leaks and loopholes of Jerusalem's banks?" He shifted his body, crossing and uncrossing his legs.

She lowered her finger and traced the paisley brocade on her armrest. "You said it well. They can't walk into a bank and request to review their clients' accounts, unless..."

He rubbed at a dull throb in his temples. Was this why she'd come along? Wasn't there a spark of interest in her about him? What did he expect? "Unless what?"

"I was thinking... Maybe Margie isn't a private investigator. She's something much more."

At her serious expression, a pleasant sensation crept up his chest. How could he focus on what she was trying to say? "Yeah?"

"Suppose..." Her touch glided along the fabric's swirls and whorls, and his naughty mind couldn't help remembering what her caress felt like. "What if Margie has the authority or is affiliated with someone who can request a bank disclose its cross-border activities?"

Whoa. He sat up straighter. As a finance major, Ann-Ann knew the banking system well. No wonder this piqued her interest. "So, what is Margie if she has so much power?"

"I don't know." She yawned and stood up. "Nana is probably done with her storytelling. I'd better get back. I didn't sleep well last night. Did Josh bring his key? If not, you ought to go back to your room too."

Chapter Thirteen

The seat belt pinched Ann-Ann's throat. Boy, it hurt.

"Auntie Ann-Ann, are we going to Jericho now?" Josh tugged at her sleeve.

Today, Nana sat with Yao and let her sit with Josh in the first row.

"Yeah." She readjusted the seat belt to make herself more comfortable and smoothed her polka-dot dress beneath it. "Why do you ask?"

"Ha, I found a joke in the newspaper this morning." He bent to search the backpack for his notebook. "It's a rewrite of the robber's story you taught us during Sunday school."

She rubbed her neck where the belt had scratched.

Josh flipped his notebook to a page, skimmed it, then tucked it away and faced her. "A man was going down from Jerusalem to Jericho, and a robber with a gun attacked him. He handed over his money and asked the robber to shoot a few bullets into his hat so he could tell his wife why he had lost his money. He then asked, 'My wife always thinks I'm a coward. Please shoot a few bullets in my coat to make it look like I fought you hard.' The robber did, then said, 'That's it. I'm out of bullets.' The man seized the robber's collar. 'Now give me back my wallet and also your money before I beat you black and blue and leave you to die by the road. Nowadays, no good Samaritans will pass this road to save you.'"

Her lips curled up. "That's such a clever twist on the good Samaritan parable."

Yao clapped. "Josh, you did it again. This joke will tickle your teacher and classmates to laugh till their tears fall." He tapped her nephew's shoulder from behind. "I'm curious. What story did your great-nana tell you last night?"

Josh glanced back at him. "The Jericho battles."

"Ah, nice," Adam, in the front seat, chimed in. "I planned to give you some background about the site we're heading to. Maybe Josh can tell us now?"

Nana waved at the boy. "Why don't you tell us? Start with Rahab."

"Rahab, the prostitute?" Josh sucked in a breath. "Well, the Israelites were ready to enter their promised land. Their leader, Joshua, sent two men to spy on Jericho. The information leaked, and the king of Jericho wanted to kill them. A prostitute, Rahab, hid them inside her house and saved them."

"Bravo." Yao applauded again. "A well-done recap. In Jesus' genealogy, two women stood out. Do you know who they are?"

Josh raised a hand. "One of them must be Rahab. The other—" He peeked at Ann-Ann.

Giddiness rising in Ann-Ann, she grasped Josh's palm and, using her finger, wrote the letters *T-A-M-A-R*.

"No cheating." Yao's voice hinted at a teasing tone.

His warm grip fell on her shoulder. She turned, and her hair slid across her shoulder. Yao's gaze locked with hers. Shudders of elation pulsed through her veins as his fingers lingered. What was going on with them?

"A prostitute in Jesus' genealogy?" Shawn's bass boomed from the last row. "Doesn't that sound hideous? Why would the Bible record such a thing?"

Because the Bible stood truthful to historical events. Yao's hand withdrew, and she couldn't find her tongue to say it out loud.

Nana's gentle voice lilted through the air. "The Bible never shies away from the truth. Besides Rahab, Tamar, another woman mentioned in Jesus' genealogy, also had a troubled past. I believe the troubling backstories of these two women illustrate God's mercy for everyone. Nobody is too sinful to be loved by God."

Two women with troubled pasts became Jesus' ancestors, and their names left a mark on human history. *Oh, Lord, thank You for Your mercy and grace. You've wiped clean my shameful past with Your redemptive work.*

Although Ann-Ann sat two rows ahead of Shawn, she heard him murmur under his breath. "Nobody is too sinful to be loved by God?"

Lord, I pray for Shawn's salvation. Your grace is sufficient even for a triad member.

Josh wiggled in his seat. "Do you still want to hear the rest of Jericho's story?"

Adam raised his piece of paper. "We're almost there. Why don't I do it when we're at the site?"

The van parked. Ann-Ann exited, and her gaze lifted toward the azure sky dotted with cotton-candy clouds. As her left foot tripped over a rock, she wobbled on her sandals.

Before she fell, a muscular arm caught her and helped her back to her feet. Yao stared into her eyes. "Are you all right?"

She nodded, heat creeping to her cheeks, and he kept his hand resting on her waist. With him standing so close, his breath tickled her ear. A thrill surged through her body, but...

Watch out, Ann-Ann Lee. Don't spoil this vacation with something you'll regret.

She drew back, put on her sunglasses, and trod to stand by Nana and Josh.

***

Why did Ann-Ann pull away? Had he set off the alarm inside her again?

"Ha, I saw how you and Ann-Ann Lee locked eyes." Shawn patted his shoulder. "Aren't you dating Daisy Dong? Have you changed your mind? I've only seen Daisy's pictures in the newspaper. No doubt Ann-Ann is more beautiful."

Yao tilted his head up. Was beauty the only determining factor between men and women? "Beauty is in the eyes of the beholder."

Shawn chuckled. "Don't get defensive. I just want to make sure I'm not competing with a friend for Ann-Ann's affection."

"Ann-Ann only dates Christians." Yao pressed his lips tight.

Shawn waved a finger in Yao's face, then sang out merrily. "How do you know I won't become a Christian? Nobody was born a Christian, right?"

Nearby, Margie dropped her camera into her purse.

Her movement distracted Yao. "Let me ask you something. Is Margie truly your girlfriend? Won't she get jealous if you pay attention to another woman?"

"Of course, Shawn is my boyfriend." Margie came over and hooked Shawn's arm with hers. "Why—"

Adam's clapping echoed around them. "Hello, everyone. The Jericho war was perhaps the most unusual battle ever won in human history. The Israelites merely marched around it and sounded trumpets, and Jericho's walls fell." He glanced at Shawn. "The skeptics may say the Jericho event had never happened."

Margie pulled Shawn forward, and Yao trailed them toward the ruin. Yeah, he'd been dating Daisy with an eye toward marriage. How had Ann-Ann affected him so much in less than two weeks since their private tour started?

Which one did he favor? Would Ann-Ann desire him?

At Mash Night in Tel Aviv, he'd revealed his innermost self to her, and she'd responded with concern and kindness. Later that night, he'd sought her out to go to the hotel's rooftop, and she'd mentioned her own wilderness experience. When he tried to delve deeper, she excused herself.

Did she know he never batted an eye at her tempestuous past? Even her living together with JT Poon, one of his business friends, didn't bother him. All those were in the past. After her return to God, she'd changed her way of living.

Adam continued his explanation, rousing him out of his contemplation. "The meticulous work of Kenyon, an archaeologist, showed that Jericho was heavily fortified and had been burned by fire. A great earthen rampart surrounded the city with a stone retaining wall, about twelve to fifteen feet high, at its base. On top of that was a mud-brick wall, six feet thick and about twenty to twenty-six feet high. The Israelites couldn't possibly penetrate Jericho's bastion."

The guide pointed at a heap of stones. "If they besieged and attacked Jericho, the wall should plunge toward the city. But archaeology found the wall simply collapsed."

"Where did Rahab live?" Ann-Ann circled her fingers around her Cartier watch. "According to the Bible, she lived in a place on the wall. Did her house collapse?"

Her clear, modulated tone plucked a string from Yao's heart. Did she think of the old scar on her wrist, the constant reminder of her suicide attempt when she'd gotten pregnant in her teens? He almost reached a comforting hand to her shoulder but dared not. His gaze fell on her, so fragile in her white dress with blue polka dots and matching blue peep-toed sandals on her dainty feet. Perhaps he needed to find out whether Ann-Ann still cared for him. *Oh, Lord, please give me wisdom.*

"Glad you asked. Evidence from excavations shows some people lived on the embankment between the upper and lower city walls." Adam scanned his notes. "The German excavation which took place between 1907 and 1909 found a stretch of the lower city wall on the north didn't fall. Rahab's house was likely located there. It makes sense since the spies could have escaped and crossed a short distance to reach the hills of the Judean wilderness."

Shawn eyed the ruins. "Even if the wall collapsed, how could the Israelites scale such a tall pile of rubble?"

"Another good question." Adam's eyes sparkled. "Excavations have shown the walls collapsed in such a way as to form a ramp against the retaining wall. The Israelites then climbed up over it into the city. Archaeology discoveries also verified a record in the Bible that the Israelites burned the entire city and everything in it."

Nana Lee's mellow alto flowed in the air. "Ah, I remember another interesting antidote from the book I've read. Archaeologists found storage jars full of charred grain here. Grain was valuable at that time, and the conquerors would have plundered it. Why was charred grain left in Jericho? The Bible tells us Joshua had commanded the Israelites not to take anything because the city and its contents were to be devoted to the Lord."

"Yes, everything fits." Ann-Ann slid her sunglasses from her nose onto her head.

Her voice brought a tingle to his chest again. Perhaps he'd ask her out to dinner once they reached the Dead Sea. She might turn him down again. If that happened, he could continue his courtship with Daisy, right?

Shawn's bass boomed over the area. "What caused Jericho's wall to come down?"

"Wow. You guys asked a lot of outstanding questions." Fingering through his beard, Adam inclined his head. "Several theories exist. Archaeologists found evidence of earthquake activity. It was still a miracle since an earthquake happened at precisely the right moment and in such a way as to protect Rahab's house. The Bible says, 'By faith, the walls of Jericho fell after the people had marched around them for seven days.'"

"Jericho is a wonderful spiritual lesson for us." Nana Lee grasped Josh's hand but glanced at Yao. "We may face enormous *walls* that look impossible to break down. If we trust in God and follow His commandments, He will perform great and awesome deeds for us."

Yao straightened his shoulders at the hint of her words. Sure. He'd at least try approaching Ann-Ann.

Adam clapped. "Our next stop is the Dead Sea, considered the world's most ancient spa. Modern science told us it's one of the saltiest bodies of water in the world, about nine times saltier than regular ocean water."

"I can't wait to soak in it, the highlight of this trip," Margie muttered under her breath.

Shawn chuckled. "I've heard nobody will sink in that water. I'll see whether I can go under."

Adam raised a finger. "Watch out for sores and cuts on your body. The water is corrosive and can cause a burning sensation. Try to keep your head above the water when you float."

Oops, there went Shawn's chance to descend into the water.

"Uncle Adam." Josh leaned forward. "Is there fish in the Dead Sea?"

"Normal marine life can't live there. The name of the Dead Sea in Hebrew is Yam ha Maved, which literally means Killer Sea." Adam waved his piece of paper. "Any fish that strays into its waters encounters instant death."

"Oh, that's why it's called the Dead Sea," Josh whispered to Yao. "I was wondering who killed the sea."

Yao patted the boy's head, then shifted to Ann-Ann's side, standing so close their arms almost brushed. What would she do if he clasped her hand? "I heard our hotel by the Dead Sea has an excellent restaurant. Should we have dinner together?"

At his low voice, her eyes stretched wide, and crimson crept up from her neck to her ears. She whispered back, "Just the two of us?"

"Would it be okay?" He fixed his gaze on the alluring rosy color on her cheeks and put his hands in his pockets to suppress an urge to hold her.

She shook her head, hid her eyes behind her sunglasses again, and strolled away.

The heaviness in Yao's chest intensified, and his shoulders slumped.

Chapter Fourteen

Inside her room at the Hod Hamidbar Hotel, Ann-Ann wagged a finger at Nana in her one-piece swimsuit. "I didn't know you can swim. When did you learn it?"

"In college. Long ago." Nana adjusted the straps with one hand. "They said it's like riding a bicycle. Once you learn it, you'll never forget it."

Someone knocked. Ann-Ann opened the door, and Josh, wearing green swim trunks, rushed in. "Are you all ready to go?" He clapped and bounced from foot to foot. "I can't wait. Let's go."

Nana patted Ann-Ann, knocking the shoulder padding on her polka-dot dress askew. "Try not to miss this once-in-a-lifetime opportunity. You may never come here again."

"Living in Hong Kong with its surrounding water, I don't know why I never learned to swim. Is it true nobody can sink in the Dead Sea?" A shiver crept up her spine, and she stifled a sigh. "Why don't you and Josh go first? I'll think about it and catch up later."

After her loved ones left, she stood in the empty room and hugged her arms around herself. In the business world, it was often said you either "sink or swim". But fear of drowning had no place in this situation. Everyone said she wouldn't sink. Maybe she should at least go to the seaside.

She slipped on her newly bought one-piece black swimwear and fiddled with the straps, remembering a scanty evening dress she wore so long ago. She'd easily slipped off the straps before Yao accused her of not being a Christian. He'd been right, of course, though his words infuriated her then.

Why did he ask to dine with her alone? She shook her head. It wasn't prudent while he was still in a relationship with Daisy Dong, right?

Yet, during the past days, she'd connected with Yao in a way she never did with anyone else, not even when she was living with JT. She'd shared her inner thoughts with JT, but JT had never revealed his. And Yao told her about his intimate personal struggles.

Outside the window, the Dead Sea's turquoise water shimmered under the late afternoon sun, luring her to join the other floaters.

Why not? Nana was right. She might never come to this area again.

Ann-Ann grabbed her sunglasses and stepped out to the hotel's sea-view sun terrace with a salted-water swimming pool. Margie, in a red bikini with a scarf tied around her waist like a sarong, sat next to Shawn on a sun bed by the pool. Nana and Josh were nowhere to be seen.

Shawn, with a cocktail in his hand, said something, and Margie giggled. Seeing Ann-Ann, Margie waggled her fingers, beckoning her closer. "We were just talking about you and your nana."

"Were you?" Ann-Ann adjusted her sunglasses and took the seat next to Margie. "Why?"

"The other day your nana, while viewing the sceneries of Lake Galilee, praised God for His wonderful creation." Margie's lips twisted up. "Shawn was offended. He said he believed in evolution. I urged him to keep an open mind."

Behind the shades, Ann-Ann stretched her eyes wide. Was Margie joking, or was she serious? She'd assumed Margie was an atheist like Shawn. Maybe she'd erred.

Shawn put his glass on the side table. "Do you Christians truly believe God created humans?"

"At least I do." Ann-Ann took off her sunglasses. When the afternoon sunshine beamed into her eyes, she put them back on.

"How about dinosaurs and fossils?" Shawn sneered. "How do you Christians explain those facts?"

Lord, please give me wisdom. She sucked in a quick breath. "Well, there are no conflicts in accepting the existence of dinosaurs and fossils and believing in creation."

Margie raised an eyebrow, crossing her arms in front of her chest. "Explain yourself."

Ann-Ann readjusted her oversized sunglasses, thankful that the dark tint concealed her nervousness. "The Bible says God created the world in six days. The evolution hypothesis proposes humans and monkeys evolved from an apelike common ancestor over about six million years. However, God's attributes are beyond our human experience and comprehension. One of them is related to time and space. While we're constrained by time, God isn't."

"You're confusing me." Shawn cracked his knuckles. "What does this have to do with creation and evolution?"

Ann-Ann rubbed her bare leg, her stomach churning. "Creation and evolution both involve the element of time, but God can't be confined by time. If God is beyond time, then to Him there's no difference between six days and six million years. The debate between creation and evolution is unnecessary because they've both overlooked a critical factor: God transcends time and space."

"Sounds logical enough." Margie dropped her arms to her side.

"The Bible isn't a scientific textbook. Genesis uses human languages that have the constraint of time and space to convey one key fact: God created the universe." Ann-Ann's muscles loosened up a bit. "The only verse in the Bible not written in our languages is the writing on the wall in the Book of Daniel."

"I haven't thought about it that way." Margie grinned. "I attended a Catholic high school and know that story. Nobody could comprehend. Later, Daniel translated for them."

So, Margie wasn't an atheist. Was she a Catholic? Maybe Margie, like her, grew up in a Catholic family but didn't fully understand the gospel.

While Ann-Ann kept quiet, Margie patted Shawn's shoulder. "You said eternal life is boring because you have no desire to live forever. But the Bible doesn't define eternal life by time. The Gospel of John states, 'This is eternal life: that they may know you, the only true God, and Jesus Christ, whom you have sent.'"

Did Margie just cite the Scripture? Ann-Ann couldn't help but blurt out, "You memorized John chapter seventeen, verse three?"

"Did it surprise you?" Shawn picked up his cocktail for a sip. "Since we started the trip, Margie has been trying to convert me into a Catholic."

Margie's smooth forehead crinkled between her eyes. "Shawn, you're exaggerating. You became intrigued after Nana Lee talked to you about the existence of God. After that, you've been pestering me to tell you more about Christianity."

Was that true? If so, why did Shawn argue with them and the guides about the biblical archaeological sites? Huh. Maybe that was his way of expressing his interest.

"Those sites we've visited fascinated me." He took another gulp of his drink. "Before we came, I didn't think things described in the Bible are still present for people to see and study."

Yao walked up, water dripping down his navy swimming trunks. "Ha, you're all here."

"Did you just come up from the Dead Sea? How did it go?" Margie pointed to a seat nearby. "Come sit with us."

"Amazing. A once-in-a-lifetime experience." Grinning, he towel-dried his body. "How about you guys? Ann-Ann? You're the only one with dry swimwear. Have you been in the water?"

She glanced at his bare chest, her heart fluttering. "I haven't."

A server swung by, and Yao ordered two glasses of merlot. "One for you." He winked. "I remember you love Merlot."

Wow. He remembered such details from their shared past. Another inexplicable feeling pulsed through her veins, leaving her unsure which she felt more—excitement or unease.

The drinks came, and he handed her a glass. "Why haven't you gone into the Dead Sea?"

"Um..." She sipped her wine, her stomach roiling. "I can't swim."

Shawn burst into laughter. "Didn't you grow up in Hong Kong surrounded by water?"

"Oh, Shawn. That wasn't funny or kind." Margie poked him in the arm. "Ann-Ann, ignore him. But you ought to try floating in the Dead Sea. Do you need me to come with you?"

A gentle warmth rose in Ann-Ann's heart. She never knew Margie was so caring.

Yao set his glass on the table. "I haven't taken a shower to rid the salty water yet and don't mind floating one more time. Maybe we can go together?"

Without waiting for a response, he stole her glass and set it aside before tugging her to her feet. "See you guys later."

Goosebumps crept up her skin as he led her toward the beach. She'd forgotten how strong and large his hand felt.

In front of her, an older man literally *sat* on the water, holding up a book above his head, while his wife took a picture. Another couple a bit farther away floated, laughing and flapping their arms, their torsos beneath the surface.

Ann-Ann sunk one foot into the water. It felt warm and oily.

"Try this." Yao dipped a finger into the sea, then brought it to her lips.

She licked it. The acid taste stunned her tongue.

"Let's go deeper." He took her hand and led her forward.

Furious stings tingled on her legs. Oops. Must be nicks and cuts from shaving.

Half immersing in the slimy salty water, she lowered her head. "Are you sure I can float? Water scares me."

"Just lean back into the water and relax." As he spoke, his gaze fell on the low cut of her swimsuit.

She stifled the urge to cringe at the unfortunate memory of their making out in his Palo Alto house. Was he thinking about their heavy petting on that day? She'd bared her upper body in front of him. Then he'd told her he had herpes, and they ended their relationship over a bitter fight.

Too ashamed to meet his gaze, she ducked farther, letting her hair shield her unease. Then her legs went limp, and she stumbled into the water. When he caught her by her waist, she gripped his broad shoulder, her gaze fixating on his bare chest.

He uttered a small groan, leaned in, and raised a hand to her face.

Was he trying to kiss her? She placed a finger in front of her lips, blocking his advances. "Aren't you engaged to Daisy Dong? Don't do something we'll regret later."

"I'm not engaged to Daisy." He let out a heavy breath but dropped his hand. "Ann-Ann, I've never felt like this before, not even when I was with May-May. Not even when we were dating in San Fran."

"We're on holiday. Maybe after we get back home, today will become another faint memory." She shifted one step away.

"Is that what you feel about us?"

His husky voice shivered over her, tingling like the water on her skin. What did she feel? Relieved because he and Daisy weren't engaged? No, not enough. He was dating Daisy and tried to court her. Wasn't that dubious, questionable behavior? She was thirty and couldn't afford to waste time and energy on mere hope.

He moved forward and tipped her face up. "Tell me you no longer care for me, and I won't bother you anymore."

The desire and longing in his eyes overwhelmed her. She turned her head sideways.

Did she still care for him? Yes. Did she love him? Maybe, maybe not. But he'd be an ideal match.

"You're quiet." He brushed a finger over her lips. "Say something."

She swallowed hard. "How much do you know about my past?"

His body went still. "Why do you ask?"

"Do you know..." Her courage failed her.

"That you used to be JT Poon's mistress?" A muscle on his cheek twitched.

Where did he learn about that part of her history? From Nana?

"Not only that..." Rubbing the cut she'd once inflicted on her wrist, she returned her gaze to his face. "I can never become pregnant."

A silence befell.

Yeah, like Stanley, he was going to drop his arm and say they weren't suitable for each other.

She looked toward the sky, preparing for his next sentence. The lingering blue luster on the western skyline soothed her somehow.

Then his voice was a whisper in her ear. "Anything else?"

Her heart skipped a beat. "What did you just say?"

A gentle wind blew over her, lifting her hair across her face.

"I asked if you have anything else to tell me." He brushed the curls away, and his eyes bored into hers. "My wilderness journey wasn't less treacherous than yours. Let bygones be bygones. By God's amazing grace, as long as we don't make the same mistake, Satan can never use them to accuse us again."

A salty sea smell whipped around, and the wind brought tears to her eyes. "You don't mind that I can't have children?"

"Should I mind?"

She stifled a sigh, breathing in to absorb the rush of gratitude. A man in his position knew everything about her past and didn't regard her barrenness as a problem. Where would she find another guy like him? Still...

He bent his lips toward her mouth.

No, she wasn't ready. She needed to know whether he'd cut his tie with Daisy.

She dodged away and fell backward into the water. Instead of sinking, her body floated.

Ann-Ann outstretched her arms and laughed aloud. "The Dead Sea is amazing."

Chapter Fifteen

At four o'clock in the morning, the van swayed from side to side as they drove north on Route 90.

Yao peered into the pitch-dark desert beyond the window. It had been a long time since that river dream visited him. Yet, it came last night. He and May-May swam in a river. The torrent pushed her away as he moved toward her. He yelled for help, and Ann-Ann jumped into the current. In an instant, both vanished.

Had Ann-Ann replaced May-May's position in his soul? How did it happen? He once thought his heart would never cease belonging to May-May.

He pressed his lips together at the thought of their float in the Dead Sea yesterday.

Why didn't Ann-Ann let him kiss her? She'd told him she couldn't bear children, as if that was the reason she refused him. Didn't she know he learned about her abortion years ago from Nana Lee?

"I'm glad you four agreed to climb the Snake Path up to Masada to see the sunrise." Adam's voice broke the stillness inside the vehicle. "After dropping you off, I'll get back to the hotel to pick up Mrs. Lee and Josh. They can take the cable car up."

"How high is the climb?" Behind Yao, Shawn yawned.

"About a thousand feet. Easy for you, Mr. Han."

"Is the sunrise special here?" The cracking of knuckles followed Shawn's question. "It'd better be, to account for having to get up so early."

"Yeah, spectacular." Adam waved from the front seat. "Another reason is to avoid the heat. By nine a.m., the temperature will hit one hundred, and it's tough to climb."

Ann-Ann switched positions of her legs back and forth. "Adam, tell us more about this site."

"King Herod built Masada at around 100 BCE as one of his palaces. Because of its isolation and the arid desert climate, the place is well-preserved. It may take a whole day to go through many of its chambers, including storerooms and bathhouses. Because of the heat, we'll try to leave at around nine to go to Ein Gedi and Qumran."

As he was talking, the van slowed. After an Israeli military checkpoint guard waved them through, they reached Masada. Sunrise was still more than an hour away, yet dim light started filling the valley below.

Even though the sun hadn't come out, an unbearable heat already surrounded them.

"Wow, it's hot." Margie fanned herself with her hand. "But it'll be worth it. I've read about the Masada story and always wanted to visit it."

Shawn huffed a loud breath through his nose. "Ha, you're not one to waste a minute of your time. So why did Masada interest you?"

Ann-Ann lagged far behind them. Yao drew his brows together. Concern for her well-being prompted him to slow down. He couldn't help going back to keep her company. "Are you all right? Do you need water?"

He handed her his water bottle.

"Thanks." She breathed hard, her chest rising and falling.

"Do you need to take a break?" He gestured toward a rock nearby.

Shawn raised an arm. "You two, hurry up. We need to beat the sunrise."

"I'm fine." Ann-Ann took a sip and gave the water back. "Let's go."

Margie waited for them to catch up. "Are you interested in hearing the Masada story?"

"Go ahead." Shawn bobbed his head. "Tell us."

"As Christians, Yao and Ann-Ann probably know that in 70 AD, the Romans invaded Jerusalem and destroyed the Second Temple built by King Herod."

Yao nodded. In the Gospel of Mark, Jesus said, "Do you see all these great buildings? Not one stone here will be left on another; everyone will be thrown down."

"Yeah, I read about it." Ann-Ann dragged a hand through her hair. "As Roman soldiers surrounded the temple, someone started a fire that soon covered the entire place. Gold melted from the roof and fell in the cracks between the stone walls. To retrieve the gold, the Roman commander ordered the temple dismantled stone by stone. The destruction was complete that day."

"We must have read the same book." Margie inclined her head with a smile. "But the story didn't end there. About a thousand Jewish men, women, and children fled Jerusalem and found refuge atop Masada. Caesar gave orders they should demolish the entire Jewish opposition. So, the Roman army besieged Masada."

Shawn, impatient like before, wagged his hand. "What happened next?"

"You like the story, don't you?" Margie patted his shoulder. "Facing an overwhelming Roman force, the Jews knew the fortress would fall."

When she halted again, he rolled his eyes.

Ann-Ann's lips curled up. Her thoughts became transparent to Yao, like the flashlight illuminating his path. Between Margie and Shawn, Margie held a clear upper hand.

How about him and Ann-Ann? At present, didn't she own the position of having power over him and their future together?

Margie retrieved her water bottle, uncapping it as she spoke. "The rebel leader, Eleazar Ben-Yair, convinced the group to commit mass suicide."

"Doesn't Judaism teach against taking one's own life?" Ann-Ann turned her head, the early morning wind sweeping her hair across her face.

Yao jammed his hands into his pockets, resisting the urge to help tuck those curls behind her ears.

"A good question." Margie sipped her water, then slid it back into her pack. "They developed a scheme to go around the Jewish laws.

Each man killed his own wife and children. Then the men drew lots to determine which ten of them would put the others to death. Afterward, the remaining men drew lots again, and one man killed the other nine before taking his own life."

"What a horrible story." Shawn scrunched his nose. "Did those women and children have any say? Wasn't it better to be a slave than to die like that?"

Yao kept quiet. As the sun crested over the distant mountains, the valley and the Dead Sea beneath him lit up. While panting, he slowed his steps to take in the view—the same view King Herod must have marveled at about two thousand years ago.

The others also turned their heads around to soak up the resplendent dawn.

"Let's keep moving." Shawn clapped a hand on his chest. "The staging area below Masada is right ahead of us."

As they climbed up the mountain, Yao gawked. The immense splendor of the ancient fortress left him more breathless than the physical strain of the ascent.

From the staging area, they followed a short stairway up to the fortress.

Margie twirled her watch into view. "It took us about an hour. Not bad at all."

"Look!" Ann-Ann pointed toward the eastern sky.

The sun peeped over the mountains, then in the next ten minutes, filled the sky.

"Wow. It's extraordinary." She sucked in a breath. "Adam was right. Definitely worth the four a.m. climb."

"Not too shabby." Shawn touched his forehead. "Now, Margie, you haven't answered my question."

"Why do you think being a slave is better than death?" Margie pointed at Shawn. "Sometimes, to die with dignity is better than to live in shame and horror."

She sounded like a philosopher. Ann-Ann was right. Margie couldn't be Shawn's girlfriend.

As if to confirm this, she turned to him. "Have you read stories by Jorge Luis Borges?"

Before Yao responded, Ann-Ann raised her hand. "I love his work. Many of his stories deal with immortality and the meaning of life."

"Yeah. One of his short stories, 'El inmortal'"—Margie pronounced its Spanish name—"tells about a Roman soldier, Marcus Rufus, who achieved immortality after drinking from a mysterious river. But as the years dragged on beyond all of those he loved, he became weary of life and struggled to lose it."

"What happened?" Shawn leaned forward. "Did he die at the end?"

"Yes, he did." She gaped into his eyes. "That story reveals one beautiful truth. Without limits, life has no significance."

Without limits, life has no significance. The words echoed in the hollowness of Yao's heart. What was life for? He'd asked that question often since he left China years ago.

A Bible verse flashed, chasing away the darkness of the lingering question like the rising sun now driving out the residual night. "I am the resurrection and the life. He who believes in me will live."

Lord, is that Your answer to my question? You are the life. With You, my life has meaning.

"That's bogus." Shawn's bass rattled Yao's thoughts. "So different from how we Chinese think. All the emperors in our history sought to live forever. Our first emperor, Qin Shihuang, was especially obsessed with immortality. He sent Xu Fu, one of his generals, to the eastern seas twice to look for secret concoctions that would help him live forever. After Xu Fu's second mission, he never returned. I suppose he didn't find anything useful and was worried about his life."

Ann-Ann shaded her eyes from the sun's glare, its golden light casting a sheen on her skin and hair even as it streaked the sky. "Some books said our first emperor not only sent out Xu Fu but also ordered everyone to search for immortality potions from frontier regions. His decree was urgent and the outcome of not bringing him what he desired was severe. Someone brought in an herb from a remote mountain." Still peering toward the horizon as if she could see that mountain, she tucked a strayed curl back up into the black mass of her hair. "He consumed it right away. But the herbal brew contained mercury sulfide. Qin Shihuang died at thirty-nine. How ironic."

"Wow, you girls are incredible! So well read." Shawn chuckled.

Yao stiffened at his companion's seeming mockery, but perhaps he should give Shawn a chance. The unruly fellow had been changing—bit by bit, yet noticeable.

"Even at his death, Qin Shihuang didn't give up his dream of resurrection." Margie echoed Shawn's laugh. "Have you heard about the discovery of his tomb? He built an enormous underground mausoleum with his Terracotta Army, containing numerous weapons and about seven thousand life-size statues of warriors and horses. He believed he would rule forever, in life or death."

"Well, for sure, nobody can live forever. Nice discussion, though." Shawn glanced at his watch. "The cable car won't start operating until eight. We still have some time. Shall we go through the ruins?"

As they explored the different sections with tile mosaics and columns from two thousand years ago, still in shockingly great shape, Yao appreciated why Herod chose the spot for his fortress—360-degree views of the world around him.

Did King Herod seek immortality like Qin Shihuang? The Masada fortress showed the king must have wished to leave a mark, a legacy, in human history.

Why did humans, limited by space and time, have the concept of eternity? Did God plant it in human hearts so they would seek Him, the eternal Almighty?

Amid the different ideas, one question emerged: What made him want to elevate his conglomerate to the next level, even at the price of entering into a loveless marriage?

Whoa. Wasn't he in love with Daisy Dong?

No, he didn't love her. He was in love with Ann-Ann. Yet he'd been dragging Daisy along. He didn't do it on purpose. Before this trip, he never thought Ann-Ann still cared about him.

Yao stole a glimpse of her. She gazed at a painted wall, indifferent to his desire for her. How could he convince her he loved her, only her?

He winced at a Bible verse. "That man should not think he will receive anything from the Lord; he is a double-minded man, unstable in all he does."

Oh, Lord, is that Your response to my question?

A woman as smart as Ann-Ann would consider his behavior dubious. He had to sever his relationship with Daisy first. But how?

Surely he wouldn't be so callous as to break the news to Daisy over the phone. No. He'd need a more prudent way to do it.

"Look at that." Margie pointed to the west side. "The Roman Ramp trail. Unbelievable. The ramp remains in remarkable shape."

Her nose scrunching, Ann-Ann scrutinized the ramp. "Quite amazing. It still works today. I can understand why the Jewish remnants would rather die than become slaves. The reputation of the Roman soldiers must have terrified everyone in the region."

"Yeah, especially for girls and women." Margie's countenance became melancholic. "They would become sex slaves like today's human trafficking victims."

Yao stretched his eyes wide. "You seem as if the subject of human trafficking consumes you." At her sad expression, he clamped his teeth into his tongue, stilling it from asking if someone she loved was a sufferer.

"Now you've mentioned it, please educate us more." Ann-Ann touched Margie's shoulder. "Have officials rescued any victims?"

"Very few." Margie exhaled hard, the puff of air ruffling her golden bangs. "Human trafficking is a difficult crime to prove. Of millions of victims worldwide, the United Nations found sixty percent of countries surveyed had no records of any conviction and the remaining had fewer than ten convictions."

Yao raised a hand. "Why?"

She turned her somber eyes on him. "In many parts of the world, prostitutes are held in disdain and considered unworthy of help, regardless of whether they're victims of human trafficking."

While Ann-Ann nodded in silence, Yao thought of *Uncle Tom's Cabin,* a book he read not long ago. Slavery was once a norm in the US. That book played a major role in the success of abolitionism. Could an ordinary person like him do something to minimize the evil of human trafficking?

"Some victims resist a change to their lives because of fear, ignorance, and concern over their only means of survival." A grim twist turned Margie's mouth downward. "After all, as recorded in the Bible, it took forty years for Israel's slave mentality to go."

Yao winced, an uncomfortable sensation squeezing his chest. Meanwhile, a new respect arose. Margie knew the Bible well. Now he was certain she wasn't Shawn's girlfriend. But who was she?

"From the convicted cases, why didn't the officials trace them to other criminals?"

"Good question." Margie lifted her chin. "The convicted is often just a cog in the machinery. Without them, the evil continues."

Ann-Ann tilted her head, the sunlight outlining her perfect profile. "Have you ever been involved in any activities to stop human trafficking?"

Good girl. He trained his gaze on Margie.

While she kept quiet, Shawn chimed in. "She has. Should I tell them what you did two years ago?" At her slight nod, he resumed speaking. "She joined forces with a Christian organization in Mongolia to track down girls trafficked out of Ulaanbaatar through China into Macau and Hong Kong. That's how we met."

"What did you uncover? Did your efforts convict anyone?" Ann-Ann spoke quieter than usual.

"No." Margie held her palms up and out. "But after that, the Mongolian government put some measures in place to protect young girls. On that mission, two government officials went with us. Before that, the government had no clue how human trafficking operates."

Yao pinched his chin, his muscles tense from strained attentiveness. "What measures did they take?"

"They informed the public about questionable advertisements and trained girls to stay away from modeling and travel agencies, international matchmaking services, massage parlors, au pair babysitting, and other employment companies promising lucrative foreign jobs." Lowering her hands, she held back her shoulders. "Their most effective measure was teaching border patrol agents to recognize potential human trafficking incidents."

Ann-Ann raised her brows in a questioning glance.

Margie's lips curled up. "For example, if they find a girl escorted by a third party—someone who holds a passport under a different surname—they have to investigate further. Through this simple step, they've stopped many potential tragedies in a short time. Unfortunately, so far, the government hasn't caught any criminals who know enough of the secret operations."

Yao looked away, thinking of the triad. Did all international crime organizations operate the same way? Full of secrets and mysteries.

Shawn mimicked Margie and chuckled. "You wouldn't believe how many discos and clubs around Macau and Hong Kong Margie and I visited. But our efforts have some impact." He rocked back on his heels. "Ah, the first cable car has arrived."

Nana Lee, Josh, and Adam strolled toward them. Adam grinned, spreading out his beard. "How was your morning hike? Was it worth it?"

"Definitely." Ann-Ann shifted to hug Josh. "Did you like your cable ride?"

"It's awesome. Auntie Ann-Ann, I've got a new joke about the Dead Sea." Without waiting for a response, Josh bounced from foot to foot. "Two kids were bragging about their fathers' achievements. One said his father built the cable car for Masada. The other kid retorted, 'That's nothing in comparison to what my dad did. Do you know what caused the Dead Sea's death? My dad killed it.'"

Yao couldn't help laughing. "Where did you get the joke?"

"I created it myself." Josh thrust out his chest.

Margie patted his head. "What a smart kid."

"Okay, everyone." Adam clapped. "We'll let Mrs. Lee and Josh walk around the site a bit. At nine, let's meet here. We'll take the cable car down together, then travel to Ein Gedi, Qumran, and Jerusalem."

Chapter Sixteen

Inside the King David Hotel in Jerusalem, Ann-Ann pored over the brochure on the desk. Wow! The hotel had been operating since 1931 and was celebrating its fiftieth anniversary this year. It accommodated many visiting heads of state and various foreign delegations.

She stood, passed Nana kneeling by their room's enormous floor-to-ceiling window, and slipped into the bathroom.

When she got back, Nana had already put on her Turkish-blue silk shirt and matching pants.

"Are you ready for breakfast?" Ann-Ann dropped her toiletry bag into her luggage. "Even in your travels, you're still practicing your No B No B every day."

"Yes, No Bible No Breakfast." Nana dipped her chin. "I've been doing it for so long. It's like brushing my teeth, a habit that sticks with me."

Ann-Ann smiled. "I wish I had your discipline. "

"You're also well-disciplined and read your Bible every day." Nana patted her arm, then pulled her to sit together on the bed. "What do you think about Shawn's comments when we visited the Qumran Caves?"

Ann-Ann wiggled her brows. "You mean his discussions with Margie about the Dead Sea Scrolls?"

"He didn't argue when she told him the discovery of the Dead Sea Scrolls was one of the most important archaeological finds in our century." Nana smoothed her fingers over her already smooth slacks. "When I talked to him about the existence of God a few days ago, I sensed he was still stuck in his atheism mindset. I wonder what made him soften up."

Ann-Ann slapped her thigh. "Must be the work of the Holy Spirit. You once mentioned that when God's timing arrives for a person's salvation, His grace becomes irresistible."

"My dear Ann-Ann, I didn't realize you'd paid such attention to what I told you." Nana gave her arm a playful pinch. "I've been praying for him and Margie since we started our travel. I hope God's mercy will fall on them soon."

"Margie may have already known God." Ann-Ann brushed aside a stray wisp of hair and relayed their recent conversation.

At Yao's name, Nana's eyes sparkled. "Before we go down to the dining hall, I have something to tell you."

"Yeah?" Ann-Ann leaned closer, her curiosity piqued.

Nana grasped her hand. "Yao came to talk to me last night."

Surely, Yao wouldn't say something about her? Ann-Ann's heart skipped a beat, but she kept quiet.

A smile tugged at Nana's mouth. "He intends to break up with Daisy Dong but doesn't know how to do it properly. He thought it unkind to tell her over the phone during his travel."

As a jittery heat surged through Ann-Ann, she withdrew her hand from Nana's. "Well, he can tell her when he gets back to Hong Kong."

"He'll tell Daisy face-to-face." Nana picked up Ann-Ann's hand again. "But he wants you to know about it now."

She swallowed hard, heat swelling her throat. "Why?"

"I think Yao is in love with you." Nana gave her fingers a tender squeeze. "On our first day of travel, when we talked about him, you said he wasn't your type. Do you still think so? Should I let him know?"

"I–I—" Her face burned, and embarrassment tied her tongue.

"My darling." Nana hugged her shoulders, and her soft white hair tickled Ann-Ann's cheek. "Yao is a good match for you. He knows your past and doesn't mind you can never have children. More importantly, I can tell he loves you very much."

She edged back and sucked in a deep breath, a vain attempt to compose herself. "Nana, he used to love May-May a lot. How do I know he isn't only thinking of me as my twin's replacement?"

Nana wagged a finger. "I saw you two lock eyes on the lakeshore the other day. No, by how he looked at you and what he told me, I believe you've somehow taken over May-May's position in his heart. In a way, Yao is a practical man and always knew May-May treated him like a brother. But you're different. You didn't grow up with him and can accept him as a lover."

Turbulent emotions roiling her, Ann-Ann lowered her head.

Nana chuffed out a breath. "Both of you have had a wilderness experience. By God's grace, you two returned to His family at about the same time. You and Yao have a lot in common."

Yes. They'd opened intimate places of their hearts to one another, revealing their true selves. But while he tried to kiss her, she'd dodged his advances because she vowed not to get involved with any man who belonged to someone else.

Was that why he told Nana about his decision to break up with Daisy? Did he intend to let her know he was free to love her? Like Nana said, they did have a lot in common. Was it enough for her to accept him?

Someone knocked. When she opened the door, Yao and Josh strolled in.

When Yao gave her a peculiar glance, heat crawled up from her neck to her ears. She moved toward the window. Outside, the morning sun shone on early swimmers in the pool, their loud laughter echoing across the green-manicured lawn.

"Great-Nana, I love you," Josh chirped, and Ann-Ann pivoted to smile at her dear nephew.

"My good boy." Nana patted his head, then stood up. "Did you sleep well? Are you hungry? Why don't we go down for breakfast?"

"Okay." He grasped Ann-Ann's hand. "Auntie, let's go together."

***

As their guide strolled through the hotel's main entrance, Yao stole a glimpse of Ann-Ann standing nearby. Did Nana Lee tell her he'd decided to break up with Daisy? Could she guess he loved her and only her?

"Okay, my friends." Adam waved his piece of paper. "We'll visit a few famous sites today. First, the Garden of Gethsemane atop the Mount of Olives. Then the Church of the Holy Sepulchre. Last but not least—the Garden Tomb."

With a snort, Shawn crossed his beefy arms over his chest, rumpling his turquoise polo shirt. "Are those sites interesting at all? Why haven't I heard of them before?"

Adam leaned forward. "All three sites are about Jesus. The Garden of Gethsemane, according to the four Gospels of the New Testament, was where Jesus underwent His agony, and later, He was arrested there."

Margie chimed in. "I believe the other two were related to His crucifixion, death, and resurrection. Am I right?"

"Absolutely." Adam's beard crinkled up. "Now, let's go."

At the base of the Mount of Olives, a sign pointed toward the Garden. Yao and his entourage entered the gate and came upon an olive grove.

Nana Lee rushed forward to touch a tree's bark. "Was this where the Lord prayed so intensely that He sweated drops of blood?"

"It could be." Margie surveyed the gnarled trees. "These are at least several hundred years old. Since olive trees can grow back from roots after being cut down, one of these might have been with Jesus back then."

"You sound like an expert." Despite his sarcasm, Shawn plucked an olive leaf. He rubbed the waxy tip between his fingers, his brow furrowing. "Why did Jesus experience agony here? If He were God, He should have known better and not fallen into distress."

"Excellent question." Nana Lee flashed her characteristic gentle smile. "As God, He foresaw what kind of torture He would need to endure."

Shawn squinted. "But He should know He wouldn't really die."

"Jesus did prophesy His resurrection." She patted his arm. "His most unbearable agony wasn't about death, but about His foreseeing that the eternal fellowship among Trinity would temporarily shatter with all sins laid on Him."

"You've got me more confused. What's Trinity?" Shawn tossed the leaf away as if trying to brush away the nonsense.

Yao fumbled with his Patek Philippe watch. Good thing he didn't have to answer such a question from a nonbeliever about a tough theological concept!

The tender smile never left Nana Lee's lips. "The God we believe in is one God with three distinct persons—the Father, the Son, and the Holy Spirit."

"How can three distinct persons be the same God?" Shawn's forehead wrinkled. "It doesn't make any sense."

"It's a mystery to us humans because we're limited by time and space. Our God, who is beyond time and space, can exist in three persons simultaneously."

Margie patted Nana Lee's shoulder, then tugged at her silk sleeve. "Wow, you said it well. I've never heard such an outstanding explanation. For sure, God is far beyond us. We can't try to use our limited mind to explain Him." Crossing her arms and widening her stance, Margie faced Shawn. "Sometimes, it's better to admit our limits and simply believe."

Shawn shook his head but kept quiet.

Yao brought a palm to his face, hiding his grin. Ha, so unlike Shawn. The rowdy giant was softening toward Christianity.

"Okay. It's time to go." Adam led the way.

They visited the adjacent Basilica of the Agony, then returned to the Old City for lunch before strolling the Via Dolorosa to the Church of the Holy Sepulchre.

Inside the ancient church, they followed a group of tourists to pass through the different sections. At the tomb, enclosed by a nineteenth-century shrine called the Aedicula, a few folks sank to their knees. Yao grasped Josh's hand and passed them in silence. They visited every point of interest and emerged from the dark interior back to the sun-drenched plaza.

Adam escorted them to a marble staircase. "According to traditions dating back to the fourth century, the location where the Holy Sepulchre sits is thought to contain both Golgotha and Jesus' empty tomb."

Ann-Ann took a seat on the nearest stair. "This place is magnificent but too dark and too overpowering."

"Ah, then you'll like the open setting at the Garden Tomb." Adam gestured for her to stand up. "If you're ready, we'll walk to the Garden Tomb."

"Now you have me intrigued." Shawn swung his arms. "Were there two places where Jesus was crucified? How could it be?"

"According to historical records, after Constantine the Great converted to Christianity, he sent his mother Helena to Jerusalem to look for Christ's tomb." Adam led them toward the Damascus Gate. "She saw three crosses near the temple of Jupiter and Venus and believed she had found Calvary. Constantine ordered a church built at the site. When the old pagan structure was torn down, they found a rock-cut tomb. That's how the Holy Sepulchre came about."

"How about the Garden Tomb?"

Adam guided them toward the Muslim Quarter. "I'll tell you when we get closer."

At its entrance, he halted. "Once inside, a volunteer will accompany you. Feel free to ask him or her whatever questions are on your mind, but please keep it brief, because another group is waiting after us."

Yao entered. Indeed, the open, spacious garden appeared in direct contrast to the Church of the Holy Sepulchre.

Under a grape arbor, a Caucasian gentleman with a slightly hunched back greeted them in a crisp British accent. "Welcome to the Garden Tomb. I'm a retired pastor, Liam Taylor."

He cleared his throat and switched to Cantonese. "Although Christians in the world commemorate the death and the resurrection of Jesus of Nazareth at many locations, where you're standing is special. This isn't because we claim to be *the* burial place of Jesus, but because so many elements here seem to match the description in the Bible. My prayer is this brief tour will make the resurrection of Jesus more meaningful for you. Please come with me to the viewing platform overlooking a hill called Golgotha."

Yao stretched his eyes wide. Where did the reverend learn to speak Cantonese? Maybe he used to work in Hong Kong?

They strolled down the pathway lined with potted flowers. Facing Skull Hill, Reverend Taylor explained why and how Jesus was likely crucified in this area. "Calvary was called Golgotha for a reason. During Jesus' time, Golgotha meant *skull* in Aramaic. It fits the description in the Gospels. Besides, the Romans always chose a site with lots of passersby to crucify criminals. They wanted to warn the public that anyone who conspired against the empire should consider the dire consequences. The main road to Damascus used to pass by Golgotha with heavy traffic. It would be an ideal site for the Romans."

From there, Reverend Taylor directed them toward the burial site and relayed the story from the Bible about how Joseph of Arimathea took Jesus' body and placed it in his own new tomb. "The most important thing is that this tomb is empty. He is not here because He has risen. Since He is alive, we can have a relationship with Him today."

Shawn raised a hand. "Do you truly believe a dead man could come back to life and is still living today?"

Their guide took a step back. "Of course I do. All Christians do."

"Explain why you believe." With arms crossed over his broad chest, Shawn leaned forward, not backing down.

Yao blinked at their friend's juvenile bullying. Or did Shawn truly want to know?

The reverend checked his watch. "Another group of visitors needs me soon. Maybe your friends can help answer your question?"

Margie stepped up. "Shawn, let's talk about that later. The reverend has to go."

Back at their hotel, Shawn grabbed Nana Lee by the arm. "Can I go to your room? You must explain to me why all Christians believe in Jesus' resurrection."

"Come with me." She elbowed Ann-Ann with a cheeky smile. "While I talk to Shawn, why don't you go to the coffee shop with others?"

Margie brought a palm to cover a yawn. "I need a nap. I'll see you later."

Was yawning contagious? Josh also let out an enormous yawn. "Uncle Yao, I'm going back to our room."

Once they left, Yao wiped his black slacks, his skin tingling. "It's a long day, for sure. Care to have a cup of coffee?"

Her cheeks flared crimson, yet she nodded.

Was she embarrassed? Why? Maybe Nana Lee told her about his feelings for her.

When he grasped her hand, she gave out a faint sigh and didn't dodge. Then her fingers coiled around his.

His heart fluttered. A surge of energy suffused his entire body with inexplicable joy and hope. Could he now plan a future with someone he loved?

Chapter Seventeen

Back in the hotel room the next afternoon, Ann-Ann took off her sneakers. "My feet are sore. We covered so many places during the past two days."

"Yes." Nana sat on the bed. "Which one did you like best?"

"All of them are interesting." Ann-Ann took a seat by Nana, sinking into plush comfort and wiggling her bare toes against an equally luxurious carpet. "I didn't know they have separate sections for men and women at the Wailing Wall. Going to Bethlehem was worth it, even though we had to pass the checkpoints. But I especially enjoyed visiting the Israel Museum to view the display of the Dead Sea Scrolls."

"Too bad Margie and Shawn didn't go to the museum with us today." Nana's brows furrowed. "Why do they have errands to run in Jerusalem? What sort of business are they in?"

Ann-Ann shrugged. No reason to stress Nana. "Now that you mentioned them, how did your conversation with Shawn go last night?"

"I suppose it went well. He asked lots of questions, showing a genuine interest in finding answers."

"Of course, it must have gone well. How could anyone resist you? Even me?" Smiling, Ann-Ann bumped their shoulders. "But how did you answer his questions?"

"Well, he questioned the Bethlehem story. He didn't think it was possible for a virgin to bear a baby."

"And?" She raised a brow.

"I told him to hold that question until later." Nana clasped her hands together, as though in prayer. "I went ahead and showed him the evidence of Jesus' death and resurrection. As you know well, the four Gospels described both events in significant detail. He asked whether other documents outside the Bible around that time talked about Jesus."

Ann-Ann traced a line on the carpet with her big toe. Those shoes had been so hot today. No way was she putting them back on tomorrow. She'd have to unpack good walking sandals. "What did you say?"

"I mentioned the writing by the first-century Jewish historian, Flavius Josephus. I also told him the most convincing evidence of Jesus' resurrection was the change in His disciples' behaviors. Not just one person, but all of them, turned from cowards before Jesus' resurrection to martyrs who willingly laid down their lives instead of renouncing their beliefs."

Nana stood up, unearthed her hairbrush from the nearby bureau, and sat back down. She worked through her wispy white hair as she spoke. "If Jesus had not resurrected and appeared to them, it was an impossibility. Besides, when the Gospel books were written and circulated, many people around Jesus' time were still alive. If Jesus' disciples weren't speaking the truth about the resurrection, then their contemporaries would have said something to dispute their claims."

Nana's brushing was too vigorous, leaving her hair flyaway in the dry air-conditioned room. Was she agitated? So unlike her. Ann-Ann hugged her, then smoothed down the staticky strands. "You explained so well. Was he convinced?"

"I don't know. I also shared my experience. How the Holy Spirit comforted me at my darkest moment during the Cultural Revolution. He lapsed into silence before taking leave." Nana scrunched up her wrinkled face. "I'll keep praying for him."

"Did you speak of the Shroud of Turin?"

"The linen cloth that many believe was used to wrap Jesus' body after His crucifixion? I didn't. The evidence is sufficient without mentioning the Shroud." She fiddled with the brush bristles in her lap. "One good thing, though. In the end, Shawn said something unexpected. He commented that if Jesus indeed overcame death to prove His deity, of course, His virgin birth was possible."

Ann-Ann bobbed her head. So true. Her own change after establishing a relationship with God through Jesus was in many ways similar to that of the early disciples. But would she willingly lay down her life instead of renouncing her faith? Didn't Nana and many Christians in China stay faithful while facing severe persecution? When the time came, the Holy Spirit would have to guide her and strengthen her.

"What are you thinking?" Nana grasped her hand. "Last night, while I was talking with Shawn, did you go to the coffee shop with Yao?"

Heat crept up to Ann-Ann's face. "Yes."

Why did she feel embarrassed? Hadn't she gone through this before with other men? Yet embarrassment was an emotion beyond her control. Was it because Yao had taken over a space in her heart that hadn't been touched before?

"What did you two talk about?" Nana flashed a smile.

"Some trivial things. He told me more about his childhood. How he and his pa went to church with you." Ann-Ann touched her lips, a delectable sensation rising in her. "He also invited me to dinner for tonight."

At the thought of their dinner date, she stole a glimpse of her watch. Almost six. "Nana, I'd better get changed and go down. I'm meeting with him at six thirty."

She pushed from the bed and took the teal dress she'd hung up to the bathroom. After a quick change and refresh of her makeup, she wiggled into her strappy white sandals by the door. Then she gave a little spin for Nana's approval. "Well? Presentable?"

"My girls are always so lovely, inside and out." Nana smoothed back the hair that swished over Ann-Ann's shoulders before stepping back and surveying her fully. "Your mother once said a pair of white sandals was all she needed to get through the summer. I suspect she insisted you packed those."

"She did. I wouldn't have wanted to walk in these all day, but I'm glad I don't need to put my sneakers back on tonight. My feet are *still* hot." Ann-Ann leaned in to kiss her nana's cheek, then shifted away. "I'd better get going."

When she entered the lobby, Yao was standing by a sofa. He strode to her side and hooked his arm with hers. "You're gorgeous tonight. This dress fits you well."

She touched his white shirt with her free hand. "You look good too."

In the restaurant, the hostess led them to a private corner overlooking the hotel's splendid garden. Ann-Ann couldn't help but move toward the window. As she took in the scene, her shoulders loosened up.

It wasn't her first time dining with a man alone. Yet, it felt like a nervous first date.

"Isn't the garden delightful?" He came to stand by her. "After dinner, we should go for a stroll."

Yao guided her back to their table where a bottle of wine awaited, as if he'd arranged their dinner in advance. He poured her a glass of her favorite merlot.

"Ah, nice." She took a sip, her tight grip on the wineglass stem revealing her edginess. *Calm down, girl. Enjoy the dinner.*

He ordered a seafood dinner. Crab cakes, oysters Rockefeller, clam chowder, seared scallops, and steamed lobsters... Instead of pairing them with white wine, he ordered her favorite red.

After so many years, he remembered her favorite food and drinks. Overwhelmed by a sudden esteem and gratitude for his tender care, she ducked her head. How was she going to return the love?

As she took one after another appreciative sip, she tried to keep her expression neutral, yet a jittery heat in her body refused to subside.

After dessert, he stood up. "Ready for the garden?"

He led her down the stairs to an oversized olive tree. Then he halted, and his fingers moved to her face to sweep aside a stray lock of hair. His touch lingered. The feathery caress sent a tingling sensation up her spine.

"Ann-Ann." He shifted his hand to her back to pull her closer.

He stood so close. She sensed his warm breath on her. His proximity felt so good, like a soothing salve. She closed her eyes, soaking in his woody and spicy cologne.

"I love you." His soft lips brushed against her forehead, glided down onto her nose and neck, then up to claim her mouth.

She clung to him and kissed him back, her chest swelling and her heart beating fast. Yeah, she was finally home.

"Don't you two know this is a public place?"

She cringed and stepped away from Yao.

"As the Chinese saying goes, a man shouldn't set his feet on two boats simultaneously." Shawn jabbed a finger at Yao's chest. "Aren't you a Christian? How can you take advantage of Ann-Ann while dating Daisy Dong?"

"Shawn, I'm glad you're here. I won't continue my relationship with Daisy because I don't love her. I'm in love with Ann-Ann. Could you serve as a witness for Ann-Ann and me?" Yao dropped to one knee at her feet. "Will you marry me? I don't have a ring with me, but will buy you one after we get back to Hong Kong."

Oh my!

She cupped her mouth with a hand, moisture clouding her vision. Was this for real? She, a thirty-year-old woman with a troubled past, had just received a marriage proposal from one of Hong Kong's most eligible bachelors.

But more importantly, they loved each other.

She nodded, and Yao's mouth stretched into an enormous smile, his usual serious expression gone, replaced by a joyful glow.

"Congratulations." Shawn sounded almost sentimental. "I'm happy for you two."

Yao, still smiling, gestured for them to shift toward a nearby bench. "Besides buying a ring for Ann-Ann, I still need to do one more thing after we get back. It's unkind to tell Daisy I want to break up with her over the phone. So, I'll have to do it in a face-to-face meeting."

"Uh, watch out." Frowning, Shawn rubbed his jaw. "She may get angry and ask her father to sabotage your business."

"I've already considered that." A crease formed between Yao's brows. "Remember our discussion at Masada about King Herod? In history, many people sacrificed everything in life to leave a legacy after their death. The fact is, after some time, no one cares about your achievements, no matter how great they are. Marrying Daisy to expand my conglomerate is foolish. Certainly not something Jesus would do."

Ann-Ann's lips curled up, and tears welled. She scooted to Yao's side to hook an arm with his.

"Well, well." With a hand still on his jaw, Shawn tapped his chin. "We have a pair of lovebirds here, don't we?"

Yao drew her to sit by him, then tilted his head toward Shawn. "Where is Margie? Did you guys find the information you were looking for?"

"Yes and no." He sat on a rock next to their bench. "Some accounts showed frequent wire transfers—with no business or apparent lawful purpose—directed to countries at high risk for human trafficking. But when we asked for the owners' names of those accounts, the bank refused."

Ann-Ann exchanged a glance with Yao. Who was Margie? Banks wouldn't reveal records of wire transfers unless...

The girl in question ambled in and wagged a finger at Shawn. "Ha, you're here. I was ready to go to the restaurant, but didn't see you anywhere."

He shot to his feet. "Margie, you've got to congratulate our friends. Yao just proposed and Ann-Ann said yes."

Margie jammed her hands on her hips and raised an eyebrow toward her yellow-gold bangs. "Wow, that was fast. Yao, aren't you dating Daisy Dong?"

"I'll fill you in with the details." Shawn drew Margie toward the door. "Now, let's go eat. After dinner, I still need to pack for our six-a.m. flight. And we have errands to run in Istanbul right away. It's brutal."

When Ann-Ann returned to their room, Nana was already asleep. How she wished to share the good news right away! To wait till morning was torture.

She went through her routine and lay in bed, gazing at the white ceiling. Moisture gathered behind her eyelids. So much to think about and be thankful for.

Lord, thank You for Your guidance. Thank You for Yao.

She drifted off to sleep.

The baby visited again. This time, she spoke and said she wouldn't come again. Before she disappeared, she said she loved her and wished her well with Yao.

The alarm clock sounded.

Ann-Ann awoke with moisture gathering behind her eyelids. Then, Yao and last night's event rushed into her head. She smiled, sat up, and plumped the pillow.

Nana kneeled before the nearby window, doing her daily devotion.

Ann-Ann reached for her Bible on the nightstand, but her mind refused to focus. Stifling a sigh, she returned the Bible to its place and whispered a prayer. "Lord, thank You for this trip. Before I came, I never expected such a wonderful outcome."

Nana stood up. "Did you say something?"

"I was just praying." Ann-Ann let out a chuckle and relayed what happened last night.

"I'm so happy for you and Yao." Nana came to sit by her. "It turns out better than I've ever expected. After we go to Turkey today, we'll be back home in seven days. I can't wait to return to Hong Kong. Have you and Yao settled on the wedding date?"

"Yao said as soon as possible." Ann-Ann brought a hand to her face, a feeble attempt to hide her unbridled joy. "I still desire a proper wedding. I hope he won't think me vain."

"My girl, of course not. It'll be your one-and-only wedding. You should do it right." Nana's dark brows pinched together. "When Jie and May-May got married, they didn't have a ceremony at all because of the Cultural Revolution. I don't want to miss yours."

"Yeah. Yao said we can have everything ready in two months. What do you think if we set the wedding date for the second Saturday of September? I'll talk to him again today." Ann-Ann glanced at the clock and got up. "We'd better get ready. Our flight leaves soon."

On the airplane, unlike before, Nana asked Ann-Ann to sit with Yao. As she sat down, Yao reached out, grasped her hand, and didn't let go. His simple gesture brought a stirring warmth to her bosom. *Lord, thank You. You love me, and Yao loves me.*

After the seatbelt signs went off, Josh rushed to their seats. "Great-Nana told me you two are getting married. Is it true?"

Heat flushed her cheeks. She withdrew her hand from Yao's and tucked loose strands of hair behind her ear.

"It's true." Yao cuffed Josh's shoulder. "Do you want me to be your uncle?"

"But you're already my uncle." Josh scratched his chin, then nodded. "Now you'll become my uncle-uncle. Ha, my uncle squared."

She couldn't help grinning. What a funny child.

"I'm so happy." Josh leaned toward Yao. "I have a joke for you. It's a real story."

Yao gave an encouraging nod. "Are you sure it's an actual story? Not something you copied from the newspaper?"

"Well, it's both." Josh sat on the armrest of Yao's seat. "My sister, Audrey, told my dad one day, 'Daddy, I love you. When I grow up, I'm going to marry you.' I told her, 'You can't marry your own father.' She then pointed to me and said, 'Then I'll marry you.' I frowned at her. 'You can't marry me either.' She looked confused, so I explained, 'You can't marry someone in your own family.' Audrey stared at me, then burst into tears. 'You mean I have to marry a total stranger?'"

Yao laughed aloud. "Bravo."

Josh hugged him, then reached over to hug her. "Uncle Yao and Auntie Ann-Ann, you're both in my family. The joke is wrong. You can marry someone in your own family."

Tears rushed to Ann-Ann's eyes. Why hadn't she ever thought about Yao that way? He'd always been a member of the Lee family.

To marry someone her family knew so well and now she loved so much was a blessing from the Lord.

Lord, thank You. Your mercy is great.

Chapter Eighteen

From his room in Istanbul, Yao surveyed the garden of the gorgeous Pera Palace Hotel, envy simmering in his chest. If only the hotels under his conglomerate could possess such lovely grounds. But not in Hong Kong, where over five million people were squeezed into 427 square miles.

At least Ann-Ann had agreed to have their wedding reception held in his Mingden Hotel, instead of the famous Peninsula Hotel. His mouth curled into a grin. In two months, she would become his wife.

Josh, standing next to him, sang out the exciting news from their guide, Emre. "We're super lucky to arrive in Istanbul while they're having the International Music Festival. I can't wait. Let's go."

"We've got time." Yao checked his watch. "Nice that our flight from Tel Aviv landed early."

He led the boy down the hallway. On the airplane, he'd told Ann-Ann about his recurrent river nightmare since he escaped from China. In return, with moisture glistening in her beautiful eyes, she'd shared about the baby girl in her dreams. He'd kissed the tears from her cheeks and reaffirmed that, no matter what happened in the past, God had forgiven them both, thoroughly, completely. His words had brought a soft smile to her lips, and she laid her head on his shoulder with a content sigh.

Josh knocked on Nana Lee and Ann-Ann's room.

The door slit open, and Ann-Ann scudded out. "Shush. Nana's taking a nap." She pulled Yao aside. "We can't go with you today. Nana isn't feeling well."

Yao's shoulders stiffened. "Is it serious? Should we take her to the hospital?"

Ann-Ann leaned against the wall and shook her head, her curly mane slipping forward. "She said she has a headache and needs more rest. These activity-packed past few days have worn her out. Since we're leaving for Ephesus, Cappadocia, and Pamukkale tomorrow morning, Nana wants to make sure she has enough energy to visit the ancient cities where Apostle Paul preached."

He whooshed out his relief, inserted both hands into the pockets of his khaki shorts, and suppressed an urge to draw her into his arms to kiss her. "Are you staying with your nana?"

"Yeah, just in case. Shawn and Margie have already left for their errands. It's only you and Josh for this free day." A meager grin quirked her lips. "Emre mentioned there would be a large crowd. Watch out for pickpockets."

"Auntie, don't worry." Josh stepped up to hug her. "I'm a little person. No one can stoop so low to pickpocket me."

She laughed aloud. "Who was talking about you? You have nothing valuable anyway."

"Um... Now you have me worried." Yao removed the Patek Philippe. "Keep this for me."

As she received the watch, he covered her palm with his.

Josh's eyes sparkled. "Ha, Uncle Yao, you're holding my auntie's hand."

Crimson crept up to her cheeks. "Well, take care. See you later." She patted her nephew's head and retreated into her room.

At the door's click, a hollowness carved out something from his heart. He'd hoped to enjoy the gorgeous day with her, even if in the company of others. Listening to classic music together would've been nice since both were learning a musical instrument.

Josh tugged at his sleeve. "Uncle Yao, should we go?"

Ten minutes later, they strolled onto a road about two blocks away from their hotel. Children ran loose through the narrow street. Someone, covered in a black burka from head to toe, walked up and sat before a grand piano in the corner. Must be an orthodox Muslim woman.

The music started, collecting a group of spectators.

"I know this one. 'Für Elise' by Beethoven. I learned it not long ago." Josh shifted closer.

A simple piece. Yet, as the mysterious performer played with such tenderness and love, the melody drew Yao in, engrossed him, and sent him back to the hotel garden in Jerusalem with Ann-Ann. He could still feel the sweet caress of her lips on his.

Applause sounded, breaking the magical spell.

"Uncle Yao, look at that." Josh drew him toward a street vendor. "I'm hot. Should we buy one?"

"Ice cream? Not a bad idea on such a hot summer day." Yao ordered two cups.

The Turkish girl behind him commented in English. "Sir, just so you know, our Turkish ice cream, dondurması, is made of goat's milk with a dash of wild orchid roots. It won't melt easily like those made of cow's milk."

"Goat's milk?" Josh goggled his eyes. "I've never had it before."

Yao took a bite of the rich, creamy, and icy-cold treat. "Nice. I like it."

They devoured the Turkish delicacy on the packed sidewalk. Afterward, Josh tugged on Yao's shirt again and yanked him toward the street's far end. A group of trumpeters, performing "God Save the Queen," led a procession with the banner of the City of Hong Kong.

"Do you recognize any of them?" Josh's high-pitched voice rose above the dazzling brass music.

"Not at all." Yao eyed the musicians one by one. "But it's nice to know Hong Kong also takes part in the international music festival."

After ambling around the nearby streets, they bumped shoulders with strangers speaking in different languages and dialects, then stopped by another street vendor.

Josh pointed at the food. "What's that? It looks like pizza, but it's cooked over wood."

A man nearby chuckled. "Kiddo, you're right. We call it lahmacun, a round pita dough topped with minced meat, tomatoes, onions, and parsley." He winked at Josh. "It's very delicious. Try it."

Yao's stomach grumbled. Hmm, just about lunchtime. "I'll take two."

After Yao paid, Josh bit into his and winced. "It's a little spicy."

"What do you mean?" Yao tried his and winced too. "Wow, didn't know this thing is spicy. Don't finish it if your stomach can't handle it."

The half-eaten lahmacun met its demise in a garbage bin. A delectable, meaty aroma teased Yao's nostrils. He turned toward a rotating vertical skewer above a vendor's cart. "There. The kebab should be fine."

They finished the lamb kebab together with pita and mixed vegetables, and sauntered into another busy street. A solo female violinist, clad in a long, flowery dress, played "Carmen" on a makeshift platform before a shop.

One of his favorite pieces. Yao hurried toward the crowd surrounding the performer and sang along with the melody, immersing in the character's emotions.

Someone shouted, "Pickpocket!"

He spun on his heel.

Behind him, a man pointed at a woman bolting away. "Stop her. She's got my wallet."

Yao shook his head and reached for Josh's hand. His jaw slackened. Where was Josh?

His gaze swept over the distance, then took in a closer range. People jammed the street, but he couldn't see May-May's boy!

Didn't Josh follow right behind him when they turned into this street?

Eight feet away, a mop of shiny black hair caught his eye, and his tight muscles relaxed. He raced over. When the child turned, Yao faltered back. It wasn't Josh.

"Josh." His voice wobbled across a group of teenagers nearby, blending with their laughter.

The violinist started another tune, the "Chaconne" from *Sonata No. 2 in D Minor*, another of his favorites.

If not because of his love of the violin, Josh would still be by his side.

Yao plugged his ears. *Lord, please help me find Josh.*

For three long hours, he circled the streets, praying and checking every child with a hint of black hair. His silent prayers rose into the cloudy sky and crashed down into his heart.

Still no Josh.

Dark clouds hung low in the sky, and as the sun sunk lower, rain poured down. The crowd dispersed, seeking temporary shelters.

He winced at an image of May-May's tear-stained face from years ago. After the Red Guards arrested Nana Lee, May-May remained mute for days. Yet, so strong was the voice inside of her that her misery appeared like an immense, invisible wheel circling in emptiness. How would she respond to *this*?

Then Ann-Ann's face overlapped May-May's.

What was he going to tell Nana Lee and Ann-Ann? Could they keep the news from May-May for long?

He slumped onto an empty bench and let raindrops pound on him. Then, regaining his strength, he stood up. Mud sloshed underfoot and stuck to his custom-made shoes. He passed by stranger after stranger, none paying him attention. Water saturated his entire body. Was it rain, sweat, or tears?

He'd lost his sense of direction. But when he turned into another street, a silhouette of a mansion, their hotel flanked by lush trees crowned in verdant leaves, loomed ahead.

One last hope. Maybe Josh returned to their hotel by himself.

Yao rushed straight to his room and drew his brows tight. Everything remained as they'd left it.

So, Josh hadn't come back.

He changed into dry clothes, walked down the long hallway to Nana Lee and Ann-Ann's room, and tapped on the door.

No response.

A painful tightness filled his abdomen.

Where were they?

He dashed toward the elevator and went up to the fourth floor. As he approached Shawn and Margie's room, sobs resounded within.

Who was crying? Why?

He knocked, his heart hammering.

Shawn let him in. "Where did you go? We've been waiting for you."

Ann-Ann sat in a corner, tears staining her face.

"I lost track of Josh and spent hours looking for him." Yao could barely breathe. "What has happened?"

Nana Lee looked up, her lips quivering. "Someone has kidnapped Josh."

He sank into the chair beside the bed, a sense of doom constricting his chest. "How did you find out?"

Margie pointed at a recorder on the coffee table. "The kidnappers sent this to the hotel."

She set it to play.

Amid blasting background noises, a child whimpered. "Great-Nana, Auntie Ann-Ann, they—"

Then he was shushed.

Josh's voice, no doubt.

Nana Lee held her hands together, tears tracing the wrinkles along her cheeks. "They may have hurt him. Oh, how traumatized the child is!"

"I feel awful to have argued with Josh about Christianity." Shawn scratched his chin, his bass voice low like in a whisper.

"Josh is such a sweet boy." Moisture glistened in Margie's eyes.

Yao gaped at her. Margie, always calm and devoid of emotions, shed tears for Josh?

Ann-Ann, raising her teary face, dropped a piece of paper on the table. "They also left this."

Crude typewriter fonts, but nobody could dismiss the message:

> We have Josh Ying. If you hope to see him alive again, adhere to the following:
>
> 1) Do not contact any authorities.
>
> 2) Get a suitcase and place in it 1,000,000 USD (one million) in unmarked, untraceable 20-dollar US bills. Bundle the bills using rubber bands into 50 stacks with 20,000 in each stack.
>
> 3) Bring the suitcase to an abandoned lot at the base of the Galata Bridge near the Sirkeci Station. Leave the suitcase in the middle of the lot.
>
> 4) This must be completed tomorrow (July 12) at 3 a.m.

5) Exception: If you can't obtain the money in time, Yao Chen must come tomorrow (July 12) at 3 a.m. as Josh's replacement.

6) If you want to see Yao Chen alive, prepare 1,000,000 USD in unmarked untraceable 20-dollar bills. Bundle the bills using rubber bands into 50 stacks with 20,000 in each stack. Place the suitcase on the spot as described at 3 a.m. on July 16.

Remember, we know you well and are watching everything.

The kidnappers thought about every detail, and their determination to get the money came through clearly on the one-page yellowish note.

"Where's Galata Bridge?" Yao muttered under his breath.

Shawn hitched his shoulders. "It spans the Golden Horn. We'll need to borrow Emre's van. But how are we going to get one million bucks before three a.m. tomorrow morning?"

"Have you talked to Emre?" Yao massaged his temples.

"Not yet. We're waiting for you." Margie put away the recorder. "Is there any way you can get such a sum tonight?"

He checked his wrist, but his watch went missing. Ann-Ann, still sobbing, took the Patek Philippe from her purse and gave it to him.

Seven p.m., July 11, Saturday.

All banks were closed on Sunday.

Nana Lee jerked her head up. "Can we even get that much US currency in Turkey?"

Margie hugged her. "Yes, not to worry. The US dollar has been the world's foremost reserve currency for almost forty years. All international business transactions need it."

"Yao?"

Unsure which woman voiced his name, he forked his fingers through his hair, pulling at the roots as if he could make his brain work. "I'm trying to think. I can't remember how much cash is in Chang-Ji's subsidiary in Istanbul—definitely *not* a million dollars. Even if the money was there, I couldn't get it now with everything closed."

He dropped his arms to his sides. "I'll call Susie."

Ann-Ann jerked up her gaze. "It's midnight in Hong Kong."

"Worth a try." He dialed her number.

The phone rang. No one picked up. He left a message, asking her to call back as soon as possible. As he replaced the receiver, an eerie hush settled over them.

He studied the note on the coffee table. One line glared at him— "If you can't obtain the money in time, Yao Chen must come as Josh's replacement."

"I need some solitude." He stumbled out of the room.

No one blocked his way.

Chapter Nineteen

Yao staggered toward the hotel's back door. His mind shifted to the past few days about Josh and his jokes.

What a funny, kindhearted boy.

He passed into the garden. As May-May's image intruded, he twisted his lips downward. If she found out someone had kidnapped her son...

The rain had stopped, and the clouds moved on. He ventured towards the twilight, still hot despite the earlier downpour. A blackbird flew overhead and circled back. She eyed a temporary pond created by the raindrops, dipped one wing into the water, then looped away.

What scared her?

Fear crept into his soul as if he was back in the Pearl River, struggling for survival, swimming toward freedom.

What was life for? He'd raised the question after he reached the riverbank in Macau.

Didn't the Holy Spirit answer him during their visit to Masada?

Should he give up his freedom and even his life for Josh? If he didn't, would he despise himself and live his remaining days in shame?

He closed his eyes and whispered a Bible verse. "'During those days, men will seek death, but will not find it; they will long to die, but death will elude them.'"

Long ago, when Nana Lee showed him his pa's last letter before death, he'd wailed at the words:

> *Yao is on his way to visit you and May-May. When you see him, please tell him, no matter what befalls me, I'm prepared to face it. Recently I've received words from Him, "Be faithful, even to the point of death, and I will give you the crown of life." I consider it a blessing. Death is our doorway to the promised land.*

Yao reopened his eyes and gazed at the gloomy clouds now releasing their burden of rain on the western skyline.

What made Pa remain steadfast in his faith journey? What promise was so great that he willingly gave up his life for it?

Someone's crooning floated in the air. A Turkish song, mysterious and sorrowful.

The waning sunlight filtered through the clouds, casting heavy shadows from the tree branches. The wind rustled through the leaves, creating a soft, gentle sound. As he wandered the open, peaceful space, his mouth soured with a bitter smile.

Lord, shall I give up my freedom and even my life for Josh?

Margie's words echoed in his head. "Sometimes, to die with dignity is better than to live in shame and horror."

If he turned himself over to the kidnappers, he might live or die.

Jesus' solemn words arose deep within him. "I am the resurrection and the life. He who believes in me will live, even though he dies, and whoever lives and believes in me will never die. Do you believe this?"

He kneeled behind a tree trunk and cried out, "Lord, I do believe."

His simple prayer reverberated in the emptiness of his mind. He shot to his feet, reentered the hotel, and went straight to Shawn and Margie's room.

***

Ann-Ann paced around their room. Did she kiss Josh before he left for the musical festival?

A sharp pain pierced her heart as Yao's words soared through the hollow of her head. "I'll go to replace Josh."

Would the kidnappers release Josh when Yao went in? Then what would happen? Would they harm Yao?

Oh, she loved them both so much. Would she lose one of them for good?

At the sight of Nana slumped in the easy chair near the bed, Ann-Ann spoke in such a loud voice that her heart skittered. "I'm sorry I didn't tell you about Shawn and Margie's actual mission on this trip before today."

Nana kept quiet but straightened to turn on the table lamp. Light filtered down in long shards from the lampshade.

She crossed to the other side of Nana's seat, casting her shadow on the carpet. "I..." Her throat closed, and her feet blurred in her vision. With each sob, her misery deepened. The salt on her lips brought no comfort.

Nana's hands trembled. "Have they hurt Josh? What will they do to Yao? It's too much to take in." She lowered her voice. "I wish I hadn't invited our boys to come with us."

An oppressive quietness lurked. Time seemed to stretch on forever. Nana spoke again, her tone gentle as always, yet a new vigor strengthened it. "Nothing we can do but pray." She patted Ann-Ann's knee. "Let's go to the Lord."

With a nod, Ann-Ann slid from the lounge chair.

Nana kneeled beside her. "Lord, once more, I ask for Your mercy and protection over Yao and Josh. I pray for those kidnappers. I don't know why they're so desperate to do such a thing. Please forgive them. Lord, please grant us Your peace no matter what our situations are."

More tears seared Ann-Ann's eyelids. How could Nana plead forgiveness for the kidnappers?

An impatient knock sounded. For a brief second, hope buoyed Ann-Ann, and she jumped to her feet. Was Josh outside? As she came back to her senses, the hot tears threatened to resurface.

After Nana opened the door, Margie marched in. "Have you seen Shawn and Yao?"

"Not since we left your room." Nana guided Margie toward Ann-Ann. "Why?"

"Yao said he would call Susie again from his room. Shawn went with him to talk to his sister—an *hour* ago." Margie clutched her chair's armrests, her knuckles whitening in their grip. "I've just tapped on his door. Nobody answered."

Ann-Ann opened her mouth but couldn't utter a word.

"No—" Nana gasped. "Did the kidnappers seize them as well?"

"Inside the hotel? Unlikely." Margie's face contorted. "Shawn may have talked Yao into rescinding his offer to replace Josh. They may be on their way to the airport."

Ann-Ann's heart sank. Was Yao that kind of man? Oh, what would happen to Josh?

Nana's black brows arched toward her hairline, but she kept her calm. "I don't think Yao would do that. Before we pass any premature judgments, let's go over our previous conversations. Margie, you said a lot of things after Yao offered himself to take Josh's place, but I can't remember any of them. My mind was in a total daze."

Those words resonated, somehow lessening Ann-Ann's turmoil. She wiped away her tears. "Me too. You mentioned the kidnappers might be involved in human trafficking...?" She waved to indicate the blankness where her memory should be.

With a gasp, Nana pressed a palm to her chest. "Human trafficking?"

Ann-Ann fixed her gaze on Nana yet looked past her. Her conversation with Yao on the Nile riverboat brought a shudder to her spine. The corpse of that poor belly dancer... Her shoulders stiffened again.

"Margie?" Nana barely whispered. "Margie, did... did I hear you mention that sometimes victims are killed to harvest their organs for sale?"

Was that why the dancer's upper body went missing? Did the murderers remove her organs for paying clients who needed organ transplants?

Nana pressed her hands together as if in prayer. "I still can't believe someone can be so cruel to kill another human being to sell the organs."

"Those people will do anything for money." Ann-Ann let tears fall down her cheeks again. *Lord, please have mercy on us.*

Margie chuffed out a breath. "It's all about money. Usually, they won't kill unless the person becomes unmanageable, or they receive an order from someone who offers a sizeable sum for a specified organ." She pulled her legs tight against her chest. "They won't harm Josh if we can deliver Yao or the money on time."

She tapped her foot. "The kidnappers thought of everything. They knew it would be difficult to seize a well-built man like Yao in public. So, they snatched Josh, a child. But Yao is their ultimate target. From the way they planned and operated, they're well experienced."

Nana kneaded her brows. "How did they know Yao was in our private tour group?"

"They must have learned from the tabloids."

"Yao is famous in Hong Kong." Nana shook her head. "Outside of Hong Kong, nobody knows him."

Margie popped up from her chair. "The kidnappers may be Hong Kong expats who read the Chinese tabloids or even people who know Yao."

"Yao's friends?" Ann-Ann jerked up her head. "Nathan and his sister, Nancy? Could that be possible?"

When Margie remained silent, Nana patted Margie's arm. "Back to Shawn and Yao. Shall we ask the front desk to let us into Yao's room? We can check for signs whether they've left."

"Such a good idea!" Admiration swelled Ann-Ann's chest.

"We can't." Margie waved as if trying to brush aside an annoying fly. "They'll ask us why. Once we tell them what's happened, they'll call the police. Josh's safety may be jeopardized."

"I still can't believe Yao would leave like a coward," Ann-Ann muttered under her breath.

Wait.

Yao told her he was learning tai chi and said tai chi helped calm him when he was under stress. Shawn was a master in Shaolin martial arts.

Her body stilled. That could mean... Ann-Ann held her breath, then blurted out, "I know where they are."

"You do?" Nana and Margie asked in unison, one in Mandarin and the other in Cantonese, their high-pitched voices and different dialects blending.

Ann-Ann bobbed her head. "They must be in the hotel gym."

Margie sprinted from her seat, and the three of them rushed downstairs to the gym.

Through the glass door, two men faced away, both shirtless, with their tanned skin stretched tight across hard muscles. As one lifted his left leg, the other followed. In a slow, smooth, and synchronized movement, they raised their right palms.

An incredible sight. Yao looked so much in control, with grace and strength. As they repeated their actions in a modulated, agile motion, Ann-Ann curled her lips into a half smile.

The men turned and stopped their movements.

She pushed the door open and rushed to Yao's side. "Hi." Her gaze flitted to his toned torso, and her cheeks burned. *What's going on? It's not the right time to think about his physique.*

"Hi," he responded, his voice soft like a gentle breeze. He grabbed his shirt from a nearby chair and pulled it over himself.

Margie stepped forward. "Um... Why are you two practicing tai chi in the middle of the night?"

Shawn bent to pick up his shirt from the floor and put it on. "Emre is coming at two. No point to go to bed. So, I invited Yao to exercise with me. It calms our nerves."

"Have you made all the necessary arrangements?" Ann-Ann glanced at them.

Yao gestured for them to leave. "Let's go to my room first."

Once inside, he strolled to the cabinet and retrieved a piece of paper from the top drawer. "Shawn and Margie, could you serve as my witnesses and sign this document?" Then he turned to Ann-Ann. "In case something happens to me, I'm leaving everything to you, my dear fiancée."

"I—" She cupped a hand on her mouth. Her stomach knotted and her chest swelled. As tears stung her cheeks, she sank onto the nearby chair. "Yao, please, you must come back."

After Shawn signed, he patted Ann-Ann's arm. "I do believe things will work out okay. Susie called back. She'll wire the money to Yao's Istanbul subsidiary on Monday. Just to be sure, she'll fly to Istanbul on Tuesday with the company's checkbook. We shall meet the deadline. We just need to make sure they release Josh tonight."

Ann-Ann rubbed her forehead, the pulse points thrumming with her tangled thoughts and emotions.

Would they hurt Yao? She couldn't help raising her gaze toward him.

Yao flashed a smile that looked worse than weeping and came to sit by her. "Don't worry. I'll be fine."

Nana touched Margie's shoulder. "How do we make sure they release Josh? Can we get in touch with them?"

"No. From my previous experiences, after Yao makes himself visible in that empty parking lot, we should see Josh there."

Her previous experiences? Ann-Ann's throat tightened. Had Margie gone through similar situations? Did she rescue the victims at the end?

Nana wobbled to a chair, then sat, her back stiff. With her brows drawn together and her chin held high, she faced Shawn. "Could you please explain the process?"

"Emre will lend us his van for the next few days. We've agreed not to seek a refund for our canceled itinerary." Shawn fingered his shirt. Sweat stains already seeped through. "After driving over the Galata Bridge toward the abandoned lot near the Sirkeci Station, we'll wait till fifteen minutes before three. When Yao and Margie get out, Yao will walk toward the middle of the lot and turn on his flashlight to make himself visible. At that moment, they shall release the child into the parking lot. Margie can bring Josh back to the van."

Nana's brows remained furrowed. A tremor ran through her lips, but she steadied them to speak. "And on July 16? After we drop the suitcase with money, if they refuse to release Yao, what can we do?"

Wow. Nana sounded like a professional and didn't miss any details.

Margie stepped forward, speaking in Shawn's place. "There's this Chinese saying, 'Pay with one hand and deliver with the other.' After Yao is with the kidnappers, he'll inform them that on July 16, the three of us will be fully armed and show up with money in our van. They shall drive a car to the empty lot with Yao inside. If we don't see Yao, we'll leave with our suitcase. Once Yao gets out of their car, we'll drop the suitcase to the ground and wait for them to inspect the money before pulling Yao into our van." She twisted her watch into view. "Did you say Emre is coming at two? We'd better get ready and go down to the lobby."

"Sorry, one last question." Nana massaged her temples. Her fingers shook before she thrust them into her hair as if to hide the sign of weakness. "You mentioned fully armed. What do you mean?"

"We'll wear bulletproof helmets and armored vests and carry guns."

Who was Margie? How could she acquire those things in Istanbul? With a chill going over her, Ann-Ann jammed her hands into her armpits. "Where are you going to get them?"

"I have my connections." Margie grinned. "By the way, when I mentioned the three of us, it includes you."

"Me?" Ann-Ann slackened her jaw, and her arms fell limp at her sides. "I don't know how to shoot."

"Margie will teach you. With your intelligence, you'll pick it up in no time. Are all of us going?" Shawn gripped Nana's shoulder. "Nana Lee, maybe you stay here?"

She wagged a finger. "I'm going. I'll pray in the van for you guys."

Ann-Ann waited for others to step out, then drew Yao into her bosom. Driven by a desperate, yearning love, she wrapped her arms around his neck and kissed him. "Please come back to me."

He cupped her cheeks between his palms and whispered, "Trust in the Lord. I'm confident we don't have to change our wedding date."

Chapter Twenty

Yao exited the van and entered the dark parking lot. Stars in the sky blinked at him, bringing him a shudder. His mind shifted toward that night of his escape from China. Was it only sixteen years ago? Back then, he was desperate, with no place to go. Now he had a choice.

A knot in his stomach tightened. With his throat dry, he clenched his jaw. How had he gotten himself into this? Should he forget the whole thing and book the earliest flight back to safety? It might not be too late. But if the kidnappers killed Josh, how could he explain such cowardly behavior to Ann-Ann and all his friends? Worse, how would he face himself? At that point, life would be meaningless.

To die now was better than when he tried to seek death and death eluded him, like what the Bible verses said in the Book of Revelation.

As he traced his thoughts to their different consequences, the familiar words emerged in his head again. *I am the resurrection and the life. He who believes in me will live, even though he dies, and whoever lives and believes in me will never die.*

A rustle rose from somewhere. He scanned around. Not a single soul. The empty lot remained as bleak and deadly as before. He was alone and helpless, just like sixteen years ago. He'd survived then. How about now?

Should he turn on the flashlight? Once he did, there'd be no return. He wiped away the sweat speckling his forehead.

From afar, blasting sirens drifted around the surrounding emptiness.

No, it wasn't empty. A silhouette of something, indistinct yet certain, perched ahead of him. Was it an illusion? He squinted at the object. Yes, a sedan, the kidnappers' car.

His heart pounding, he chewed the inside of his cheek and clicked the flashlight on. A circle of light appeared on the unpaved ground. Then a different luminescence emitted from the sedan's interior. Its door opened, and a child stepped out.

Soft thuds echoed through the silence. "Josh?"

A powerful force pulled Yao's arms behind his back, and a warm breath blew on his earlobe. "Listen here." A heavy Middle Eastern accent laced the man's words. "If you cooperate, all of us will be better off."

When did they come from behind him? Why didn't he detect their approaches? He thought he had his fear under control. Maybe not.

He gritted his teeth in a vain attempt to stop his legs from shaking. "I'll cooperate only after the boy is safe with my friend."

"Look again." A familiar twang tinted the new speaker's English.

Was it a hallucination? The accent sounded Asian.

A tall figure from his friends' van rushed toward Josh and carried him back to safety.

Then something slammed into Yao's head, and his world went dark.

***

Early in the afternoon, Ann-Ann followed Margie into the elevator to travel to the fifth level.

She yawned and covered her mouth. They'd hurried back to their hotel with Josh in the early morning. Though exhausted, none of them could sleep.

Josh kept silent at first. Once inside their room, he sobbed so hard that he hiccupped. They couldn't console him, no matter how they tried. At last, Nana kneeled by him and prayed aloud. Minutes later, he quieted. He'd fallen asleep.

But sleep had eluded Ann-Ann. Lacing her fingers behind her head in the darkness, she thought about Yao, their intertwined past,

147

and the future they might share if he came back safely. Would Susie wire the money in time? Could they obtain small, untraceable bills to that amount here?

Her musing went awry at the sound of the elevator doors sliding open. A young woman came forward and led them to a room. "Have you ever handled a gun before?"

"I have." Margie gestured toward Ann-Ann. "But she hasn't."

"No problem. My name is Debra. Call me Debbie." She placed a rifle on the table. "This is a lightweight semiautomatic rifle, an AR-15." She explained its mechanics. "Now, let's go to the practice area."

Twenty shooting lanes extended before them. Guns and various tools lined the walls.

"Some basics first." Debbie took two identical guns off the wall and gave one to Ann-Ann. "I'll show you how to load it."

It seemed easy. Ann-Ann pulled back the charging handle and loaded in a round.

"You're doing a great job." Margie crossed her arms over her chest. "One more tip. When you shoot, the gun will kick back. It's the recoil, the backward movement a shooter feels when the bullet is discharged. Pure physics. When a gun launches a bullet forward, the bullet will exert an equal force in the opposite direction on the gun." She wiggled a finger. "There's no way around it. If you grip the gun with both hands and extend your arms, the intensity may lessen a bit."

"Now, prop the rifle against the shoulder like this. Properly positioning the rifle butt helps your shoulder absorb recoil. Otherwise, kickback can hurt." Debbie did a demo with her own weapon. "Some prefer closing one eye and looking through the scope with the other. I prefer to shoot with two eyes open. It doesn't matter as long as you can line your eye through the sights to view the target."

Boom! A loud noise erupted.

Ann-Ann dropped her gun and plugged her ears with both hands but couldn't stop her body from trembling.

Debbie's bullet hit the middle of the bull's eye, creating a gaping hole. She laid down the gun. "I forgot to mention it's going to be loud." She grabbed a pair of earmuffs from the nearby table. "For you. Just in case."

Ann-Ann's shoulders stiffened, and a knot tightened in her stomach. "Are you sure I can shoot this thing and not get hurt?"

Both Debbie and Margie bobbed their heads.

Beads of sweat slicked Ann-Ann's forehead. She picked up the dangerous machine, aimed through the scope, exhaled, and squeezed the trigger. Her body jolted. An earsplitting bang and the acrid smell of burned gunpowder assaulted her senses as the gunstock rammed her shoulder.

The bullet hit the target, but not quite near the center.

Margie applauded. "Nice job. Keep trying."

Ann-Ann aimed. This time, the bullet smacked the target away to the left. On her third try, she readjusted and hit the dead center.

"Bravo." Margie patted her back. "You're a born natural. After tomorrow, you'll shoot as well as I do."

At her praise, Ann-Ann dipped her chin, unsure whether to cry or laugh. Her arms felt sore. No, her whole body felt like she had been hit by a truck. Then her thoughts turned to Yao. She was doing this for the man she loved and must make sure she didn't fail when the time came. Her future happiness depended on him. She'd once called him a jerk and tried to avoid him for years. When did he find a way into her heart and capture it?

Determination tautened her muscles. She raised the rifle and shot again.

***

One face blurred into another, one scene to the next. Muffled sounds echoed in the hollowness of Yao's mind.

Was he dreaming?

He fluttered his eyelids. Shadows shifted before him. His head ached, his muscles stiff. Fire seared his body.

He blinked. Dim light seeped through an iron-bar window, casting gloom on the floor.

Where was he?

He sat up and blinked again, adjusting to the dismal room.

A slab of bread and a bottle of water waited on a table against a wall. A portable hiker's foldable toilet claimed a corner.

His stomach rumbled, and an overwhelming need to urinate urged him to move.

He pushed against the ground to stand up, but the room tilted to one side. He fell back on the hard cement.

His body jerked at the scraping of a door opening, a dog barking, followed by human noises. It wasn't the door to his room. Were the kidnappers inside the adjacent room?

Before anyone enters, I'd better finish what I need to do.

After crawling to the toilet on hands and knees, he managed to complete his undertaking. Then he consumed the bread and water. Another feat.

The dog barked again. A woman spoke in English yet with a distinct Hong Kong accent. "You shouldn't have hit him so hard."

A man responded, also in accented English, the same accent as the guy who seized him in the parking lot. "We don't want trouble. Also, we can't let him or anyone know where we live."

"It's no trouble. I told you he'll cooperate."

Hot. Unbearable heat. Sweat soaked Yao's shirt, forming rivulets between his shoulder blades. Nancy? Impossible. The concussion was playing tricks on him.

Yeah, no air-conditioning in July. In his youth in Beijing, they didn't have air conditioners either. Somehow, he'd not only survived but also grown tall and healthy.

Of course, he would survive this time.

A deep cough rattled his body. He slapped a palm on his mouth. Too late.

Someone pounded the door open. Two people, covered in black from head to toe, including gloves, entered. Were they two orthodox Muslim men? Probably not, because a Muslim man wouldn't wear a burka to disguise his identity regardless of the situation. Wasn't it summer? How did they bear the heat? Or maybe they enjoyed the cool air in their room.

Yao scratched his neck. How could he think of those trivial nonsenses under the circumstance?

"Good. You're finally awake." The tall one walked up. His Middle Eastern accent gave away his identity—the same man in the parking lot. He gestured toward the shorter one standing by the door. "Ready?"

Ready for what? Yao's leg muscles tightened, his heartbeat racing. What did they plan to do to him?

The short fellow kept quiet but waved a Polaroid instant-film camera. Yao focused on the exposed wrist of the raised arm. A woman's wrist, he was sure of it. Was she the same woman who spoke English with a Hong Kong accent?

The man reached into his burka and pulled out something.

A dagger!

Were they going to kill him? Didn't they want the money? Or did someone hate him so much to desire his life?

The man deflected the blade. "Okay, start."

He kicked Yao's shin.

The woman pressed the camera shutter.

Pains shoot from Yao's joint up to his lower body. He shifted backward on his hands and butt, a feeble attempt to avoid another assault. When his back hit the wall, he winced and braced for more havoc.

The guy moved closer. Instead of kicking him again, he pointed the sharp edge to Yao's throat. "Ready? Another one."

He pushed down and pierced Yao's skin. The camera clicked once more.

Yao contorted his face but stifled a scream.

Okay, stay calm. They just want snapshots of my misery to be sent to my loved ones.

Still, as warm blood drops slithered down the length of his neck, chills shivered up his spine.

He hadn't been present when the Red Guards murdered his pa, but the messenger told him a teenage boy hit Pa with a hammer on the neck and killed him. On the night Yao escaped from China, he'd visualized Pa's blood spurting from his ruptured artery. What flashed across Pa's mind at that moment?

"Done." The man moved toward the door.

Yao blurted out, "Wait."

Both turned toward him.

With the heat, Yao's throat felt like closing in, but he must convey the message. He pushed his body up. "You know the people in our group well. Shawn and Margie are triad members and have connections." He swallowed hard. "On July 16, they and their friends, fully armed, will show up with money in the van. They asked you to drive a car to the empty lot with me inside. If they don't see me, they'll leave with the money. You shall park your car near their van. Once you let me out of your car, they'll drop the suitcase on the ground and wait for you to inspect the money. Then I'll get into their van."

The man raised a hand. "Anything else?"

Yao shook his head and slumped back against the wall.

R. F. Whong

Chapter Twenty-One

Yao sat in one corner, keeping the farthest distance from the toilet. Was it only one day? Why had the smell become so repulsive?

The nick on his neck no longer hurt, yet his body ached from lying all night on the cement floor. Sweat now soaked not only his shirt but also his pants.

A cold shower would be...

Voices rose from beyond his window. What language was it? Turkish?

Curiosity getting the best of him, he dragged his sore body to the window and leaped onto it to take in a glimpse of the outside world. Underneath a tall brick wall, two dark-skinned girls stood by a tree, their faces dull.

So, maybe it wasn't a free world out there. They looked like teenagers without a trace of the liveliness typical of youth. Were they confined like him? How long had they been here? Were they victims of human trafficking?

A burned smell drifted into his nostrils. Perhaps someone overcooked a steak. He eyed the empty plate on the table, and his stomach growled with his thoughts of the seafood dinner he and Ann-Ann enjoyed a few days ago. Would be nice to have a lobster. A bowl of rice would do too.

Did the kidnappers plan to starve him to death? No. They wanted money, not his life.

He huffed, returned to his previous spot, and sat. With nothing to do and no one to talk to, time stretched on.

One of his favorite short stories by Tolstoy, "How Much Land Does a Man Require?" flashed across his mind.

A farmer received an offer he couldn't resist. For a fixed sum of money, he could walk around as large an area as he wished from daybreak to sunset and mark his route with a spade along the way. All the land he'd walked on and marked would be his. The only condition was that he must return to his starting point by sunset. Of course, after setting off, he sprinted and demarcated the land in lightning speed. As the sun started to set, he raced back to the starting point just in time. Exhausted from the run, he dropped dead, and his servant buried him in an ordinary grave—only six feet long.

What did a man need to survive? Food, water, shelter, and clothing.

Yao scratched his forehead. Nowadays, why did everyone's life become so complicated? Sanitation, education, healthcare, careers, retirement, all kinds of gadgets and devices... The list kept growing.

The cement floor numbed his rear. As he tried to stand, someone unlocked the door.

A tall fellow entered. He set down a bottle of water and a slab of bread on the empty plate.

Yao swallowed to bring saliva to his dry mouth, unable to hold back the impulsive urge to talk. "Sir, it's boiling in here. Could you please bring me a fan?"

The guy's long black robe rustled. He didn't respond and trudged out of the room. The lock clicked.

Great, he just shrugged and left. Yao's lips curled up into a grin, and he started chuckling.

Insane. How could he laugh under the circumstance? But he couldn't help it as he shifted to the table and devoured the meager food.

Definitely not enough. His stomach growled again.

When had he been hungry the last time? As a child back in Beijing? Food was scarce. People in their shared house, including Nana Lee and May-May, converted the yard into a small farm.

Tomatoes, cucumbers, and beans replaced the flowers. They all raised chickens to supplement the meat shortage.

Yet, he was happy, especially when May-May received food packages from her mother in Hong Kong and cooked his favorite dish—sautéed ginger threads together with a mixture of soybeans, canned bamboo shoots, and red carrots. Through those supplies from abroad, he didn't starve at all when he was growing up. Perhaps one reason both he and May-May grew tall and strong. More importantly, he was surrounded by people who loved him dearly.

What did a person need to live happily? Food, water, clothing, shelter, and love. Maybe love was the driving force for him.

Before this trip, he was foolish enough to focus on expanding Chang-Ji even to the point of marrying someone he didn't love. He'd been desiring Ann-Ann all along, and now she returned his love. *Lord, thank You for releasing me from my blind ambition.*

His heart swelled over their wedding plan. September 12, the second Saturday of the month. Ann-Ann would become his wife if he survived.

He splayed out his legs on the floor and gazed at the ceiling. A fly zipped past him.

Go away. There is no food here.

Did all those trafficked victims lack food? He only had to starve for four days. How long did other victims have to suffer?

Amid the height of the Cultural Revolution, with all the surrounding oppression, he'd questioned whether God even cared about humans. If He did, why didn't He intervene when good people were persecuted unjustly?

Years later, he found his answer. Yes, God cared. Otherwise, He wouldn't have sent His own begotten Son to this dark and treacherous world. On this earth, Jesus had braved intense sufferings, including crucifixion, the most terrible form of death. The Lord knew the pain and promised to walk with anyone willing to accept Him.

Ann-Ann grew up in Hong Kong, but she also went through a scary wilderness. Yeah, sometimes a prosperous environment could become even more treacherous than persecution.

The door opened again. The same man walked in and put down a basin of water and a white hand towel. "No fan, but this shall help."

As soon as the man left, Yao sprang into action. What a treat to wash his sweaty body with cold water. *Praise the Lord.*

***

Ann-Ann set down her rifle. Okay, day two at the shooting range. "Do we need to come again tomorrow?"

"Nope." Margie flashed a thumbs-up. "We're good to go."

Mission accomplished. Exhaling her relief, Ann-Ann twisted her Cartier watch into view. About lunchtime. Somehow, the sight of the old scar on her wrist no longer bothered her. "Margie, thank you for helping. Care to go to lunch together? My treat."

Margie shook her head and picked up her backpack. "I'm meeting with Shawn. We still have some errands to run."

"Ah, I almost forgot. You two need to get the bulletproof helmets, armored vests, and guns." Unable to suppress her curiosity, Ann-Ann tilted her body forward. "Where are you going to borrow those items?"

Margie waved as if to brush her aside. "How is Josh? Did he sleep well last night?"

Ann-Ann swallowed back her next question. Margie still guarded her information. No way would she answer whom she worked for. "Last night, he woke up from nightmares three or four times and howled."

Her buried emotions surged to the surface, and she blinked down the heat behind her eyes. "Josh whimpered that he was scared. When we asked him who those people were and what they did to him, he couldn't answer but pleaded to go home, where kids don't get carried away by strangers. The danger is over. Why does he still experience panic attacks?"

Margie halted her steps. "Have you heard about PTSD?"

"Post-traumatic stress disorder?" Ann-Ann wrinkled her nose. "Doesn't that only happen to soldiers returning from a war zone?"

"Well, any sort of trauma will induce it, especially when an event leads to a difference between everyday routine and a life-and-death situation."

"Is that what he's experiencing?" Poor child. "Margie, how can we help him?"

"It takes time. Once we get back to Hong Kong, take him to see a psychotherapist. Professional help will speed up his recovery."

Margie resumed walking. "I'd better get going. See you back at the hotel."

So prayers alone wouldn't help Josh recover?

Ann-Ann parked the van inside the hotel parking lot, the heaviness still weighing hard on her sleep-deprived body.

Her nephew's condition stressed her, but Yao's perilous state stirred up unimaginable pain. How did she develop such a strong attachment to him in mere weeks?

Or perhaps she'd grown to care about him in the years since they'd gone out. Yeah, he'd been a constant presence at their family gatherings. As Josh had said, he was a member of the Lee clan.

They had so much in common. Nana and Mama always hinted he was an ideal match for her. Yao had also more than once extended an olive branch. Yet, bitterness from their fight blinded her to her true interests.

Now she was ready to give herself to him, to integrate herself into his world... And this happened. *Lord, please let Yao come back to me safe and sound.*

The Mediterranean sun glared. The warm wind blew across her face, and two adorable sparrows chirped in the nearby branches. Instead of entering the lobby, she sat on the lawn.

During a recent conversation, Yao shared a childhood incident in Beijing related to sparrows. As his woody and spicy cologne drifted into her nostrils, she delved deeper into his past. Then he mentioned something absurd, scary.

His words echoed in her head. "Nonstop political campaigns shadowed everyone's life. The Great Leap Forward prohibited private farming, and the Four Pests Campaign aimed to eradicate rats, flies, mosquitoes, and sparrows. One afternoon, our teacher took us to a field to kill sparrows. We brought tin cans and other utensils. She commanded us to generate loud noises to frighten the birds off and stop them from settling. The sparrows would fly nonstop, become exhausted, and eventually drop dead. I started giggling at the funny idea. The teacher grabbed me by my ear and slapped me hard."

She'd gasped and covered her mouth. "How terrible."

He'd shaken his head. "I was lucky. Back at home, after I told Pa what'd happened, his eyes became clouded with moisture. He said it was fortunate we belonged to the categories of poor and lower-middle peasants, workers, revolutionary soldiers, revolutionary cadres, and revolutionary martyrs. Otherwise, both of us would have been locked up."

"Hi, Ann-Ann." A bass voice roused her. Then Shawn's large shadow fell over her. "Why are you sitting alone here? Are you all right?"

"I'm fine, thanks." She stood. "Are you leaving to meet up with Margie?"

"Yeah. How did the shooting go? Do you need to go again tomorrow?"

"Margie said we're good to go." The sparrows stopped chirping. She stole a glimpse of them. The birds flapped their wings against the wind and flew away.

"Do you have a few minutes?" He gestured toward a garden bench nearby. "May I ask you a question?"

Her curiosity piqued, she cocked her head to eye him. "Of course."

He waited for her to sit, then took the empty spot next to her. "You grew up in a Christian family, right?"

She nodded, waiting.

"I–I—" A tint of crimson mottled his cheeks.

Was he embarrassed? Why? "Yes?"

He sucked in a breath. "People who weren't born into a Christian family... Well, how do *they* become Christians?"

All those years ago, she'd argued with Yao about what a Christian was. Now she knew. "Growing up in a Christian family, I received baptism when I was a child. I attended worship regularly and memorized Bible verses. But I didn't become a Christian until I was in my twenties."

His eyes stretched wide. "How can that be?"

As she reminisced about her conversation with Yao, tenderness flooded her heart. "Religious activities are important, but they didn't make me a Christian."

He drew his eyebrows tight, appearing to pay great attention.

"A Christian is a person who has established a link with God through Christ." She motioned her arm. "I used to think that, since I was baptized, I must be a Christian. After my nana helped me connect with God, I realized I was just a so-called cultural Christian."

Shawn kneaded his brows. "I'm confused. If reading the Bible and attending church isn't sufficient, how does one connect with God?"

"God is holy. He won't connect with anyone who harbors sin. We must confess we're sinners and accept Jesus' sacrifice on the cross as the only way to be saved. Then the Holy Spirit will help us establish a personal relationship with God. Do you want to confess your sin to the Lord today?"

"I–I—" He dipped his chin. "I need to think about it more."

"I understand." She stood up. "I also have a question for you. Can you tell me where you and Margie are going to borrow the bulletproof helmets, armored vests, and guns?"

He shot to his feet, then waved. "I'd better hurry lest I be late and upset her again."

Like Margie, he guarded their information tightly.

Ann-Ann watched him leave, then strolled inside. When she entered their room, Nana rushed toward her. "You're back. Josh is finally asleep. Let's go inside the bathroom and look at the pictures. The front desk delivered them to our room about an hour ago."

What pictures? She followed Nana into the spacious bathroom and shut the door. By the sink lay two black-and-white pictures of Yao. The first one showed his contorted face as someone kicked him. The second, blood dripping down from a wound on his neck, exposed the horror in his eyes.

Ann-Ann clenched her fists and hissed out a breath. "Is Yao dead? Did they kill him?"

"Don't panic. I think he's okay."

As Nana hugged her, Ann-Ann nestled close, breathing in the soft feeling of comfort. She curled up her fingers, her whole body shaking. "But the pictures..." Her throat seized up, and a tear escaped.

"The kidnappers used them to warn us that they can take drastic actions if the money isn't there in time." Nana drew her to sit on the bathtub rim. "I believe they won't kill Yao."

Ann-Ann wiped her face with the back of a hand. "You think so?"

Nana bobbed her head.

"The money." Ignoring the tears now heating her cheeks, Ann-Ann rubbed her neck to focus on what needed to be done. "Has Susie wired the money into the subsidiary's account yet?"

"She has." Nana got up and tore a piece of toilet tissue to dab Ann-Ann's wet cheeks. "She called Shawn after you and Margie left for the shooting range. But the bank may hold the funds according to its policy since it's such a large amount. We'll know better when Susie arrives tomorrow."

One more day of waiting. Yet, what else could she do? She squeezed her eyes shut but couldn't lift the feelings of misery.

"Have you had lunch yet?" Nana cupped her palm to the side of Ann-Ann's face. "You have dark circles under your eyes. You didn't sleep well, did you?"

"I'm not hungry." Images about Yao and his childhood kept intruded her mind. "Nana, Yao told me something about sparrows when he was a child in Beijing. Do you remember those incidents?"

"Oh, that." Nana dropped her arm. "He must have been referring to the Four Pests Campaign. What a disaster. The extermination of sparrows enabled the proliferation of locusts, leading to crop damage. Food was scarce." Nana's eyes took on a faraway look. "If your mama didn't send us supplies from Hong Kong, May-May and I might not have survived."

Ann-Ann shivered. She'd grown up resenting the focus and money Mama spent on Nana and May-May. At the time, she hadn't comprehended the significance of her mother's endeavors. "Yao said you were generous and often shared the supplies with others. He believes that's why he grew tall and healthy."

"It's the least I could do under the circumstances." Nana raised her chin and patted Ann-Ann's back. "Since I became a Christian, the assignment from God has always been to love people around me, seek their spiritual growth, and help them enter God's family so they can enjoy a relationship with Him."

"Nana, I love you." Warmth soothed Ann-Ann's chest, and her shoulders loosened up a bit. "You've gone through so much, but you're still full of grace, faith, and courage. I hope I can be like you."

"You're growing fast in your faith journey as well." Nana's lips parted in a grin.

Ann-Ann leaned her head against Nana's bosom. "My faith is little, like a mustard seed. I remain apprehensive about Yao's well-being."

"Don't worry." Nana hugged her. "I've received the words from the Holy Spirit. Yao will come back to us safe and sound."

Was Nana right? Would Yao come back to her safely?

Chapter Twenty-Two

Ann-Ann trailed Shawn and Margie, and they scurried into Istanbul's international terminal. All around her, people's relatives and friends craned their necks to view passengers.

"There she is." Shawn rushed over. "How was your flight?"

"Uneventful." Susie hugged him, Margie, then Ann-Ann. "Glad to see you all here. How are Nana Lee and Josh? Any more news about Yao?"

"My nana is fine. She has such great faith. No matter what situation she's in, she's always full of peace and hope. Josh still shows signs of PTSD. Last night, he awoke from nightmares, crying and pleading to go home." Ann-Ann pressed against her tight-knit stomach and narrowed her eyes to suppress her tangled emotions. "Margie said it takes time. Once we get back to Hong Kong, we'll take him to see a psychotherapist."

"Yeah, it's tough, especially for a child." Susie's hair slipped forward as she looked down at her luggage. "I admire Nana Lee a lot. She's remarkable. Did Josh say anything about the kidnappers?"

"He still couldn't tell us what kind of people seized him. He only said they all wore long black robes." Shawn took his sister's suitcase. "Let's go to the van first. We can talk more back at the hotel."

Outside the airport, the morning sunshine cast elongated shadows across the cement pathway toward the parking lot. After settling into the Chevy van, Ann-Ann handed Susie two pictures. "The kidnappers sent these to the hotel yesterday." Her voice cracked. She wiped her hands on her black slacks but couldn't lift the oppressive feelings.

Susie tilted the photos toward the window to gain more light. "Yao doesn't look good. Why did they abuse him?"

"It's a tactic the kidnappers use often," Margie responded. "They want us to know they're serious and will take drastic actions if necessary."

"My nana said so as well." Ann-Ann reclaimed the pictures and traced Yao's contorted face with a finger. Even knowing the validity of those words, she couldn't relax. With trembling lips, she pressed the photos against her heart in a desperate attempt to pacify her trepidation. "Susie, how many bank accounts does your company's subsidiary have? I worry we can't obtain such a sum from one bank."

"Good thinking. Only a chief finance officer would think about those details." Susie retrieved an envelope from her purse and slid out a piece of paper. "According to my record, they have three different bank accounts."

"Most banks have cash in the vault to meet the requirement of reserves. Many banks hold US dollars for international business transaction purposes. Hope the banking system here operates the same way." Ann-Ann slid the pictures into her purse and crossed her arms over her chest, wrinkling up her blue cotton T-shirt. "I suppose we'll find out soon."

"But small, untraceable bills? That's a lot of twenties." Shawn spoke from the driver's seat.

The van approached a bridge. Ann-Ann sighted something at its base, and a pang shot through her. This wasn't the Galata Bridge, was it? She shifted her thoughts back to the discussion. "Well, banks' reserves are calculated by multiplying total deposits by the reserve ratio. For example, if a bank's deposits total ten million dollars and the required reserve is twenty percent, that bank's required minimum reserve is two million dollars. Some large banks also hold extra reserves." She tilted her face up toward the sky to avoid the sight of the bridge. "Bank reserves are kept to prevent the bank-run panic. Most likely, the bank will give us only part of the million dollars Susie wired in yesterday."

"Now you got me worried." Margie tapped the seat in front of her. "Does the subsidiary have an account with the largest bank in town? Instead of going back to our hotel, shall we go there now?"

The van crossed the bridge and turned onto the main road toward their hotel.

"I have no idea where the banks are. Look at this street's name. Refik Saydam Cd? Are all street names so long and difficult in Istanbul?" Susie knitted her brows tight. "We'd better go to the subsidiary's office first."

"Tell me the address. I'll locate it." Margie opened the map on her lap. After Susie spelled out the address, Margie jabbed at a point on her map. "Ha, we're in luck. It's not far away from our hotel."

Praise the Lord! Ann-Ann's taut muscles loosened somewhat as if that small thing evidenced God's provisioning for them. "Nice that our hotel is located in the town center."

Twenty minutes later, they left the subsidiary's office with the addresses for all three banks. Their first target was Ziraat Bank, the largest of the three. While they trod into its downtown office, a long line queued up before the counter.

Margie moved to the head of a line and flashed a badge. The bank teller dropped the deposit slip in her hand to rush into the back room.

Susie's eyes stretched wide. "What—"

Ann-Ann raised a finger to her lips. "Shh. Let's talk later." She wrinkled her nose, her spirit buoyed. She'd guessed it right. It appeared Susie had no idea who Margie was and simply relayed to Yao what Shawn had told her.

A tall man with a mustache strode out to usher them into his office. After Susie mentioned the million dollars she'd wired into the subsidiary's account, the manager tapped his desk. "Based on our reserve guidelines, the most we can give you is eight hundred thousand."

"But—" Susie halted as Margie wagged a finger at her.

Margie leaned forward. "Can you give us unmarked, untraceable US twenty-dollar bills?"

The manager gave her a questioning glance. Undeterred, Margie placed a palm on the desk. "If you don't have enough small bills, could you please ask your employees to scour them from other banks?"

The manager frowned. "That's a lot of work."

"I know, and I appreciate your help." She curled up her lips. "It's important."

"May I ask why?"

"Sorry, we can't tell you at this point." She dipped her chin. "You already know whom I work for. Confidentiality is crucial."

The manager glanced at his watch and let out a long breath. "It's unlikely we can get it done this afternoon. Will tomorrow morning be acceptable?"

"Sure." Margie pushed against the desk to stand up. "See you at ten o'clock tomorrow morning."

As she led them out of the bank, Margie checked her notes for the other addresses. "The next two banks should have two hundred grand."

Indeed, they obtained a hundred and forty thousand in small US bills from one bank and another sixty thousand from the other. While they walked toward the parking lot, Shawn halted. "Look, a luggage shop. Let's go buy a suitcase. We also need some rubber bands."

***

Yao yelled, "Ann-Ann, don't go near the riverbank! It's slippery. If you fall, the rapid current will sweep you down the river."

"Yeah." A smile spread across her face. "I know how to swim now. I'll be okay." She hunched forward and plunged into the water.

"No. Don't..." He grabbed her arm in a vain attempt to pull her back.

A crescendo of noises exploded from nowhere. Yao opened his eyes.

Where was he?

Rays of light shone on his face. He sat up, his gaze drawn to the iron-bar window.

Right. He was inside a cell somewhere in Turkey. After they seized him, he hadn't been sleeping well. Fragmented dreams, always with a river scene, kept interrupting his slumber.

What was today? Yes, Tuesday.

He glanced at his wrist. Empty, of course. He'd given his limited-edition Patek Philippe watch to Ann-Ann. Not only the watch, but he'd also given everything he owned to her should something dreadful happen.

Bittersweet feelings flooded him. Sweet because God was still by his side and his beloved Ann-Ann would work alongside his friends to free him. Bitter because he couldn't unburden his fear that he might lose everything, including his life, in two days if —

"Lucky, go fetch the bone."

He stilled at the sound beyond his window—the voice of the man in the abandoned lot who'd abducted him.

"Good doggy. Come get your treat," the man praised. "Now, sit."

The accent was not only Asian but also Cantonese, and the tone sounded like Nathan's.

Yao hadn't seen his friend for a while, but the resonant voice was unmistakable. Could it be possible? Would his friends set up a scheme to kidnap him?

His body tensed up. Moving the table under the window, he climbed on it and peeked outside.

Like the others, the person disguised himself in a burka but didn't wear gloves. He squatted to pat a German shepherd puppy.

Yao trained his eyes on the man's left hand. Was there a scar on his index finger? He squinted and still couldn't figure it out. The man stood too far away.

With heat pulsing through his veins, Yao got off the table and paced around the small room.

If Judas forsook Jesus for thirty silver coins, why wouldn't his friends betray him for a million dollars?

Was money so important that men would do anything in pursuit of it?

He flattened his lips as flashbacks of his past entered his mind.

To protect themselves, how many sons and daughters turned against their parents amid the Cultural Revolution? During an accusation meeting against his math teacher, didn't he run up and slam his fist into the old man's body? His classmates attached burning cigarettes to the teacher's face and shaved off half of his hair with a razor.

The next day, their math teacher couldn't face the humiliation and jumped to his death.

Was there any difference between him and Nathan?

He clenched his teeth against the pain, then spread out his legs into the first stance of tai chi. With his body standing still, he slowly raised both arms, then dropped his left hand to form a posture of holding a large ball between two palms. Step by step, he moved through the entirety of the twenty-four tai chi forms.

Afterward, he slumped against the wall but couldn't subdue his despondency. Wasn't tai chi supposed to calm his nerves? Why didn't it work?

He'd sinned against many in his past. Could he truly claim Jesus' redemption for all his wrongdoings?

Lord, what'll happen next? Will I survive this ordeal? Please help me.

Had Susie wired the money to his company's Istanbul subsidiary? If not, what would happen to him? Could he try to negotiate with the kidnappers?

If Nathan and Nancy learned that he'd figured out their identities, they would take drastic measures. No, he'd better keep quiet and trust in the Lord.

He closed his eyes and clenched his fist. *Lord, I have little faith. Please help me.*

A low, guttural noise sounded. The dog was angry. What had Nathan just done? Did he try to break the puppy's spirit?

Strange. Margie had talked about the very subject. Her words reverberated in his mind. "Do you know how trainers break a puppy's spirit? Take the food away while he's eating, lock him in a small space for inordinate amounts of time, and punish the dog by brutal force for any sign of disobedience. Human traffickers break a girl's spirit the same way. On top of all those tactics, they arrange for different men to rape the victim day in and day out until she's numb to sexual assaults."

The puppy barked, then howled. What did Nathan do to him now?

"Few women escape from sexual slavery. For those lucky ones, even after being free for years, they still faced serious health issues, psychological trauma, and unfair social stigma." Margie had gone on to describe a rescued Mongolian teenager sold into prostitution by an agency that had promised to help her get an au pair job in Hong Kong. "She told me more than twenty men raped her on her first day inside a club. Afterward, she developed incontinence, the direct result of brutal sexual abuse."

Oh, why were humans so cruel? Was money the only motivation?

Lord, if I regain my freedom, I'll seek Your will to do something against the evil of human trafficking.

Chapter Twenty-Three

A tap sounded on the door. Ann-Ann dropped the face towel in her hand. "Who is that?"

She glanced at her watch. Almost eight. Who would stop by so early?

"Me," Susie called out.

Didn't Susie say she would meet them downstairs in the lobby? Ann-Ann unlocked the door. "Jet lag? You look tired."

"Yeah, brutal." Susie strolled to the sofa in the sitting area and plopped down. "How is Josh? Did he have nightmares last night?"

"A little better." Ann-Ann peeped into the bedroom to check on Nana and Josh. "You know about Old Master Q?"

"The lead character in a popular Chinese comic? What about him?"

"Josh has to complete a summer project, including having pictures taken of him and Old Master Q together on this trip. He's been so excited about it everywhere we visited." Ann-Ann took a seat on the sofa as well. As she thought about her last chitchat with Josh, her shoulders relaxed a bit. "Last night, he mentioned Old Master Q for the first time since his ordeal. It's an encouraging sign."

"Morning, Susie." Nana ambled in from the bedroom and sat by them. "Have you had breakfast yet?"

"I have." Susie turned her gaze toward the bedroom. "Is Josh still asleep?"

"He's drawing flowers in his notebook. A good thing. He hasn't done that since the day he was kidnapped." Nana brought a palm to her chest. "How about you? Did you sleep well last night?"

Susie wagged her head. "I was awake most of the time." She leaned back in her chair and feathered through her hair. "Margie took the equipment with her to Yao's room and let me stay with my brother. So, we chatted almost all night."

Ann-Ann grabbed the washcloth from the sofa to wipe her face.

"What do you think about Margie?" Susie touched her forehead. "Yesterday, the bank teller looked so surprised when Margie showed her badge. Shawn told me she was his girlfriend. Now I wonder who she truly is."

Nana's eyes stretched wide. While Ann-Ann gave her a brief account of yesterday, Nana gawked. "Is Margie a law-enforcement officer?"

"We aren't sure." Ann-Ann tilted her head sideways, the towel resting on her cheek. "She never gave us a direct answer when we questioned her. I've been wondering who she is all the time. No matter what, having her here with us is part of God's protection. If she weren't here, how could we handle our situation?"

"I agree. I'm convinced she isn't my brother's girlfriend." Susie yawned. "He kept me company last night, and we discussed certain serious subjects."

Ann-Ann raised a brow. Could he be serious about Christianity and ask his sister more about it?

Susie looked up at the ceiling. "I don't know whether I've mentioned this to you. Shawn is very stubborn. Before, whenever I tried to share with him about God and Jesus, he would make an excuse and leave. I didn't expect any difference when I saw him yesterday and thus avoided talking about my faith. Oddly enough, he's changed. He asked how I became a Christian."

Ann-Ann exchanged glances with Nana. Wasn't the work of the Holy Spirit astounding? The tough giant took the initiative to learn how to become a Christian.

Nana poured water for them. "What did you tell him?"

"I shared my testimony. He became quiet. Then he told me how the validity of the recordings in the Bible surprised him as you guys visited the Holy Land." Susie took a sip of the water. "He described how the genuine kindness your group showed him touches his heart. No matter how poorly behaved he is, you guys and little Josh always love him."

They sat in silence, sipping their water. Susie broke the stillness. "Yao's willingness to sacrifice himself for Josh, even though he's on the verge of planning his wedding, shocked Shawn the most."

Pain zipped through Ann-Ann's heart. "Yes, Yao proposed a few days ago. We were so happy. Now..."

"Don't be anxious." Nana drew her into a tight embrace. "Yao will return to us safe and sound."

Ann-Ann dipped her chin and re-focused on Susie.

Susie clattered her water glass onto the green marble coffee table. "Shawn asked me if someone can be so sinful that God won't forgive him." She turned her cup around, frowning at it. "I'm a new Christian myself and don't know how to respond."

An inpatient knock interrupted them. Nana's lips arched up. "Sounds like Shawn."

Ann-Ann let him in, yet her eyebrows refused to relax. Had he changed, as Susie said? Or would he be argumentative and yak nonsense, as always? Josh was just beginning to improve. Any disturbance in their safe setting could spiral the child back to fearful confusion.

With a cup of coffee in hand, Shawn took the single armchair next to the sofa. "You all look rather somber. Are you talking about Yao? Don't worry. I trust Margie. Things will work out okay."

Susie let out a small laugh. "Believe it or not, we were talking about you."

"Me?" He tapped his fingers against his mug. "Why?"

Nana directed her gaze at him. "Susie brought up your question about whether someone can be so wicked that God can't forgive him."

"I–I..." He set down his cup, ducked his head, and forked his fingers through his hair.

Nana didn't break her intense gaze on him. "Think of the robber who was crucified with Jesus and consider the apostle Paul, who used to persecute Christians and even kill them. They were saved. The Bible tells us everyone has sinned. By God's grace, no matter how sinful we are, we're justified because of Jesus."

Ann-Ann's chest swelled. Right. Nana, like Yao and other Christians in China, knew the Bible well.

His wide nose scrunching, Shawn peeped at Nana. "I can't believe you've ever sinned."

"You would be shocked if I told you about my past. Even now, I may not sin by commission, but I often sin by omission."

"What does that mean?" He massaged his temples.

"I may not do things that displease God. I often don't do things that please Him, which is equally bad." Nana clutched her fingers together. "According to the Gospel of John, 'All that the Father gives me will come to me, and whoever comes to me I will never drive away.' Nobody is too sinful or beyond the reach of Christ's redemption. The key is whether you seek Him."

Moisture glistened in Shawn's eyes. "I've done many evil deeds. I've engaged in deceitful and dishonest conduct. I've had numerous women."

"If you go to the Lord, He will accept you." Nana stood up and gathered him into her bosom. "Do you want to confess your sin to the Lord now?"

"I do."

Nana gestured for them to kneel together and pray. As Ann-Ann said her amen, the phone rang.

Susie picked it up. "Hello?" A crease formed between her brows. "Okay. I understand. See you at three."

"Who called?" Ann-Ann grabbed Susie's hand, a chill creeping into her heart. "What's the matter?"

"It's the bank." Susie kneaded her forehead. "They won't see us at ten but promise they can get enough small bills by three."

Three o'clock? "That's close to the end of the bank's business hour. What if...?"

Ann-Ann shut her eyes, refusing to entertain the possibility.

"My girl, don't worry." Nana hugged her. "The Lord is still in control."

An eerie hush stretched across the sitting area. At the same time, love, and yes, even peace, flowed through Ann-Ann like a gentle stream. *Lord, thank You for Nana.*

Josh's voice broke the silence. "Uncle Shawn, you look different today."

As the boy entered, Ann-Ann stole a glimpse of Shawn. His face shone with a new, peaceful glow.

Nana flashed a gentle grin. "Josh, God has answered your prayers. Your uncle Shawn has accepted Christ as his personal Savior and become a Christian."

Josh rushed to wrap his thin arms around Shawn. "Uncle Shawn, I love you."

Shawn's cheeks flared a bright crimson, and he muttered under his breath. "I'm thankful for your prayers." Then he stooped to Josh's level. "Kiddo, I found a splendid joke from the newspaper in the lobby for your summer project. Are you interested?"

"Tell me." Josh retrieved the notebook from his pocket.

"Remember the desert in Egypt? Two men, Kevin and Mike, traveled through the scorching desert, looking for food and water. As the sun reached the middle of the sky, they saw a mosque. Kevin said, 'Muslims are there. They may help us if we say we are Muslims.' Mike responded, 'No way. I want to be honest, even though I'm super hungry and thirsty.' They entered the mosque, and an Arab greeted them." Shawn paused and winked at Josh.

Josh drummed his pen. "Yeah? What happened?"

Eyes aglow, Shawn slapped his thigh. "Kevin thought of a Muslim name and said, 'My name is Muhammad.' But Mike told the guy his real name."

Josh tugged at Shawn's arm when he stopped again. "Come on. Tell me the end of the story."

"You really want to know, don't you?" Shawn chuckled. "The Arab man said hello to Mike and asked the servants to give him food and drink. He turned to Kevin and said, 'Hello, Muhammad, happy Ramadan. Let's fast and go to the prayer room.'"

"Ha! Uncle Shawn, that's a good one." Josh jotted it in his notebook. "I wish Uncle Yao were here. He always laughs at our jokes."

When was the last time Josh shared a joke with them and Yao applauded? Tears came to Ann-Ann's eyes again. Then she forced a smile. At least her nephew seemed to improve. And Shawn, who often taunted them with vulgar language, had accepted Christ as his Savior.

Lord, please let everything go well tonight and let Yao come back to us safe and sound.

***

Bang! Bang! Bang!

Three blasting gunshots interrupted Yao's nap. He sat up.

Was it day three or day four? He tried to focus, yet his mind failed him. Had his body weakened so much during the past few days?

Bang! Bang! Bang!

Three more shots cracked through the air. He plugged his ears with both hands but couldn't stop the intruding memory.

As he shut his eyes, his mind transported him back to that thicket by the Pearl River in Guangdong. The only thing separating him from his freedom was an empty field. Guards patrolled the area. If he left the haven of the wood with dawn breaking, he could get shot. If he tried to wait till the evening, his body couldn't handle the long swim ahead without food for another day. His stomach churning, he sprinted toward the river. Shots rang out. As his foot pushed off the riverbank, pain ripped into his side. He'd been hit.

Bang! Bang! Bang! Bang! Bang!

More deafening noises jolted Yao back to the present. He survived back then. He wouldn't die this time. Or would he?

When he prepared to leave that thicket by the Pearl River, he'd calculated his probability of survival to be fifty-fifty. How about now? Even if his friends brought the money, would the kidnappers let him go unharmed, or would they want more money?

He'd told the kidnappers his friends would be heavily armed. They must believe him, or they wouldn't be practicing their shooting now. But were they preparing themselves to fight? If so, caught between two armed groups, his chance of survival dwindled.

Lord, have mercy on me.

He dragged his tensed body forward. Like yesterday, he moved the table to the window and stood on it to peek outside.

The midmorning sun shone into his eyes. He blinked and refocused on the four individuals, all disguised in burkas. They took turns in their practice. Although he squinted hard, he still couldn't see whether one of them had a scar on his index finger. He shivered at what he could see—two shotguns and two rifles.

What would his friends get? Rifles?

Five versus four, *if* he counted Susie and himself, but only three of them would be armed.

Had Ann-Ann learned how to shoot by now?

Warmth soothed his thudding heart. His girl would pick up a gun because of him. He'd told her to trust in the Lord that they didn't have to change their wedding date. Why did he have so many doubts now? Had the lack of food, water, and sleep, plus excessive sweating, weakened not only his body but also his mind and soul?

Bang! Bang! Bang!

He emitted a long, low breath and got off the table.

Lord, please help me trust in You.

Chapter Twenty-Four

After dinner, Ann-Ann's stomach roiled as she entered Yao's room, now Margie's accommodations. She placed her bowl of uneaten soup on the table, clutched her abdomen tight, and took in slow, steady breaths. Still, the light food she'd forced down threatened to come back up.

Which one of them would leave the van to set down the suitcase? If the kidnappers grabbed Yao and the money, then what?

She dragged shaky fingers through her hair.

"Great. You're here." Susie flashed a tentative grin. "Are Nana Lee and Josh staying in the room?"

"I told Nana to take care of Josh in the hotel." Ann-Ann sat next to Susie but couldn't help kneading her temples. "And you? Are you coming with us?"

"Okay, one million." Margie let out a low whistle. "Susie and I have both counted it. Good enough."

"You probably don't need to be so precise." A crease formed between Shawn's brows. "Most likely, the kidnappers will just flip through it."

"You may be surprised." Margie moved toward the pile of equipment. "We can't leave any chances and jeopardize Yao's safety."

Ann-Ann surveyed the cash, her fingers whitening from clenching the sofa armrest. "Fifty stacks will take them just minutes to count. Assuming they know each stack with a thousand twenty-dollar bills is about four inches thick, they can eyeball the whole thing in less than twenty minutes." She ground the armrest's scratchy fabric beneath her palm. "Margie, shall we have a rehearsal?"

"Ah, how about it, guys? Come and get your equipment." Margie demonstrated the right way to wear them. "If you need help, let me know."

As Susie remained seated, Margie waved at her. "I've also got a bulletproof helmet and an armored vest for you."

Ann-Ann adjusted hers, much heavier and bulkier than she expected. "Wow, the law-enforcement people wear this stuff every day? How long does it take them to get used to the weight?"

With a shrug, Margie led them back to the sitting area. She pointed at the sofa. "Let's assume our car parks there. Ann-Ann, please go sit down and keep the rifle by your side. You'll be our driver tonight. Shawn, take the front passenger seat." She raised her unloaded rifle. "Susie, you and I will sit together in the second row. You'll sit behind Shawn."

Did that mean Susie would be the one to drop off the suitcase? Ann-Ann bit her lower lip, her chest tightening. Could Susie handle it? Unarmed?

"Ann-Ann, park with the passenger side facing the kidnappers' car, then grab your rifle and get into the shooting position. Susie and Shawn will get out with her taking the suitcase since he'll be carrying his rifle." Margie put down hers as if it weighed her down. "Once we see Yao and the kidnappers exit their car, Shawn, you will approach Yao, and Susie will trail you. With Yao and our opponents also approaching, you guys should meet between the two vehicles."

Margie pulled the suitcase over. "While the kidnappers inspect the cash, Shawn will stand by Yao, shielding him and ensuring they don't seize him again. Their companions in the car shouldn't dare to shoot. In case the kidnappers who escort Yao try to attack you in hand-to-hand combat, practice your Chinese martial arts. I know you're an expert."

Shawn chuckled. "I also have these." He flashed two daggers. "One is for Susie. Margie, you probably don't know my sister and I learned martial arts from the same master. Susie is as much an expert as I am."

"Nice." Margie grinned. "When the kidnappers carry the suitcase to their car, you, Shawn, walk backward to our van with Yao and don't take your eyes or gun off the kidnappers. You're taller and wider than Yao. If they dare to shoot, we'll count on them aiming for your center mass and your protective gear doing its job. But as they know we're well armed, I bet they won't shoot and will take leave right away."

Ann-Ann winced. Bet? As a finance major, *bet* was a dirty word to her. But what else could she do? *Lord, please protect us.*

"Is it clear to everyone? Let's rehearse." Margie picked up her rifle again. "In the first round, Ann-Ann, you play Yao, and I'll play the kidnapper. Let's go to that wall and pretend their car parks there."

Ann-Ann put down her rifle and moved to her position. Margie stood behind her and shoved her forward. They went through the motions without an issue. The subsequent rounds proceeded smoothly as well.

Lord, thank You. Please let everything go as planned.

But would the kidnappers play their roles as rehearsed?

"The past few days have been hectic." Susie flopped onto the couch and chuffed out a breath. "I never had time to ask about Nathan and Nancy. Have you found any information about them?"

Ann-Ann eyed Margie. "The other day, you mentioned the kidnappers might be involved in human trafficking. Do you still think so?" A chill crept up her spine. The corpse of that poor belly dancer... "You also suspected the kidnappers may be Hong Kong expats who read the Chinese tabloids or even some people who know Yao. When I asked whether Nathan and Nancy might be involved, you didn't respond. Could you please let us know what you think?"

Susie's eyes opened wide. "Our friends Nathan and Nancy? How could it be possible?"

"People will do anything for money." Margie scrunched her well-shaped nose. "I don't have any direct evidence. As I've said, the kidnappers know our private group well and have thought of everything. They first seized Josh, an easy victim, but their final target is Yao."

"Yeah." Shawn inclined his head. "Yao is well known in Hong Kong. Outside of Hong Kong, nobody knows him. The kidnappers must have read Hong Kong tabloids to learn his whereabouts."

Margie gazed back at Ann-Ann. "When you talked to Josh, did he mention what the kidnappers looked like?"

"Josh did say something rather odd." Ann-Ann squinted. "I'm not sure why I didn't think of it before. He said there were four people, all covered in black from head to toe. When he cried and pleaded for his mama, the shortest one came to hug him. Josh must have pleaded for my sister in Cantonese. The person understood Cantonese and showed pity for my nephew."

"What an important piece of information!" With hands on her hips, Margie halted before Ann-Ann. "So, there are four kidnappers. Probably the shortest one is a woman because women would be more likely to be moved by a child's plea for his mother."

"Prejudices, prejudices." Shawn made a face with a cross between a smile and a frown. Then his tone turned serious. "Let's assume two of them are Nathan and Nancy. Why did they become involved with the human traffickers? Did they join voluntarily?"

"I suppose we'll never know for sure. After Yao comes back to us, maybe he'll give us more clues." Margie checked her watch. "Almost two a.m. Are you all ready to go? Let's take action."

Air whooshed from Ann-Ann's chest, and her heartbeat kicked up speed. This would be no rehearsal. Their painstaking preparation might not bring desired results.

Lord, have mercy on us.

After she passed the Galata Bridge and drove into the empty lot, her van's headlights revealed a silhouette of a sedan facing south. As instructed, she parked about a hundred feet away, facing the opposite direction.

She turned off the headlights, and the desolate darkness descended. Even in the pitch blackness, she intuited Margie was beaming. Someone rolled down the van's passenger window. Without turning her head, Ann-Ann sensed Margie's movement.

Boom! An explosion erupted. A spark flashed, and smoke filled the air. The bullet bounced off. Margie had launched a shot into the ground, displaying their firepower.

Shawn and Susie opened the doors and turned on a flashlight. Guided by the dim torch beam, they trod toward the other car.

***

Tonight was the night, right? Yao lay on the cement floor, trying to guess the time. Night had fallen. Like the past few days, the streetlight's yellowy glow filtered through the window, casting long shards on his body.

He tried to sit up, but his leg muscles twitched and refused to cooperate. Was his fear so intense that his body failed him?

An image of the Milky Way flashed across his mind. In that thicket by the Pearl River, he was so fearful and had run in darkness for hours until weakness brought him down. As he collapsed, the Milky Way with its myriad of stars blinked through the branches above him.

He was eighteen then, with nothing other than the clothes on his back. Now he was thirty-one, with a sizable fortune and a lovely fiancée.

Yet today, he had nowhere to run.

From afar, the mosque's last call to prayer drifted through the night. Must be midnight. If the kidnappers lived outside of Istanbul, they'd need to act soon to meet the three-a.m. appointment.

His lips trembled, and his shoulders tightened even more.

What would happen? Did his friends get the money? Even if they did, would the kidnappers let him go? Was it possible they wanted more money?

The lock turned. Two people entered, still arrayed in black burkas. The tall one flashed his torch on Yao. "Get up," commanded the man who brought him food and water every day. "Time to go."

Yao bit his lips, pushed against the floor, and fell back down.

The shorter one rushed to his side and jerked him up.

The tall guy clattered his flashlight on the table. "Put your hands behind your back."

The two worked together to tape his wrists, mask his eyes, and gag his mouth. "Now, walk."

One of them yanked his shirt. The other pushed him hard. Almost losing his footing, he slammed his head on something. Four hands dragged him forward. A dog barked, a car door opened, and the same man's voice ordered him to get in.

He shuffled in. After the engine ignited, the car started moving, then picked up speed. The drive felt like an eternity before the car reduced its speed, made a turn, and stopped.

An eerie hush descended. Only the steady breathing from the two individuals at his sides interrupted.

"They're here." A stranger, likely the fourth fellow whom Yao hadn't encountered, spoke.

Boom!

At the gunshot, he didn't smell any smoke. So, it must be from his friends.

Someone snatched his eye mask away. The guy to his right side opened the rear passenger door. "Follow me."

Yao got out, flanked by two kidnappers, each holding a gun.

His friends—Shawn and Susie, with her pulling a suitcase—advanced toward them. Once they came face-to-face, she dropped it.

When Yao stepped forward to pass the suitcase, Shawn moved to stand back-to-back with him, facing the opponents. Yao turned his head sideways. In his peripheral vision, the two kidnappers unzipped the suitcase to inspect the cash.

Minutes—more—passed before the two fellows stood up. "Good enough. Let's go."

They trudged backward into the sedan. Then the car sped away.

"Don't relax just yet." Shawn's voice sounded lower than usual. "Let's walk back to the van. Yao, you sit in the front."

At last, Yao slumped his exhausted body into the seat. Ann-Ann's fingernails scraped his cheeks as she clawed his gag free and, teary-eyed, wrapped her arms around his neck. "Praise the Lord, you're safe and sound."

"Except he stinks." Shawn made a teasing tsk sound. "Yao, you're dirty and sweaty."

Ann-Ann giggled. "Who cares?"

When she covered his mouth with hers, Yao kissed her back and whispered, "Maybe untie me first?"

***

Dogs barking, doors slamming, dark shadowy figures walking, men and women talking...

Ann-Ann opened her eyes. The room was bright and quiet. The noises must have come from her nightmares. After they came back this morning, Yao shared his experience from the past few days. Those tidbits had somehow found their way into her dreams.

She shifted her position in bed—a bed she hadn't intended to fall asleep in. The plush queen mattress squeaked, the made bed beneath her, and a throw blanket draped over her.

How did it get there?

A warm, large palm touched her cheek. "You're awake."

Ann-Ann lifted her gaze to meet Yao's. He was sitting on a chair by the nightstand.

"What's the time now?" She covered his hand with hers, her voice sleepy, half-muffled.

"One in the afternoon." Soft lips fell on hers.

She kissed him back, pulling him into her arms. Oh, how nice to have him back! "I slept straight for almost seven hours?"

"Yeah. My sleeping beauty." He lay next to her and his lips continued to caress her earlobes and throat, then back to her mouth again.

Heat spread throughout her body with a familiar ache between her legs. She let out a pant and parted her lips. Yao pushed his tongue in. She closed her eyes, desire coursing through her veins. As their tongues tangled into an intimate dance, flames crept up from her toes to her head, melting her, boiling her.

A strong hand moved up to her chest.

"Oh no." As if scorched by fire, she wrangled out of his embrace to sit up. "We shouldn't."

Whew. She almost gave in to her body's desires and did something they would both regret later. Where did her willpower come from?

Thank You, Lord.

"I'm sorry." He edged away. "I missed you so much. Not seeing you in the past few days was torture."

"I missed you too." She leaned forward to stroke his chin. "Be patient. In less than two months, we'll be husband and wife."

He drew her into his arms again. "I can't wait. I wish we were back in Hong Kong and today were September twelve."

"Of course, you can wait." She chuckled and tried to get away. "Now that you mentioned it, we're leaving Istanbul tomorrow morning, right? Have you packed?"

"Not really. Don't go." He placed another tender kiss on her lips. "Cuddling with you is more important than packing."

A tender love crept in once more. This morning, they got back to the hotel around four thirty. Margie went to stay with Shawn and Susie. After Yao showered, Ann-Ann served him the bowl of soup she'd saved from last night's dinner. The soup was lukewarm, but he devoured it as if it was the most delicious food ever created. Right at that moment, the compassion she'd never felt for anyone flooded her heart. Now, that same feeling returned.

She shut her eyes and immersed herself in this precious moment. In less than two months...

Oh, Lord, thank You, thank You.

Epilogue

Hong Kong
September 1981

After the wedding ceremony, Yao ambled into his Mingden Hotel's banquet room for the reception. Six years ago, they'd had another similar event, albeit at a different location—his mansion. The same gorgeous sunny day, perfect for a wedding. The same beautiful group of people, ideal for a celebration. Except that Ann-Ann's mother and stepfather filled the roles of bride and groom back then, and now, the title was bestowed on him and his Ann-Ann.

During the preparation, she'd insisted on wearing her mother's wedding gown. "I can never forget it. On that day, Nana helped me return to God's family."

With her bountiful energy and typical determination, she'd rummaged through his house to retrieve her mother's reception décor from six years ago. "These look new. They've been used only once. You've just lost one million dollars. Let's save funds to help that Christian organization Margie is affiliated with."

A pleasant warmth embraced his heart. His bride supported his funding activities to fight the evil of human trafficking, even to the extent of sacrificing her dream wedding. Still, he'd convinced her to accept a diamond ring and matching necklace.

Yao paused in the doorway, flanked by porcelain flower vases nearly as tall as he was, their images reflecting on the polished marble floors. One of Chopin's classic piano solos, "Nocturne No. 2 in E-Flat Major, Op. 9," glided through the air. Chandeliers cast gilded light over the recycled décor, lending a striking beauty to this grand occasion. Draped in exquisite cream-tinted fabric, festooned with the Mingden Hotel insignia, the newlyweds' table was further beautified by cobalt hydrangeas set on glassware. The words *Wishing Yao Chen and Ann-Ann Lee lots of love and happiness* gleamed from a red banner on the wall, the only updated décor they'd added.

"Congratulations again, Yao." In a pink gown, Daisy Dong sauntered over to greet him, her heeled pumps striking the floor with soft clicks.

"Thank you for coming." He shook hands with her, then closed his other hand over their clasped ones, and held hers there in an attempt to convey the depth of his gratitude.

After his return to Hong Kong, he'd shared his trip experience with her. Her eyes stretched wide at his retelling of the incredible journey. She'd expressed her understanding of how such an experience would change anyone's outlook and forever connect him to those who'd shared it. Now she drew him into a warm hug. "I'm happy for you. Finding someone you love dearly isn't easy. Wish me well. If I hope to meet my Prince Charming soon, perhaps I should plan a trip to the Holy Land and Turkey."

"Well said." He chortled. "The Holy Land is a must for Christians. You won't regret it."

After she left, Shawn rushed over. "Ha, the flower in your tuxedo is tilted downward." He adjusted it, then slapped Yao's back, almost knocking the boutonniere loose again. "You and Ann-Ann look awesome together. You two are meant for each other."

"You're charming too. Thank you for being our best man, and I must thank Margie." Yao craned his neck to find her. "Where is the bridesmaid?"

"I talked to her minutes ago. Maybe she went to help Ann-Ann change?"

"Makes sense. I'll let them be. How is your new martial arts academy going?" A gentle heat spread through Yao's entire person. *Lord, thank You, thank You.* "How many students do you have?"

"More than I can handle." With a chuckle, Shawn pointed toward his sister across the room. "See Susie over there? I may steal her from you to help me out."

"Absolutely not." Yao wagged a finger, then gripped Shawn's arm. "I admire you. Your changed lifestyle has impressed everyone. What made you shut down your casino? Did you lose a lot of money?"

"Not really." Shawn shrugged. "Quite a few individuals bid to buy it out. I received a decent deal."

Yao patted his friend's shoulder. "The Lord is full of mercy to all of us."

With a glance around them, Shawn pulled Yao toward a corner. "After we came back, both of us got sucked into different activities. I never did ask—Do you think Nathan and Nancy were among the kidnappers?"

"I have my suspicions but no direct evidence." Yao exhaled, pushing out the sudden weight on his chest. "Why do you ask?"

"I can't get over the fact my childhood friends would do such a thing."

"I concluded that if Judas forsook Jesus for thirty silver coins, then likely my friends could betray me for one million dollars." Yao surveyed the guests in the spacious room. "Look at all those people. Without God and Jesus' love, each of them, including you and me, is capable of committing a grievous evil."

"Right on!" Shawn inclined his head. "You amaze me once more. I'm glad you're my brother in Christ."

"Same here. I'll never forget how you shielded me from the kidnappers with your own body."

Jie, May-May's husband, strolled toward them. "Yao, congratulations. Now you're officially a member of the Lee family."

"Thank you." Yao looked behind Jie. "Where are Charlie, Josh, and Audrey?"

"They went with May-May to check on their auntie Ann-Ann."

"Jie, you and May-May did a wonderful job raising a child like Josh. He's funny, kind, and courageous." Shawn leaned forward. "Is he fully recovered from his ordeal in Istanbul?"

"I believe so. The kidnappers didn't hurt him, but he's still experiencing trauma, mainly from being snatched from his loved ones and fearing the ordeal could happen again. As the psychotherapist explains, such things take longer to heal than physical wounds." Jie shook his head, then smoothed back the hair that flipped onto his forehead. "May-May prays with him every night. Many at church are praying for him. I'm convinced the power of prayer goes beyond human comprehension."

"Indeed. I'm proof that God can work wonders! He is all-powerful and can accomplish anything according to His will, even things that seem impossible to us." Shawn's eyes sparkled. "Your daughter is so cute. As the flower girl and the ring bearer, she did an excellent job."

A few steps away, Ann-Ann's grandfather and her stepfather, Uncle Duan, waved at them. They shifted over.

Uncle Duan asked, "Where are all the ladies?"

"They must be with Ann-Ann in her room." Jie's eyes took on a mischievous glint. "I think they're having their own party." Then his tone turned serious. "At the touching moment when you walked into the sanctuary with Ann-Ann, May-May wept."

"Your grandma wept too." Grandpa grasped Yao to pull him into a hug. "Seeing you and Ann-Ann come together has always been our sincere wish. But we never thought it would happen. God's grace, as Shawn said, is astounding."

Yao eased back from the older man's hold and grinned again. "Nana Lee also played a crucial role. Without her help, Ann-Ann might have still shunned me."

"Nana Lee?" Jie laughed aloud. "Now she's your nana as much as she's mine."

"Everything worked out well." Shawn swung his arms. "Pastor Mang's sermon touched me a great deal. I may consider switching to your church."

"I'm glad you and Ann-Ann will honeymoon in Hong Kong." Uncle Duan spread out his hands. "After your dangerous trip, every one of us shall stay put for a while."

"For sure?" Yao winked. "Didn't Mama mention last night that she plans to go to the Holy Land later this year? Aren't you going with her?"

***

Ann-Ann scrutinized her reflection in the mirror. Mama's bright-red dress fit her well.

"You look gorgeous in this dress." Nana touched her bare shoulder. "I'm glad you had it altered to feature a more modern look."

"I'm so happy." Grandma pulled out a handkerchief to dab her eyes. "Tell me again about your visit to the Mediterranean. You speak of Egypt and the Holy Land, but everyone hushes up about Turkey. What happened there?"

Ann-Ann exchanged a glance with Nana. "Grandma, nothing too serious. Didn't we all come back to Hong Kong safely?"

"Yao proposed in Turkey." Nana winked and pointed at Ann-Ann's diamond necklace. "He was generous to have given her this. It must cost a small fortune."

"The necklace is spectacular." Grandma put her handkerchief away. "Oh, such a happy ending. All the suspense and uncertainties are behind us."

"I'd better go." Nana checked her watch. "Certain church friends need my attention."

"Let's go together." Grandma hooked her arm with Nana's.

After the older ladies left, Mama strolled in and came to hug her. "Ann-Ann, your wedding ceremony was delightful."

With mischief sneaking in, Ann-Ann scrunched her nose. "Aren't you relieved I finally settled down? Before our trip, you kept nagging and asking me why I couldn't find any guy to go out with."

Mama ducked her head, her grin turning sheepish. "You always gave me such a weird reason, claiming you had an enjoyable life and enough loved ones to keep you from feeling lonely. You even insisted singlehood was better than being ensnared in a messy marriage."

Did she say that? She might have. "You worried nobody would take care of me when I grew old."

"Well, all that was in the past." Mama gave her shoulder a tender squeeze. "Nobody suits you better than Yao. He once confided in me it was tough to find a girl who loved him instead of his money."

Ann-Ann touched her forehead, cringing over when she and Yao first dated. Back then, she loved his money. Maybe he knew it, and that was why he commented she wasn't a Christian.

Lord, thank You for Your great timing. If we'd gotten married back then, our marriage would be miserable.

She wrinkled her nose again. "Mama, I still don't know when Yao learned about my abortion and barrenness."

"Your nana or I may have told him. Nana and I always treat him as one of us." Mama waved. "It's not important. I'm so pleased he's officially a member of the Lee family."

"Don't most guys, like Stanley, care about having children of their own? Why is Yao different?" Unfiltered words rolled off her tongue.

Mama brushed a wisp of hair back from Ann-Ann's temples. "Like you, Yao has experienced lots of pain and suffering. After his return to God's family, he established a set of standards for his future wife. To him, finding someone who loves him instead of his money is more important than having children."

"Bravo!" Still, Ann-Ann brought a palm to her chest, in an attempt to hold in the emotion threatening to burst loose in a squeal. "And now... after all the twists and turns, two desolate souls found each other."

Margie strode into the room. "You're still here."

"Margie, thank you again for being Ann-Ann's bridesmaid." Mama hugged her. "I'll leave you two here for now. With May-May's restaurant catering for the reception, she may need my help."

Ann-Ann waited for Mama to leave. "Margie, when are you leaving for your next assignment? Where is it this time? By the way, in Istanbul, you said no need to file a police report because you would inform your organization directly. Have you done it?"

"Very soon." Her sensual lips crinkled up. "Somewhere in Asia. And yes, I've submitted a detailed report to my boss."

"You're as guarded as before." Ann-Ann flashed up her eyebrows, yet at least her friend squeezed out time to come to her wedding. "After what we have gone through, I thought you'd let me know whom you work for."

"My dear friend, it's more for your protection than mine. The less you know about me, the better off you are." Margie picked up Ann-Ann's hand and tipped the ring to the light, tilting it to catch the flare of prisms. "I'm tickled Yao gave you a three-carat diamond ring to replace the pendant you gave up in Egypt."

Ann-Ann surveyed the gigantic rock sparkling on her ring finger, giggled, then turned her hand to grip Margie's. "If you need it, don't hesitate to let me know."

"You're generous, but Yao will give me a hard time if I dare to ask for this ring." Eyes as sparkly as the diamond, Margie shook a finger at her. Next, her tone dipped. "You and Yao are so kind. The Christian organization fighting against human trafficking told me you sent sufficient funding to cover their expenses for the next few years."

"Oh, that's the least we can do." A mist formed in Ann-Ann's eyes. "That belly dancer in Cairo and what you told us about the trafficked victims' horrid stories... I sincerely hope the evil of human trafficking can be eradicated."

"It may take a lot of effort." Margie tapped her chin, her red nail polish a perfect match to her lipstick. "We just do our part and pray for God's will to be done."

"Pray, yes. Yao and I will keep praying for you. And, as long as we can, we'll support the fight against human trafficking."

May-May walked in with Josh and Audrey in tow. Dressed in an azure gown, with a slim figure, a perfect oval face, and flawless skin, she could pass for a teenager, not a mother of three. "Ann-Ann, seeing you in Mama's red dress... such an emotional moment! I couldn't help crying over how all of us have found the mates God created for us. And Yao has been like my brother since childhood."

"I was just about to say the same—how wonderful it is to have found my soulmate." Ann-Ann hugged her, pressing her face to May-May's silky-smooth hair and breathing in the slight scent of ginger from whatever dish her twin had been helping prepare. Then she held May-May at arm's length. "I'd say how lovely you look, but since we're identical, it always feels like I'm complimenting myself. Still, I must say that light blue fits you well. Where is Charlie?"

"He went home." May-May huffed a heavy breath, her shoulders sloping beneath Ann-Ann's grip. "He's afraid of having another asthma attack. Please continue to pray for him."

"Of course. Everybody in the family is praying for him." Ann-Ann released her hold of May-May. "By God's mercy, he'll outgrow his asthma."

Margie eyed them up and down. "You two are identical. How do your husbands tell you apart?"

May-May winked. "It's never a problem."

Audrey rushed toward Ann-Ann. "Auntie."

She picked Audrey up and kissed her chubby cheek. "Thank you for being our flower girl and ring bearer. In this beautiful dress, you look like a princess."

The girl wrapped both arms around her neck and kissed her back.

Josh patted her arm. "Auntie Ann-Ann, I need one more photo with Old Master Q for my summer project. My teacher gave me an A already. But after I told her about you and Uncle Yao, she said she would give me an A-plus if I manage to get your wedding picture. Can we have it here?"

Music floated into Ann-Ann's ears. The live band had started to play Nana's favorite hymn, "Amazing Grace."

She set Audrey down and looked up. Yao was leaning against the doorframe. "The reception is about to start. Are you all ready to come?"

"Josh, maybe we have a group picture taken at the reception?" Ann-Ann took Yao's arm, resisting the urge to kiss him. "My dear hubby, let's go—we have all our friends waiting and our whole lives ahead of us."

The End

Have you read *Blazing China* (https://www.amazon.com/dp/B0CD9P49HW), the prequel of *Detour to Agape*?

Dive into a mesmerizing tale of loyalty, redemption, and transformation by Whong, named a 2025 Featured Author by the Minnesota Anoka County Library and a 2026 Featured Author by the Suffolk Virginia Authors Festival.

A Note from the Author

Hello and thank you for sharing this journey with me. Writing this book was a special and emotional experience, and I cannot say how honored I am that you joined me through these pages. If you like the book and have a moment to spare, I would appreciate a short review. Thank you for your help.

About the author

Although I grew up in Hong Kong and Taiwan, my family members live in different parts of the world, a common phenomenon for most Chinese my age because of political conflicts.

I work for a small biotech company and have published 120+ scientific books and papers (under my legal name).

While I am relatively new to the realm of creative writing, I'm thrilled that I was chosen as a featured author by the Minnesota Anoka County Library in 2025 and by the Suffolk Virginia Authors Festival in 2026.

One of my books, *Echoes over Stormy Sea*, has won several awards, including being recently chosen by readers as a winner in the HOLT Medallion Contest.

Amazon Best Sellers

Our most popular products based on sales. Updated frequently.

I currently live in the Midwest with my husband, a retired pastor. We served together at three churches from 1987 to 2020. Our grown son works in a nearby city.

Check out my other books.

The Way We Forgive (Women's fiction): https://www.amazon.com/dp/B0BQ5LNLNB

Blazing China (family saga): https://www.amazon.com/dp/B0CD9P49HW

Detour to Agape (sequel to *Blazing China*; contemporary romance): https://www.amazon.com/dp/B0CD9P29GJ

Prestige of Hearts (contemporary romance): https://www.amazon.com/dp/B0CV4FL3CH

Center of Enigma (Paradise PA Mystery Book 1; mystery/suspense/thriller): https://www.amazon.com/dp/B0D9R2M134

Essence of Illusion (Paradise PA Mystery Book 2; mystery/suspense/thriller): https://www.amazon.com/dp/B0DFVPKW3N

Allure of Elegance (Paradise PA Mystery Book 3; mystery/suspense/thriller): **https://www.amazon.com/dp/B0FCP1BV32**

Series Page: https://www.amazon.com/dp/B0DFNXPSGW

Love Under Holy Skies (contemporary romance): https://www.amazon.com/dp/B0F362Q7T8

Echoes over Stormy Sea (Action/Adventure; Dual-time Odyssey Book 1): https://www.amazon.com/dp/B0DPGQ6TZP

Thunders over Idle Land (Action/Adventure; Dual-time Odyssey Book 2): https://www.amazon.com/dp/B0F49GFHW6

Fire Between Two Skies (Action/Adventure; Dual-time Odyssey Book 3): https://www.amazon.com/dp/B0G2YZZ8LG

Series Page: https://www.amazon.com/dp/B0F4LKXS2W

Nonfiction (under Ruth Wuwong):

Are your health and finances linked? A Christian Entrepreneur's Quest:
https://www.amazon.com/dp/B0BQ5JXFYY

Wander Or Not: https://www.amazon.com/dp/B0CXJ79MWF

To connect with me, please go to www.ruthforchrist.com.

Follow me on social media:

Amazon: https://www.amazon.com/author/love.respect.grace
Goodreads:
https://www.goodreads.com/author/show/42632055.R_F_Whong
Bookbub: https://www.bookbub.com/authors/r-f-whong
Twitter/X: https://twitter.com/RWuwong
Instagram: https://www.instagram.com/ruthwuwong
Facebook: https://m.facebook.com/ruth.wuwong